Win a 5 Carat Diamond!
Each book has a random number inside the back cover.
Once 20,000 books are sold the winner will be announced.
For more information go to
www.KT-Banks.com

"STAND AND PROTECT"

"STAND AND PROTECT"

A Novel

K.T. Banks

iUniverse, Inc.
New York Bloomington Shanghai

"STAND AND PROTECT"

Copyright © 2008 by K.T. Banks

iUniverse books may be ordered through booksellers or by contacting:

iUniverse
1663 Liberty Drive
Bloomington, IN 47403
www.iuniverse.com
1-800-Authors (1-800-288-4677)

Because of the dynamic nature of the Internet, any Web addresses or links contained in this book may have changed since publication and may no longer be valid.

This is a work of fiction. All of the characters, names, incidents, organizations, and dialogue in this novel are either the products of the author's imagination or are used fictitiously.

ISBN: 978-0-595-50904-1 (pbk)
ISBN: 978-0-595-61689-3 (ebk)

Printed in the United States of America

Thanks to our Family & Friends for all their love and encouragement.

And to all the people in the Multi-Family business. May God Bless You All!

PROLOGUE

▼

New England

1993 ...

The bright gold and red leaves cascaded through the air against the crisp blue and white autumn sky, accompanied by the delighted laughter of the two young girls. The big, old school building loomed grandly in the background. "You know they'll just make us rake all this up again, don't you?"

Shannon Murphy just grinned at Jill Barrington, as the multi-colored leaves settled on both of their heads, one blonde, and one red. "Only if they catch us. I bet I can throw 'em higher than you can!" Neither of the little girls had an inkling of the tragedy that was soon to befall them.

The click of the camera was heard as they watched the next batch of leaves descend. Startled, knowing they were caught, Shannon spun around to see a man taking pictures of them. She grabbed Jill by the shoulder and whispered in her ear, "Great, now we're busted." Both girls got very still trying to decide if there was anything to be afraid of. Two pairs of blue eyes, one dark denim blue and the other a bright cornflower blue, were opened wide.

"Oh don't stop now," the man complained. "I'm just taking your pictures for tomorrow's paper. You would like to see your pictures in the paper wouldn't you?" He was tall and skinny, wearing blue jeans, a New England Patriots sweatshirt and a baseball cap. "My name is James Earl Cabot. Like I said, I'm with the local newspaper. Two pretty little girls like you, in the middle of all of these leaves make a great picture!" He smiled broadly and winked at the girls.

"In the paper? Then we would be busted for sure!" whispered Shannon.

Jill looked more worried then ever. "And my Dad will kill me. You know I'm not supposed to ever get in trouble!" Tears were starting to gather in her eyes. "Now they'll make me go back to that private school," she said with a shaking voice.

Jill's parents were in politics and had reluctantly agreed to let her go to a public school, thinking it might look good for their image. Her father was the District Attorney, with a lot of ambition, and her mother was a former prosecutor, from a very wealthy family, now the perfect politician's wife.

Getting angry on behalf of her friend, Shannon jumped up and stalked over to the man with the camera.

"Look Mister, we don't want our picture in the paper. If you do put it in, we, uh … we'll sue you. That's what her parents do!" She jerked her thumb back towards Jill. With hands on her hips, she stood glaring at him.

"Hey, no problem, I'll just take some pictures of the school and find some other kids to take pictures of. It's such a beautiful day. No hard feelings, right?" he held out his hand to shake hers.

Shannon noticed that his smile didn't reach his small brown eyes. A small shiver raced up her spine. Backing away, she said, "Okay then, no hard feelings." She reached Jill and took her hand to start pulling her away.

"Wow, you were great Shannon. I love having you for my best friend. You just stand up to anybody! I wish I could be more like you." She looked at her friend with love and gratitude in her eyes. Shannon didn't reply.

She thought she could still feel the man's eyes on her back. As she turned to glance back at him, sure enough he was still standing in the same spot, watching them walk away.

✳   ✳   ✳   ✳

That night, still bothered by the earlier episode, Shannon was trying to decide if she should tell her father about it. They had a very close relationship, made even closer because when Shannon was three years old; her mother had decided that being a wife and mother was boring.

She had left both husband and daughter to go off and 'find' herself. They hadn't seen her since then, but they did get an occasional phone call, especially if her mother needed money.

"Hurry it up, honey; we have to be at the field by six o'clock. You know we're playing the Bobcats tonight. Speaking of wild animals, what's wrong with you? You've hardly said a word and you're just pushing the food around on your plate." Sam looked at his daughter inquiringly and put his hand on her forehead. "You okay?"

Shannon was so proud of her big strong father. He was the head football coach at Kennedy High School. She knew tonight's game was especially important because the two teams were going into this undefeated. Seeing the concern in his eyes, she decided he had enough to worry about. "It's nothing Daddy; I'm just excited about the game. My stomach is all fluttery!" She grinned up at him.

The sweet innocent little face had his heart swelling as he thought for the millionth time how lucky he was to have her. At thirty-three years old, he couldn't believe how fast the last ten years had gone by.

Knowing that the games were just as important to her as they were to him, Sam thought he understood her lack of appetite. Glancing at his own plate, he saw he hadn't eaten a lot either. Like father, like daughter he mused. Sometimes he worried about her being raised without a mother. She was such a little tomboy, more interested in sports than dolls. She never had any close friends until Jill started going to Jackson Elementary with her last year.

Because Jill was from a very wealthy and well-known family, the other kids had been intimidated by her. Sometimes they made fun of her, especially her bright red hair. They were usually lead by the school bully, Hoyt Chambers. On one such occasion, Shannon had jumped to her defense and they had been the best of friends since then. Sam was relieved to have some female influence in his daughter's life. "Well kiddo, let's go win this game."

*   *   *   *

"Oh shit, she forgot her lunch again." Knowing he was running late, Sam decided to bring it by to her just before lunchtime. He thought nothing could ruin this day. He was still high on the big win last night. They had blown them out by a score of thirty five to six. Shannon was so excited last night she almost couldn't sleep. Which explains why she forgot her lunch. Again.

Or it could have been when he made her go back up to her room to change clothes. Today was picture day and he had wanted her to wear her new light blue dress instead of her usual jeans. He had even talked her into wearing her hair down, the long golden curls reaching almost to her waist. Sam thought his daughter looked like a little angel. He chuckled when he thought about all the trouble she was always getting into.

*   *   *   *

Standing by the lunch table, Sam glanced at his watch as he explained to his daughter why he couldn't stay for lunch.

"That's okay, Daddy. I'm going to go find Jill anyway."

As they were about to walk out into the hall, a loud scream pierced the air, followed by a popping sound. Sam quickly pushed Shannon back into the cafeteria. "Stay here honey; I have to go see what's going on." He put his face down to the same level as hers, looked her straight in the eyes, and repeated, "I mean it, stay here, no matter what." Then he ran down the hallway.

One of the teachers was yelling for everybody to get down under the tables. Shannon got underneath the nearest one. It got very quiet because no one knew what was going on. She could actually hear each tick of the clock above the door.

After a while some of the children began to whisper, "Are we having another fire drill?

"Maybe it's a real fire."

"Maybe it's a bomb!"

"We're all gonna die!"

The girl closest to her began to cry. It was starting to feel like a long time had gone by. Shannon wanted to go check on her father. And where was Jill? Getting more worried by the minute, she jumped up and ran out the door. It was too late for the nearest teacher to stop her.

As she moved swiftly down the deserted hallway towards Jill's homeroom, she saw some black shoes sticking out of a doorway. Sneaking up to the door, she was horrified to discover a policeman lying on his back with a pool of deep red blood spreading across the floor. His eyes were open, staring blankly across the room. Flyers that had fallen around him had the smiling face of a dog in a trench coat talking about crime prevention. Now she knew she had to find her Dad and Jill to warn them. Her heart was beating so hard; she thought she might throw up. She took a deep breath to try to steady herself and crept along the hallway, staying close to the bright blue metal lockers. Everything felt surreal; she had never seen the school this deserted and quiet. It reminded her of a scary movie that she and Jill had watched late one night, when Jill's parents had thought they were asleep.

*　　*　　*　　*

Suddenly she heard her Dad talking in a low voice. "Come on man, she didn't have anything to do with putting you in jail. She was practically just a baby at the time. You don't want to hurt her." He was speaking with authority, like he did with his football players, but Shannon thought she could hear desperation in his voice. As she turned the corner, she could see her Dad standing in a doorway. She could hear someone crying.

"Shut-up and get out of the way!" The voice seemed to snarl, making Shannon jump. "Mr. D.A. has to pay for what he did to me. I'm not going to hurt her so long as he pays, and I know he has plenty of money coming from a family like that. I'm only telling you one more time, get out of my way."

As it dawned on Shannon that he was talking about Jill, she heard her father say, "I can't do that." He took a step further into the room just as a loud boom went off. She watched—it seemed in slow motion, as her father's body flew backwards out of the doorway.

Even with the loud boom still echoing in her ears, she could still hear Jill screaming in terror. The man was yelling at her and trying to pull her out the door. Still feeling like she was in slow motion, Shannon turned and walked back the way she had come. She went to the schoolroom with the body of the dead policeman and bent over him to get the gun out of his hand. She wiped the blood off the gun with the bottom of her new dress and went back down the hallway.

As she rounded the corner, she saw the man pulling Jill around the body of her father. He looked up and saw her standing in the middle of the hall with the gun pointed at him. He laughed and sneered, "Well, look what we have here." Then his face hardened, "Get out of the way little girl, or I'll just take you with us."

With numb recognition she realized it was the man from yesterday, the one with the camera. Holding the heavy gun as straight as she could, she said in a low voice, "You just killed my Dad, and I'm not gonna let you hurt Jill too." She looked into Jill's horrified eyes for a split second. The little girl dropped to the ground just as Shannon pulled the trigger. With disbelief, the man grabbed his left arm.

"You little bitch, you shot me!" With a loud snarl he raised his gun to aim at her. Shannon fired the gun again and he fell to the floor, still cursing. As Jill watched from the doorway, Shannon walked up to the man and shot him twice more.

CHAPTER 1

▼

Dallas, Texas
October, 2007

"Shannon, I need you to baby-sit for me again tonight. I have a date with that new guy in twenty two seventeen. You know the one with the black BMW? I'm going to leave early to get ready. And since its Thursday, you're going to have to do the reports again too. Oh, and be sure to check out those three apartments that are moving in tomorrow. They have to be perfect; you know how people love to bitch. Make Larry go with you in case you find something wrong. I wish I had time to get my nails done, but I'm the only one that gets anything done around here." With that, Heather sauntered out of the office.

Shannon was a leasing agent at the Sherwood Village apartments in Dallas Texas. She sat at her desk with a worried look on her face. "How am I supposed to get all that done and be home in time to baby-sit? I wish just once she would ask one of the other girls to help out." She glanced over at the other two girls, Camille and Amber, as they laughed and gossiped with a resident.

Amber was of medium build with bright strawberry blond hair and hazel eyes. Camille had short, kind of spiky black hair, with dark brown eyes and high cheekbones. Dramatic make-up with dark red lips gave her an exotic look. Camille leaned her long thin body invitingly into the man from ten-twenty eight. She had already gotten into trouble last month for sleeping with a resident, but it looked like she was at it again. Heather said it was probably why she leased so many apartments.

"Who couldn't lease an apartment at a place like this? Not only are the apartments beautiful, the community is like a resort." She thought about the huge fitness center, four sparkling pools, and a billiards room with a beautiful long, antique looking bar. A theater room that could seat about forty people and had a freestanding, old fashioned looking popcorn machine and heavy red velvet drapes across the movie screen with large, potted dark green palm plants in each corner. Even tanning beds, in case you couldn't get enough of a tan in the hot Dallas sun. And that was only some of the amenities they offered! There were six hundred and eighty units, spread out in two story buildings that had been designed in an old English village look. Even the intersecting driveways throughout the parking lots were made of cobblestone.

The buildings were made of stucco and stone, and many of them had English Ivy creeping up the sides. They spent several thousand dollars a month just in landscaping, with an abundance of flowers everywhere. There wasn't a day of the week that didn't have a least a few landscapers on-site. The place was so beautiful they stayed leased up most of the time. It seemed like the only time people moved out was to buy a house or for a job transfer. When they had first opened the office, some of the buildings weren't even completed yet, and they had had a staff of eight just to run the office and show apartments.

The apartment business was a big industry in Dallas. The Apartment Association of Greater Dallas (AAGD) had over ten thousand members including the product and services vendors. Besides the individual associations, there were also the Texas Apartment Association (TAA) and even bigger, the National Apartment Association (NAA).

Not for the first time Shannon told herself how lucky she was that they got to live here. They even had a handi-cap unit to make it easier for her Dad. And her son Bryan had lots of friends to play with. Their three bedroom apartment was almost fifteen hundred square feet. It was worth putting up with the long hours and a difficult boss.

I just wish I didn't have to baby-sit for her so often; Shannon thought and then immediately felt guilty.

Heather's son had a behavioral disorder. There was actually a long name for it, but what it meant was that he was pretty hard to deal with. Plus she was always afraid he was going to get hurt. One time he crawled up the front of the china cabinet in one of the model apartments and the whole thing had come crashing down on him.

Heather had a date that night, so Shannon had rushed him to the hospital for three stitches above his eyebrow. The doctor had said he was lucky it didn't kill him. Travis will be five next month though; maybe he'll start to outgrow it? Shaking her head, Shannon got to work on the weekly report. Her hand froze for just a second before she could write the word October.

CHAPTER 2

▼

Shannon could feel the sweat droplets on her top lip as she looked down the hallway. As always, she wanted to scream at her father not to go into that room. Just as she heard the gunshot, she awoke with a scream in her throat. Luckily she held it back. This time she wouldn't wake up Dad and Bryan. At least now the nightmares only came in October. For years, it was an every night occurrence.

The therapist thought moving to a far different climate would help. After all, they said Texas only had two seasons, summer and winter. It turned out that it did help for the most part and Shannon loved it here. Bryan was born here. Even Dad liked the fast pace of Dallas. There was always something going on. Plus, some of the best sports in the country. All you had to say to put a smile on Dad's face was, "How 'bout them Cowboys!" Meaning the Dallas Cowboys football team, of course.

Shannon realized her thoughts were rambling, trying not to dwell on that October day almost fifteen years ago. It was a tough time. The great news was that her father didn't die, although he would never walk again. Of course Jill's parents sent her away to a private school. The two girls never saw each other again. And to make it worse, the other kids couldn't get over the fact that she had killed someone. They had all stared at her, and would get really quiet when she entered the room.

Two boys, including Hoyt Chambers, had been peeking out of a classroom door and had watched the whole thing. Word had spread about how many times she had shot the man. How calm she had seemed. There had been blood dripping from the ends of her long blond curls, from leaning over the dead policeman. No wonder they were afraid of her. She was afraid every time she thought about it. To make it worse, it made national headlines. They called her a hero.

She couldn't go anywhere without people pointing at her. All the talk shows had wanted her to be on T.V.

Instead, she was at the hospital for weeks, willing her Dad to live. He was in a coma for thirty-two days. Her mother showed up, trying to capitalize on all the publicity. She had even made quite a bit of money doing magazine interviews, enough money to leave as soon as Dad came home from the hospital. For a while a nurse came to the house every day, to teach Sam how to live his life from a wheel chair. Shannon's love for her Father grew even more as she saw how hard he struggled to keep his good attitude. She knew he did it for her.

Glancing at the clock on her nightstand, she saw it was almost six o'clock in the morning. It was time for her to get up and start the day. She stretched her arms over her head and took the time to look around her room. She loved her room. She had decorated it like something from the Ernest Hemmingway era. She had a queen size four-poster bed with white curtains around it, which billowed gently beneath the ceiling fan. There were palm plants on the floor and ferns hanging from the ceiling.

Bryan and her Dad had bought her three little golden monkeys that sat on her dresser. The one in the middle held a candle that looked like it had bamboo on the sides and made the whole room smell like vanilla. She caught a glimpse of herself in the mirror and, as always felt a momentary surprise to see herself with dark hair. As a young teenager, she had started using a temporary brown dye on her bright blonde hair to disguise herself. She had to color it every five weeks or so to keep the blonde from seeping through, but she couldn't seem to bring herself to use a permanent color. She always thought she might feel safer in a few weeks and would let the natural color return, but so far she couldn't do it. They had even changed their last name to Walker.

Even moving around the country she had still been recognized sometimes and even once was too much. With the brown hair and a pair of glasses she didn't need, no one ever recognized her. Being a grown woman now, and with so much time passing, she could probably get by without the disguise. But she liked the lack of attention she got by just blending in. She had read in a magazine that people tend to notice blondes more.

All of a sudden, her bedroom door flew open and a warm little body jumped into bed with her. "Mom, Mom, I woke up before you! That means I can start staying up later at night, right?" Bryan's eyes were shining. What an unexpected joy he was, she thought. She had gotten pregnant with him while still in college. The professor she had an affair with turned out to be married with two other children. That was when she had dropped out of college in her senior year and they had moved from Austin to Dallas. So far, Bryan had never really asked many questions about his Father. He just seemed to accept that he lived with a Grandfather instead.

*   *   *   *

In his own room, Sam was also waking up. He could hear Bryan and Shannon laughing. Like everything else in his life, he had taken it pretty well when Shannon had gotten pregnant. He was happy to have someone else to share their life with. He philosophy was, what was meant to be, was meant to be. Although he did wish she was happily married and worried secretly that he was the reason that she wasn't. She had changed so much since the tragedy of 1993. Where as before she was feisty, now she let people walk all over her.

She didn't know that he had gotten a certain college professor fired before they left Austin. It would be a cold day in hell before that professor ever taught again. The man, Doug Collins, had made so many threats Sam had to put out a restraining order against him and they had relocated to Dallas. He might be stuck in a wheel chair, but that didn't mean he was helpless. Sam ran his hand through hair that was now more gray than blonde. He was still a handsome, athletic man at fifty years old. He had played wheelchair basketball for a number of years.

He was also coaching Bryan in baseball. The boy was a natural. He had been playing for a year now and showed ability far beyond his seven years. He was tall for his age too, maybe a little on the thin side, but there was time for filling out. He looked over at the picture of Bryan next to his bed. With his bright blond hair and a scatter of freckles across his nose, he looked almost just like Shannon had at that age. His thoughts were interrupted as Bryan knocked on his door, "Grandpa, are you ready for breakfast?"

*   *   *   *

Later as they were about to finish eating, Shannon had a smile on her face. "I have a surprise for the two of you!" She had to laugh at the looks on their faces. They both stopped what they were doing and looked at her with their eyebrows raised. It was the same exact expression on both their faces. "How would you like for the three of us to go to the Cowboy game this Sunday?"

As Bryan jumped up and down, squealing, Sam asked, "How did you get tickets to this game? It's against the Giants and has been sold out for weeks."

Bryan suddenly got quiet as he waited for her answer. Shannon pulled the three tickets out of her purse. "I've had them for weeks. I just didn't want to tell you until I knew I could get the weekend off."

Bryan looked worried. "Mom? Are you sure you'll get the weekend off? They won't try to make you work will they? Like they usually do?"

This was the reason she had waited so long to tell them about the tickets, but with only two days to go, she felt pretty good about it. "Well, Bryan, I haven't taken a day off in over two weeks. I really don't think there will be a problem," she smiled at him to reassure him. "Come on now and finish getting ready for school."

CHAPTER 3

▼

Shannon was already at her desk writing work orders from the messages left with the answering service overnight. Ms. Norman's disposal was stopped up again. Larry, the maintenance man, was going to be irritated about that. She missed the old maintenance man, Robert. He had married and moved to California the year before. He was always in a good mood and had really gotten along well with both the residents and the staff. Actually most of the maintenance men she had worked with were great guys. Larry didn't have the best personality, but he did get a lot of work done.

She looked at the clock wondering where everyone was, when the front door opened and Heather rushed in. She stopped when she saw that Shannon was the only one there.

All the lights were on and she could smell the coffee. "Where are Camille and Amber? Don't tell me they're late again. Have you called them to see where they are?" When Shannon shook her head no, Heather snapped at her, "Well don't just sit there, call them! Have you opened the models yet?" Shannon nodded as she was dialing Camille's phone number. When Heather was in a bad mood, it didn't do any good to try to get a word in.

"Hello?" Camille sounded like she was still sleeping.

"Hey, Camille, Heather wanted me to call ..." before she could finish what she had been about to say, Camille was yelling.

"Oh, shit! Don't tell me you didn't cover for me. Tell her I'm out opening the models. I'll be there as fast as I can." When Shannon didn't say anything, Camille said, "Oh, you probably told her you already opened them didn't you? I should have known Miss Goody, Goody. Well you're a lousy liar any way; get Amber to tell her I'm out on property."

"Well, Amber's not here yet either." Shannon wasn't sure what to do.

Camille was letting out a string of curses. Then she got quiet for a minute. "Well that's okay, she'll get over it. Hey, um, Shannon," her voice suddenly sounded cajoling, "since you got me in trouble today, can you do me a favor? I have a date Sunday and I need you to work for me."

Shannon's stomach knotted in dread of having to turn her down. "Oh no, I'm really sorry Camille, but I have plans for this Sunday too. I have tickets to go to the game with Bryan and my Dad."

Camille's voice got hard, "But Shannon, this is a date with Marc in fifteen twenty two. You know how long I've wanted to go out with him." Shannon knew his wife had just moved out two days ago. "That's more important than just some stupid family thing. You can do that any time. Please?" she said sweetly. "You owe me."

Shannon wasn't sure what she thought she owed her for, but she knew she couldn't disappoint her family. "I'm sorry, but I promised ..."

"Well fuck you!" Camille slammed the phone down.

With a sigh, Shannon replaced the receiver. She knew there would be hell to pay later. When she noticed that her hands and feet start to get cold, she willed away a panic attack. She had been having them since '93, but after years of therapy and even some medication, she had learned to control them to some extent.

Heathers' high heels clicked as she returned to the room. She was petite, not quite five feet two inches tall and always wore the biggest heels she could find. She also wore her light brown hair up in a clip on the back of her head to give herself added height. "Shannon, are you day dreaming again? No wonder I'm the only one around here that ever gets any thing done. Listen, I've got to … uhm, run some errands today. Think you can handle things around here alone until Camille and Amber drag their asses in?" Before she could respond Heather interrupted again. "Oh yeah you need to walk twelve thirteen this morning. I think that bitch has skipped out on me. She still hasn't paid her rent and today is the sixth." She was still mumbling about people taking advantage of her as she left the room.

Shannon wrote it down in her day planner in the ever-growing tasks column. Amber hurried into the room, looking down the hall to see if Heather was in yet. "Does she know I'm late again? Where is Camille? Let me guess she's late again too right?" As Amber rambled on, the phone rang.

"Thank you for calling Sherwood Village, this is Shannon." There was no reply. "Hello?—Hello?" Still no reply. As she started to hang up she thought she heard someone breathing. "Hello, is anyone there?" Then she heard a weird laughing sound that sent chills up her spine.

"Oh, I'm here all right—Shannon." A low male voice replied, laughing again as he hung up the phone.

As Shannon replaced the receiver she just stared at it for a couple of seconds. "That was weird," she said under her breath. When Amber asked her what that was all about, Shannon explained it to her.

"Oh man, maybe we're going to start getting those obscene phone calls again. Did he ask you what color panties you're wearing? Let me answer it next time!" Amber was laughing, with a mischievous look on her pretty face.

"Be my guest," was all Shannon had to say.

The front door opened as Camille strolled in. She gave Shannon a dirty look as she went down the hall to Heathers office and shut the door.

"Jeez, what's wrong with her? I'm staying away from her today." Amber stared down the hallway.

Shannon just shrugged. She knew Camille was still mad at her because she didn't want to work for her on Sunday. Trying not to even think about what must be going on behind the closed door, she got out her guest cards to do some follow up. She didn't really like doing follow up because she felt like she was just bothering people. Luckily her closing ratios were so good she didn't have too much to follow up on.

After a few minutes, Camille came out of Heathers office with a satisfied smile on her face. She gave Shannon a look of superiority, then actually stuck out her tongue at her. "Heather wants to talk to you," was all she said. With her hands and feet starting to get cold again, Shannon went to Heather's office.

Heather was looking into the mirror, fussing with her hair as she walked in. "Shannon, Camille told me how rude you were to her on the phone this morning. I must say I am disappointed in you. All she did was ask you to work on Sunday. It's only twelve o'clock to five o'clock. I mean really, it's not like you have a life or anything." She turned around from the mirror. "I told her you would work for her this Sunday, and I don't want to hear any arguments from you about this."

At Shannon's look of dismay, she hurried on, "Oh come on! You know you're my best leasing agent anyway. We have four more move outs this month. We need to get those leased up. I want to win Manager of The Year at this years Christmas party. Last year they gave it to that bitch Beverly. She makes me sick. How could they choose that fat cow over me?"

"I … I can't work this Sunday. I already told Camille that I have plans with Bryan and Dad. We're going to the Cowboy game. I've already bought the tickets and it's a sold out game." Shannon had already worked six straight weekends even though they were supposed to alternate.

Heather looked incredulous, "Are you arguing with me? If the game is sold out you can make extra money by selling the tickets. Or your Dad can ask one of his friends to go. Plus, Camille is already gone. She took a couple of vacation days because this is so important to her. She needs to go shopping." Heather picked up her purse, "I have to run do those errands I mentioned earlier, don't forget to check to see if twelve thirteen skipped out. I can't believe that bitch would do that to me," she muttered as she hurried out. "Oh yeah, take Larry with you so he can check how much damage might have been done to the apartment.

With her head down Shannon knew she was going to have to disappoint Bryan and Dad again. Grabbing the key to twelve thirteen out of the key box, she decided to go check it first to see if indeed the girl, Kimberly Orwell had moved out. If she had, she could make notes about any damages herself and not have to bother Larry. He had been irritable lately since he had to fire Mike Reynolds, his assistant maintenance man. Now with only a porter and a temp, he had more than enough work to do until they could hire someone else.

*   *   *   *

Even though it was near the back of the property, Shannon decided to walk to building twelve instead of taking one of the golf carts they used to tour apartments. She figured it would help relieve some of the stress she was feeling. It really was a beautiful day. Dallas didn't really have much of what most people considered fall weather. But at least it wasn't as hot as August. Above the apartment buildings the big Texas sky was a piercingly bright blue. She waved to Ephram Peters, one of her favorite residents. As she turned her head to the West she noticed storm clouds in the distance. The wind was also picking up.

"Good, I hope we get some fresh rain. They keep saying in the news how much we need it." She was trying to think of anything besides how much she was going to upset Bryan about the Cowboy game. The apartment was on the third floor and she nimbly ran up the three flights. She was trying to remember if she had ever met Kimberly before.

She knocked on the door a couple of times and waited. Finally when there was no answer, she just used the key she had grabbed from the key box. As soon as she opened the door she heard music coming from inside. "Hello, Ms. Orwell?" The apartment was dim because all the blinds were closed. There was some light coming from the bedroom though.

"Ms. Orwell? Anybody here?" The music was also coming from the bedroom. It sounded like a slow mournful song from Pink Floyd. The apartment had a strange, kind of metallic smell that had her head spinning. She walked hesitantly towards the bedroom.

There was a small lamp on, on the night stand that cast shadows around the room. A chill ran up her spine. When she saw the girl lying on the bed she jumped. "Oh! I'm so sorry. I thought you would hear me knock. Didn't you hear me calling you? Ms. Orwell?" As she moved closer to the bed she froze, she could see something was very wrong.

The girl had long blond hair spread out over the red pillows. She was nude upon the red sheets. Shannon's brain was taking all of this in before she could really comprehend the situation. She noticed only the top half of the sheet was red. Closer to the bottom it was pale pink. Was the red? … was she? … is she dead?

It was then she noticed with screaming horror—the long oozing gash across the girls' throat. When she heard a noise behind her she jumped again and came out of the daze. "Oh my God! Oh my God! She's dead!"

As she stumbled out of the apartment her mind flashed back to blood on the schoolroom floor, the dead policeman, and her father lying there in a pool of blood.

With her heart pounding and feeling lightheaded she ran all the way back to the office as it started to rain.

CHAPTER 4

▼

Hours later she was still at the office, long after closing time. She was seated on a sofa in the clubroom with a blanket around her shoulders and her feet tucked beneath her. She occasionally had shivers that were hard to control and she was freezing despite the blanket.

The detective questioning her, Detective Blake, was being very patient but it seemed like he kept asking the same questions over and over again. The detective was a black man, well under six feet tall and balding with a little bit of a potbelly, although he had an unmistakable air of authority.

"Ms. Walker, you said you heard a noise. Was the noise in the apartment, or coming from outside? Can you describe the noise at all? Do you think someone was still in the apartment?" He could tell by the look on her face that she hadn't even thought of that. She started to shiver again. "Look it's getting late, why don't you go home and try to eat some dinner, try to relax and tomorrow you can come down to the police station. Do you live alone?"

Shannon was so grateful to be able to leave at last that she stated to babble," No, no I don't live alone. I live with my father and my son. I know they must be worried about me and I really do need to get home. I need to go home now. I just live a few buildings away." She jumped to her feet and the blanket fell to the floor. She looked beseechingly at

Detective Blake, "There wasn't anything I could do for her, was there? I wasn't really thinking at all, I kinda, kinda just froze. Then I ran." She lowered her head as tears fell again.

Detective Blake patted her shoulder awkwardly, "Hey, I promise you, there wasn't anything you or anyone else could have done at that point. You did the right thing." He motioned to a nearby police officer. "Cunningham, please escort Ms. Walker to her apartment." He stood for a minute and watched them walk away. Poor little thing, she looked so shaken and dazed. He knew this sort of thing would take a long time to get over. As an idea formed in his mind he reached for his cell phone.

*   *   *   *

Shannon walked on trembling legs beside the young policeman. Actually he stayed a couple of steps behind her. The night was dark and she glanced behind her to make sure he was still there. He was glancing right and left as though he too was a little spooked.

"You don't think the mur-..." she stopped and had to swallow a couple of times, "the man who did that could still be around do you?" Shannon's heart started to accelerate again.

Officer Cunningham stopped and looked at her seriously, "Well, you can't be too sure, can you mam?" Then he looked a little abashed, "I've just been out of the academy a short while and they drill it into us to stay on the alert at all times. I'm sure you'll be fine tonight though." When she looked doubtful he added with a small smile that was probably meant to be reassuring, "Take my word for it." He stood up straighter; she thought to look more professional.

Still feeling weak and sick, Shannon was almost pitifully grateful when they finally reached her apartment.

CHAPTER 5

▼

As soon as Shannon walked through her front door, Bryan started asking questions so fast she couldn't even keep up with him. "Mom, is it true that somebody's dead? Was it a girl or a guy? Was it really a murder? Bobby said Caitlin's mom told Mrs. Rivers, and he heard Mrs. Rivers tell his mom that you found the body. Did you mom? Find the body I mean." Confusion crossed over his expressive little face for a minute. He noticed how tired his mother looked. Her eyes looked different, kind of red and swollen. "Aw mom, was it gross? Are you okay?"

Sam interrupted, "Come on Bryan. I'm sure your Mom will tell us all about it. You promised me you would take a shower when your Mother got home. You go on and jump in the shower while your Mom eats some supper. She's probably starving and needs some strength to answer all you questions." Surprisingly—quietly, the boy did as he was asked, with a last lingering look at his Mother.

"Thanks Dad. I do need some time." She avoided her Dad's eyes because she really hadn't had time to decide how much to tell him. She knew he worried about her. He had told her before not to walk vacant apartments alone. He didn't know she did it all the time.

"Come on and sit down Shannon. I made pork chops, steamed vegetables and macaroni and cheese." He wheeled himself into the kitchen and returned with her plate on a tray across his lap. "So, do you want to talk about it? There are so many conflicting stories going around this complex, I'd like to know how much of it is true. But if you're too tired we can talk later."

As always he put her needs ahead of his own. She reached over and took his hand. For the first time since she found the body, she started to thaw out a little. She smiled at him in reassurance. "It has been pretty awful. I went to see if someone had skipped out because she hadn't paid her rent yet. And yes, I did go alone. Larry was busy so I didn't want to ask him. At first I just thought she was asleep. As soon as I realized she was dead I just ran back to the office. I don't even remember the trip back. One minute I was in the apartment, the next minute I was back in the office. Almost like I morphed there or something." A hysterical laugh escaped her lips. Horrified she clapped a hand over her mouth as she fought back tears. How could she laugh at anything after that poor girl had just been killed like that? Besides she couldn't let herself cry again. Bryan would be out any minute.

"Come on honey, eat something. I kept it warm for you. We'll talk more about it later. You know what they say, this too shall pass. I'm sure the police will take care of it." Sam made up his mind to call the police tomorrow morning.

*   *   *   *

Detective Blake was back at the crime scene. The Medical Examiner had finished and they were about to transport the body. "Hey, wait just a minute guys. Manning is on his way. I want him to see this."

The girl's body was laid out on the bed as if posed. Both legs were straight down and her hands were folded across her chest. Her throat had been cut. The long blond hair spread out across the pillow had turned out to be a wig. Her real hair was dark auburn.

They had found a Kleenex on the nightstand that looked like she had used it to wipe off all her makeup.

Blake thought that was a little weird because his wife always removed her make up in the bathroom, in front of the mirror. The rest of the apartment was in perfect order. It was very clean, nothing looked out of place.

None of the door and window locks looked like they had been tampered with. He thought again of the maintenance man that had recently been fired. Had he keep any keys? As Manning came through the door Blake turned to talk to him.

CHAPTER 6

▼

The next morning as Shannon prepared for work, she fretted that her eyes still looked a little swollen. Her head was hammering too, so she took a couple of aspirin and hoped they would kick in soon. She jumped as the phone rang shrilly beside her.

As usual Heather's voice sounded pissed off, "Well Shannon, it looks like you got your way. Rita called from the corporate office and said she wants you to take a few days off. She's afraid the reporters will hound us more if you're here because you found the body and we're under strict orders not to talk to them. You're not to come back to work until Monday. So it looks like you've got yourself a three-day weekend while the rest of us have to do all the work. Camille is not happy that she had to cancel her plans because of you."

Nonplussed for a minute, Shannon didn't know what to say. She knew she could really use the three days off but it still made her feel guilty. "I'm, I'm sorry Heather. Tell Cam" … she stopped when she heard Heather slam down the phone.

    ✳   ✳   ✳   ✳

Hearing Sam and Bryan in the living room she went to tell them the news. "Well, guess what? That was Heather on the phone. She said the corporate office wants me to take the next three days off." It was such an unusual statement; the two guys were quiet for a moment.

Then, "Yippee! That means we can go to The Cowboy Game for sure!" Bryan was ecstatic. With a jolt Shannon realized she had completely forgotten about the game. Good thing she had not gotten around to telling them she wasn't going to get to go.

She looked at her Dad. Knowing what she was thinking he smiled at her and Bryan. "We sure can! Bryan you better hurry. The school bus will be here any minute. Don't forget your binder again today." After Bryan had kissed them both goodbye he left for school with a big grin still on his face.

Sam turned to Shannon, "I know what you're thinking. You're wondering if it's right to go have fun at the game, at a time like this. Shannon, I think if we've learned anything, it's that life goes on. And you know how Bryan would feel if we had to miss the game."

"Yeah, I know you're right. I wouldn't do that to him. But I almost had to." She told him about the stunt Camille had pulled yesterday. "Anyway, I better call Detective Blake. I have to go into the police department today. They asked me tons of questions yesterday, but maybe today I can be of more help. Some of the shock has worn off and my mind feels a little more clear." She went into her bedroom to make the call.

A few minutes later she came out again looking relieved. "Guess what? I don't have to go in today after all. He said they'll call me if anything else comes up." She looked around the apartment. It didn't look as if it needed much cleaning. With a smile she looked at Sam. "Wanna watch All My Children?"

CHAPTER 7

▼

Sunday dawned bright and clear. "The high today is only supposed to be seventy two degrees, a perfect day for football!" Sam announced as he folded the newspaper and put it next to his seat. Shannon laughed. It was hard to tell who was the most excited between Sam and Bryan. Although she knew she was right there with them. Football must run in their blood. She was driving the van with her Dad and Bryan in the back seats. Sam's seat was next to the sliding van door and equipped to make it easy to get his chair in and out.

As they got closer to Texas Stadium, they could see the parking lots were already starting to fill up, even though they were really quite early. After unloading everything and everyone from the van, they joyfully began the walk to the famous stadium.

Years before, after playing at The Cotton Bowl in Dallas, The Cowboys wanted a stadium built exclusively for them. Construction began in the late nineteen sixties. The cost even then was around thirty five million dollars.

Although they're still called the *Dallas* Cowboys, the stadium was built in Irving Texas, a suburb of Dallas. So they just named it Texas stadium. Opening day came on October twenty fourth, nineteen seventy one. The stadium is partially domed, with a hole in the middle of the roof that is supposed to keep the rain off the fans and still allow the field to be open to the elements.

There are over sixty five thousand blue seats around the gridiron. The stadiums amenities include three hundred eighty one glassed in, and most importantly air conditioned, luxury suites. There is a stadium club for parties and banquets, usually with lots of food, drinks and entertainment. Shannon had once been to a meeting there for the Dallas Apartment Association.

It was hard for Sam to believe that they were already building a new stadium. This one was to be in Arlington, Texas. It was to have a re-tractable roof, and really be state of the art.

"Wow, smell that? Why is everyone bar-b-queuing in the parking lot?" Bryan's head swiveled from side to side as he tried to see everything at once.

"They're having tailgate parties Bryan. Remember, you've seen it on T.V." Sam ruffled the hair on his grandson's head.

"Oh yeah! But I didn't know it'd smell so good. Mom, I'm hungry. Can we tailgate party next time we come?" Bryan was so thrilled to be there, that he all but danced all the way to their seats. They were sitting in a special section where Sam could just park his chair next to Bryan's seat. They had a great view of the field. There are five flags hanging from the roof celebrating the Cowboys five Super Bowl championships. Shannon enjoyed watching all the people and the pumped up atmosphere. "Oh, look there's the quarter back!"

"Grandpa? Are they really gonna build a new stadium?" Bryan rocked his seat bottom up and down.

"That's what they're saying. It's going to be in Arlington near the Ballpark at Arlington where the Rangers play baseball, and Six Flags Over Texas amusement park. I'll bet it's really gonna be something."

Shannon agreed, "I think it's a perfect location, halfway between Dallas and Fort Worth. That way it'll be easy for everyone to get there." Although it was called the Dallas/Ft. Worth metroplex, there was a huge difference between the two cities. Ft. Worth was nicknamed 'Cowtown' from the early years in the 1840s while Dallas was considered by most as much more sophisticated.

Dallas was started as a new settlement in the early 1840s as well, by a man named John Neely Bryan. He named the settlement 'Dallas' after a friend, but it has really never been known just who that friend was. It wasn't incorporated as a town until 1856.

Outlaws were common during the 1870s, like Doc Holliday and Belle Starr. Doc came to Dallas trying to improve his health. He opened a dentist's office, but then turned to gambling. After killing a man in a gun fight in 1875, he had to leave Dallas in a hurry.

Belle Starr began her adventures in Dallas as a saloon girl that sang and danced. She later harbored outlaws and stolen horses.

When most people think of Dallas, depending on their age they either think of November 22, 1963, the day President John F. Kennedy was assassinated, the television series called Dallas about the lives of the rich Ewing family, or the Dallas Cowboys.

She looked around the stadium, delighted to be there and that she got to watch everything going on.

*   *   *   *

Not too far away, someone else was watching. *"There she is. There they are. Just look at them. Like they don't have a care in the world. How quickly they forget. That's okay; let her have her fun for one day. Her little world is about to change. Big time!"* From his vantage point, he could keep the binoculars on them most of the time and it would just look like he was looking at the field. Although he did study Sam and Bryan and even look at some of the action on the field, he just couldn't help himself and kept them trained on Shannon most of the time.

Shannon felt the fine hair on the back of her neck stand up. For a moment she felt startled and alarmed. Then she laughed at herself thinking it was just the adrenalin of being there. They still had almost an hour before kick-off and she was determined to make the most of their day. The sun was shining through the famous hole in the roof of the enormous stadium, with fluffy white clouds drifting by. The apartment complex and the murder seemed unreal and very far away.

*   *   *   *

That night Shannon was happy, as she was about to drift off to sleep. The Cowboys had beaten the Giants. Not by much, but a win was a win, especially since losing Troy, Michael and Emmitt. She missed watching the triplets, as they were called, and thought it might be a long time before the Cowboys reclaimed the Super Bowl. But she hoped it would be sooner than later. After all, she thought, they are America's Team.

CHAPTER 8

▼

Shannon was just opening the door to the office the next morning when she felt a presence behind her. The man had walked up so quietly she hadn't heard him until he was right next to her. She jumped and tried to suppress a shriek. "Sorry, ma'am. Didn't mean to startle you." The man reached around her and held open the door.

"Oh! Oh. Well, we're not really open yet. We don't open until nine o'clock." Feeling nervous at his close proximity, she took a couple of steps back from him.

He gave her a slow, lazy smile, as he looked straight into her eyes. "You must be Shannon. I'm Luke." He held out his hand. She took it automatically, but he could tell by her expression she still didn't know who he was. "I'm the new maintenance man. I'm taking Mike Reynolds place. I started last Friday."

Feeling a little bit silly at being so obviously scared of him, Shannon blushed. "I'm sorry. No one told me we had hired someone. I know Larry must be happy to have some help at last. Come on in. Larry is probably out on the grounds or in his office around back."

"Yeah, he is. I was just talking to him. He gave me my own set of keys, guess that makes me official." He held up his hand with at least four or five keys on a key ring and jingled it back and forth. "I took call for him this weekend, so today is actually my fourth day on the job. I heard about what happened last week." He took her hand in his once again. "Are you okay?"

Shannon thought that he looked genuinely concerned. She smiled at him, "Yeah, I'm doing better, thanks."

They took a moment to study each other. Luke was surprised. From the way the other girls talked about her, he had thought she was going to be unattractive. She was really pretty when she smiled at him like that, with a shy dimple at each side of her mouth. She had long dark hair pulled back in a tight braid. Her glasses where a bit librarian looking, and didn't sit quite right on the small straight nose, but behind them were big blue eyes, more wide then round. Her skin looked soft and smooth, and was beginning to blush again as he continued to look at her. She didn't look like she wore much makeup besides some slight lip-gloss and mascara. That was unusual in Dallas.

Shannon felt a strange warmth creep over her as she looked up at him. He was tall; she'd guess about three or four inches over six foot. His hair was kind of a caramel blonde color, a little long, like he was overdue for a haircut, but she thought it suited him. His eyes were crystal blue, lighter than her own and seemed to look deeply into hers. But it was his mouth that really held her attention. It was full, and actually beautifully sculptured like in the romance novels she occasionally read. She suddenly realized that he was still holding her hand and pulled hers away quickly as she heard the door open. He was fascinated that what had been a slight pink blush on her cheeks now turned into a bright red.

Heather was coming in at the same time as Camille. "Well, I see the two of you have met. Shannon you haven't even turned on all the lights or made the coffee yet. That's okay, Camille can do it. I need to talk to you in my office." Then she turned her attention to Luke. The tone of her voice changed one hundred percent. She all but purred, "Good morning Luke. Did you have any problems this weekend? You know I told you, you could call me anytime."

"Oh, he didn't need you Heather. He had me!" Camille slinked up to Luke and put her hand possessively on his shoulder. She smiled at Heather like she had scored some kind of victory. Luke just stepped back, and let Camille's hand fall.

"I have everything I need, ladies. If you'll excuse me I'll see you later." He turned back to Shannon. "It was really nice to meet you." He turned and left the room. As soon as he was gone, Heather and Camille stopped smiling and stalked away. Calling over her shoulder, Heather reminded Shannon to come to her office.

"Why didn't you call me as soon as you found the body last week? This is my property and I was almost the last to know. Do you know how that made me look? I know you liked all the attention, but I had a right to be the one to handle everything. By the time I got here, that Detective Blake just—dismissed me. Me! I'm the Manager here. Not you. From now on when anything happens, you notify me first." Heather was clearly angry.

"I'm sorry Heather. All I could think of was to just call the police. I was panicked and upset. Larry was asking me a lot of questions, then the police got here so fast, and it's all kind of a blur. I promise …"

"Yeah, I saw how helpless you looked., surrounded by all those men. No one paid me any attention at all. Didn't they think I was upset? I am the Manager here," she repeated. "Anyway, stay away from Luke. I saw how you two were looking at each other. I promise you, missy, he is more man than you could handle. Now go help Camille open up. Oh yeah, yall need to get started on the Halloween party."

Amber had arrived while she was in Heathers office. "Hey, Shannon. You doing okay? God, I know that must have scared the shit out of you last week. I'm glad it wasn't me. I heard it was really gory, with blood everywhere from where her throat was slit open. We're never going to be able to lease that apartment again. Anyway, I felt sorry for you and I'm glad you got the weekend off. It had the added benefit of pissing off Camille. She bitched about you the whole weekend." Amber had the ability to be friends with who ever was in front of her. Shannon knew without a doubt that Amber must have joined in the bitching.

"Thanks, Amber. I feel a lot better now. I just hope they hurry and find out who would do something like that." Shannon put her purse in the desk drawer and opened her day planner. She felt a little lost after taking three whole days off.

Amber came over and sat on the corner of her desk. "You know who I'll bet it was? Mike. Remember how weird he was and how pissed off he was when he got fired?"

"Weird? I thought you had a thing with him." She looked up at Amber to see how serious she was.

Amber managed to look guilty. "I did not have a thing with him. I just said I thought he was cute. He came over for dinner once. Just think, I could've had a killer in my own home! Did you know they found pictures of us in his apartment? All of us, even you. He was a weirdo all right. Hey, speaking of men, have you seen the new guy yet? Oh—My—God! I've never seen anyone that sexy in real life. He kind of reminds me of Brad Pitt.

"Brad Pitt? He does not, you think all good looking men look like Brad Pitt." Camille had walked back into the room as they were talking. "Besides, I think he's gay." She plopped herself into the chair behind her desk and tried to look bored.

Their office was actually like a big reception room. They each had a desk and there was a big round table for sitting with clients while they signed all the paper work. There were expensive paintings on the walls, beautiful thick rugs on the tile floors and big lush plants everywhere. It was almost like working in a mansion.

Amber was indignant on behalf of Luke. "He is not gay! You're just saying that because you threw yourself at him all weekend and he didn't even flirt back. I think he's nice. And he has the cutest butt I've ever seen. I just saw him strap on a tool belt and almost creamed my jeans, if you know what I mean," she laughed.

Knowing they could spar over Luke all day, Shannon told them Heather wanted them to get started planning the Halloween party. "Ugh, just think how many kids are gonna come out of the woodwork for that. They'll tear this place apart. Too bad we can't have all adult properties like the good old days." Camille hated having anything to do with children. "Why don't you plan it Shannon? You have a kid yourself so you know what makes them happy."

"Hey, I know! We have two clubhouses, why don't we have a kid's party at the one by the playground, and the grown up one here?" Amber's face was bright at being the one to come up with the idea.

Camille even jumped on board. "Amber, I think you're on to something. Now that sounds like fun. We can have a costume party with a prize for the best costume. Shannon, you can be in charge of the one for kids and I'll be in charge of the one for the adults."

"Hey! It was my idea. Why can't I be in charge?" Amber was starting to pout. The rest of the day was spent planning the parties and showing apartments. Luckily the murder the week before didn't get too much news time because on the same night there was a Presidential Address on all the networks. No one asked about it all day.

CHAPTER 9

▼

As the week went by things felt like they were getting back to normal, with the exception of Luke being around. Even some of the female residents were finding reasons to come in and ask about him, he was causing quite a stir. Although he maintained a polite distance from Camille, he was friendly to Amber and for some reason; he was extra nice to Shannon.

One day Shannon was out walking the property in the afternoon and saw him bending down talking to Bryan at the playground. When Luke saw Shannon, he gave Bryan's baseball cap a tug and stood up to wave her over. "Hey Shannon. You didn't tell me you had a jock for a son. He says he plays football and baseball."

"Yeah, Mom. Luke said he played baseball when he was little too. He's gonna pitch to me sometime. He even has a Nolan Ryan rookie card, but his Dad gave it to him when he was little so he can't trade me for it. I told him I have over four hundred baseball cards, don't I Mom?"

Shannon felt a pang as she watched the two of them. Sometimes she felt guilty that Bryan didn't have a Dad. She nodded seriously, "He does have quite an extensive collection. Some of them were my Dads when he was young. I wasn't aware that the two of you had met." She looked inquiringly at Luke.

"Well he does look a lot like you, except for the blond hair. It's easy to see where he gets his good looks." Luke wagged his eyebrows at her, making Bryan laugh.

"Hey Mom, let's invite Luke to eat dinner with us tonight. He can meet Grandpa and I can show him my baseball cards. Please?" He looked up at Luke. "Mom's a real good cook."

Shannon was caught off guard for a minute. She wasn't sure she wanted Luke to come to her house. She didn't feel like she really knew him well enough and it would be sure to cause talk if anyone found out about it. On the other hand she knew it would be fun for both Bryan and Sam to have someone else to show those cards to.

Seeing her hesitation Luke grinned and said, "A home cooked meal? Sounds great! I am getting pretty tired of take out." He had such an easygoing way about him that Shannon relaxed. Standing there with the bright sunlight shining on his hair and in his clear blue eyes she realized that it wasn't really that he looked so much like Brad Pitt, they just had the same kind of—well, male beauty.

"Well okay, how about seven o'clock? You do like tofu and bean sprouts don't you?" The confused and slightly repugnant look that crossed his face had Bryan and Shannon both laughing. "I'm just kidding. We're having spaghetti." Luke sighed with relief.

"Well, I'm going to put this notice on a resident's door. I'll see you at seven o'clock?" At Luke's nod she turned to walk away. Luke stood where he was and watched her. All the girls in the office wore a uniform consisting of khaki shorts, pink polo shirts and white tennis shoes. As he admired the muscles in her legs and the gentle sway of her hips, he noticed Bryan staring up at him. He had never seen a man look at his mother that way.

"Do you think she's pretty?" He demanded. "Cause I do, but no one ever asks her to go on a date. I know the other girls in the office date a lot cause I hear them talking about it all the time." He thought for a minute, "Maybe she should wear more makeup?"

Luke laughed. "Bryan, your mother is beautiful. My guess is that she doesn't want to date because she would rather spend her time with you. She probably turns down lots of dates you don't know about.

"Well, why don't you ask her out? I can tell she likes you 'cause she teased you about the tofu. She doesn't usually joke with anybody but Grandpa, and me, and sometimes my friend Timmy. But he's too young to ask her out."

He looked so serious that Luke had to ask, "Why do you want your Mom to go on a date?"

"Because Grandpa said she should. I heard him talking to his friends about it one night when they thought I was asleep on the couch. They said it's not good for a woman her age to be without a man. Grandpa thinks it's because of him, but I think it might be me. A lot of guys don't like kids. But you do, I can tell." He grinned up at Luke with all the openness a boy of seven years can have." But I want to get to know you better first. That's why I want you to come to dinner. To make sure you're the right guy."

Luke was perplexed for a minute. "Hey, wait a minute little man. I appreciate your honesty, but you're moving a little too fast. There is a lot more involved here. What do you say we just take it slow and see what happens? And you're right, I do like kids. I used to be one. Are you sure you're just seven years old. It seems like you've been doing some pretty serious thinking."

"I'm seven and a half." With a steadfast look on his young face Bryan looked straight into Luke's eyes, "I love my Mom and I want her to be happy." Luke didn't know if it was the freckles across the small nose or the crooked baseball cap, but at that moment he felt his heart squeeze. This was a fantastic kid.

CHAPTER 10

▼

Shannon didn't know why she felt nervous that night as she prepared for dinner. The sauce had been simmering for a couple of hours and the apartment smelled delicious. Sam and Bryan were in the living room playing a game of chess and there was nothing else to do in the kitchen for the moment. She took the time to go back to her bedroom and see how she looked, which she knew was silly. This wasn't a date. He was just coming to dinner and to see Bryan's cards. He must be lonely. She realized she didn't really know anything about him. She just assumed he was new in town because he said he hadn't had a home cooked meal in a while.

She noticed her braid was coming a little unraveled and long tendrils and curls were starting to escape. Quickly and efficiently she re-braided her long hair. Because she thought she looked tired she added a little more makeup than usual. She hesitated as she reached for her favorite bottle of perfume. Then firmly pushed the bottle away. "This is not a date stupid," she muttered to herself. She looked at her jeans and t-shirt and decided they would be just fine.

When she heard the timer for the fresh bread go off she hurried into the kitchen. Just as she had everything ready, the doorbell rang. Since Bryan and her Dad were just about to finish their game she went to open the door. She was stunned when Luke held out a single white rose. He had a sheepish grin on his face as if he too were slightly embarrassed. He also brought a bottle of wine.

"Hi," he held out the bottle, "I thought this would go with the spaghetti." Bryan had started to run to the door, when he saw Luke standing there with a rose and the wine; he stopped suddenly, not wanting to intrude. Oh boy, this was perfect. He was glad he had had that little talk with Luke. When he noticed how awkward the two seemed he said, "Hey Luke, come on in. You're just in time."

Realizing that she had just been standing there staring at him, Shannon felt like a fool.

"Well, how lovely." She took the rose. "Thank you Luke. Please, come in." When Luke entered the living room he saw the man in a wheel chair. "Luke, this is my Dad, Sam. Dad this is Luke, uh … I'm sorry Luke I don't know your last name.

"Johnson. Lucas Johnson." The two men shook hands. Sam was giving him the look typical of fathers everywhere when meeting a man interested in their daughter. Looking around Luke said, "Wow, something smells great!" he saw the table beautifully set with a large bowl of spaghetti, another large bowl of tossed salad and wonder of wonders a big loaf of freshly cooked bread. When his stomach gave a loud growl, Bryan hooted with laughter and Sam smiled broadly.

"Shannon let's feed this man, I'm starving too. When I know she's making spaghetti, I don't eat lunch so I can save room. Nobody makes it better than Shannon."

The meal and the whole evening passed with so much laughter and teasing, it felt like they had all known each other forever. Sam was delighted to see the blushes on Shannon's cheeks and the sparkle in her eyes. Bryan smiled so much his face hurt. But Sam did notice that whenever he tried to question Luke about his family and past, he usually changed the subject. Being an expert on doing the same thing, he had to wonder why.

As Luke was about to leave there was a knock on the door. Timmy was standing there with a worried look on his face. "Hello Ms. Shannon, I'm afraid I'm in a little bit of trouble."

He looked so miserable Shannon was concerned. "What is it Timmy? Is there anything I can do?"

"I was supposed to water Ms. Springer's plants for her today 'cause she's out of town, but I forgot to go by the office and get the key before yall closed. She's real picky about her plants and she's been out of town for four days. I'm afraid if I wait until tomorrow some of them might die." His eyes watered as he thought of failing his responsibility.

He was a good kid, which was why she was so glad he and Bryan were such close friends. Bryan was standing beside her, "Mom, can't you get him a key tonight?"

"Well, you know what Timmy, it's almost dark outside. I'll just go get the key and go water them myself. You and Bryan should be getting to bed soon anyway."

Timmy was so relieved he gave her a big hug. "Thank you so much! I'm so sorry I forgot. I'll never do it again." Saying goodbye to Bryan he took off for home.

"Hey, Shannon, I'll go with you. After that meal, I could use the walk. It was really nice meeting you Sam. Bryan my man, you do indeed have a baseball card collection to rival the best of collectors. Thanks for inviting me over." Luke shook hands with Bryan like a grown up. Nothing could have pleased the boy more.

"Go ahead you two, I'll get Bryan to bed. You don't want to keep Ms. Springer's plants waiting. Come on Bryan; let's clear these dishes real quick before bedtime. I'll race you!" He took off in his chair with a giggling Bryan following.

CHAPTER 11

▼

Luke opened the door for Shannon as they headed outside. It was a glorious evening. The full moon was huge, and a bright orange. It was still low in the deep blue velvet sky. The wind was picking up a little and the smell of all the flowers lining the walkway was intoxicating. The evening was quiet except for someone's nearby wind chimes blowing back and forth.

"You have a wonderful family. Is every night that much fun at your house?" Luke very much wanted to take her hand in his as they walked along but knew it was too soon for her. She was so different from most of the single women he knew in Dallas. He was full of curiosity about Bryan's father and about Sam's wheel chair, but as no one had brought either subject up, he didn't ask.

Shannon gave a long sigh. When was the last time she had felt like this? So content and relaxed, walking in the moon light with a man. And what a man, she thought with a small smile. "Yeah, it's always pretty crazy at our house. Between Bryan and my Dad there is always something going on." As she looked up into his eyes, and then at those gorgeous lips, she felt her heart give a quick leap. She stumbled a little and he reached out to steady her by putting his arm around her waist.

They stood where they were, just staring at each other. The wind picked up even more and Luke moved his hand to push back the loose curls out of her eyes that were escaping her braid. Unconsciously her mouth parted and she licked her lips, she couldn't seem to quit staring at that wonderful mouth. He brushed his calloused thumb over her petal soft bottom lip.

"Ceily? Ceily? Where are you little girl?" Shannon turned to see Mrs. Martin hurrying towards them. Mrs. Martin was at least eighty years old and could probably run circles around women half her age. She was about five feet five inches tall and had on black leggings with a leopard print tunic over it. She wore her hair in a light brown bob that suited her perfectly and made her seem twenty years younger.

"Shannon, have you seen my Ceily? She was throwing such a fit to go out I couldn't even get the leash on her." She held up the rhinestone-studded leash. "I've never seen her act like this before. I saw her run this way." She was craning her neck and squinting her eyes to see into the oncoming darkness.

"No, Mrs. Martin, I didn't see her. Did you Luke?" Luke had been so preoccupied with Shannon he knew a whole kennel of dogs could have ran by without his noticing. Then he noticed that Mrs. Martin was looking at them with speculation in her warm brown eyes, as Shannon must have too. "Mrs. Martin, this is Luke Johnson. He ..."

"Oh that's okay dear, I've met Luke. He fixed my ceiling fan last weekend. It was making such a dreadful noise; I couldn't hear my television shows. He fixed it in two minutes. That last boy tried to fix it twice and never could get it right. As I always say, it just takes the right man." She looked up at Luke and actually batted her eye lashes at him.

Shannon was amused to see that he even had that effect on girls of any age. It was a wonder he didn't have to carry a large stick to beat them all off. At that moment she knew she would have to guard her heart closely. With her limited experience with men she knew she could never compete for a man like him. It was a good thing Mrs. Martin had come along when she did.

"Hey, what's this?" Luke bent down to pick up a small dog with white and red hair. She happily began to lick his chin. Shannon rolled her eyes and thought, even dogs? Mrs. Martin's dog, Ceily, was a prized Cavalier King Charles Spaniel. So many movie stars owned them, that lately people were calling them "Snob Dogs". She was very well trained and usually well behaved.

"There you are you naughty girl. What's gotten into you tonight? She almost never wants to go out this time of night. Well let's be on our way so you young people can go back to courting." She began to move off with Ceily in her arms.

Shannon was mortified, "Mrs. Martin, we are not courting. Luke is just going with me to the office to get a key."

Mrs. Martin just smiled. "Shannon, I'm not so old I can't see the obvious. If I was just a few years younger I'd give you a run for your money," she laughed with a broad wink at Luke.

Even with the moon glowing so brightly, the romantic mood was gone. They began to walk faster and soon reached the office. Luke just shook his head, amused at Mrs. Martin. "That is quite a woman. I would love to have known her in her youth."

Shannon laughed, "I'll just bet you would. Wouldn't it be fun to look through her photo albums? I'd love to take the time to sit with her and listen to all her stories. I keep telling myself that I will someday, but I just stay so busy I keep putting it off."

As she unlocked the front door, they could hear the phone ringing inside. As it kept ringing Shannon realized it must be the back line, or someone forgot to put in on the answering service for the night. When she reached the desk she could see that it was indeed the back line. "Hello? This is Sherwood Village apartments" she paused then tried again, "Hello? This is Shannon."

"Shannon, I have another surprise for you." The singsong voice was low and deep, Shannon felt chills race over her skin. She had heard that voice before. *"Did you know you have a whole building without outside lights tonight? You better check it out before someone ... else, gets hurt."* He laughed as he hung up the phone.

Shannon dropped the receiver as her fingers went numb. At the look of horror on her face, Luke grabbed her by both arms. "Shannon, what is it? What's wrong?" She didn't know what to say, couldn't seem to find any words. "Shannon", he shook her a little bit hoping to snap her out of it.

"It was the same voice. Th ... the same as the day I found Kimberly Orwell" She looked at Luke with eyes almost blank with shock. Her pupils were so large her eyes almost looked black.

Luke felt his own heart speed up. "What are you talking about? You never said you talked to anyone strange that day."

"I forgot about it. I just forgot about it after I found Kimberly's body. Amber thought it was another obscene caller like we had before. But this was the same voice, Luke, the same voice." Her own voice was rising because she wanted to scream as it all came back to her. "He said he has another surprise for me, and that we have a building with no outside lights. Why would he say that? What does he mean another surprise for me?"

"Shit!" Luke had a feeling he knew what it meant. "We better call Blake." At Shannon's blank look he said, "Detective Blake. I saw his card on Heather's desk. Just sit here a minute while I go get it." Shannon sat and started to pray while Luke went down the hall. She could hear him on the phone, but concentrated on her prayers.

"The police are coming. Damn, I want to go check for buildings with no lights on but I don't want to leave you. What do you think he meant that the present was for you? Does he use your name?" When she nodded Luke felt a fist grip his stomach. "Well, that really doesn't mean anything. You said your name when you answered the phone. You always say it when you answer the phone." She felt some measure of relief at his words. Luke was pacing back and forth in front of the windows as he kept watch for the police.

He didn't want to alarm her any further but he was wondering why the man had called at that time of night. How did he know anyone would be in the office? For that matter, how did he know the number to the back line? He saw a cruiser pull quietly up to the curb. "They're here." He went outside to meet them as Blake's car also pulled up. After just a few words the cruiser left to check out the buildings and Blake came into the office with Luke.

Shannon looked small and alone as she sat waiting for the men. She hadn't moved an inch since Luke had first told her to sit down, before he called the police. Detective Blake sat next to her while Luke continued to stand. The detective took her hand, "Well, hello again. Look, let's not panic here. This was just a phone call. Maybe someone is just trying to scare you. I understand you had a similar call before?"

Shannon related everything she had told Luke. "This was the exact same voice. It's creepy; I can't believe I had forgotten about it. He kind of whispers, but there is laughter in his voice at the same time." The door opened and a uniformed policeman hurried up to them. "You better come see this." The man had a sad and wearied look on his face. Shannon's shoulders slumped. She knew. She knew they would have found another body, but she had still had a small shred of hope that they wouldn't.

Detective Blake looked at Luke. "Please take Ms. Walker home and then meet us back here. We may have more questions." They left and Shannon and Luke locked up the office. They walked back to her apartment quickly and quietly. The romantic walk just a short time before seemed like a dream.

When they got to her door, she turned and looked up at him. "Let me know what happened. Tonight Luke. I know I won't be able to sleep anyway. I'll go in and talk to Dad. He'll wait up with me."

Luke kissed her forehead. "I'll be back as soon as I can." He hated leaving her looking so frightened. "Uh, drink some warm milk or something okay? There's nothing you can do, sweetheart." He drew her into his arms to hold her close for a moment. He couldn't help but notice how perfectly she fit against him.

She laid her head on his shoulder and felt like she had come home. He smelled so good, she nestled into his comforting warmth and felt his heart beating steadily.

Feeling guilty at finding any comfort at all while someone lay dead not far away, Shannon moved back. They looked into each other's eyes for a few seconds before Shannon walked through the door and shut it behind her. Luke walked away only after he heard the lock click in place.

Luke headed straight for the crime scene. It wasn't hard to find because by this time more cop cars had pulled up and they had their lights on. He walked into the apartment and straight to the bedroom where Detective Blake waited for him. The detective handed him a pair of latex gloves. "Bout time you got here Manning. What took you so long?"

CHAPTER 12

▼

Detective Sergeant Lucas Manning didn't answer as he looked at the body on the bed. It was exactly what he was afraid of. The nude body was laid out just as the last one had been. Blond hair spread out over the pillow. Pink Floyd on the stereo. But this time, the fatal stab wounds were to the mid-section instead of the throat. He walked to the nightstand and with gloved hands picked up a tissue smeared with makeup.

When Kimberly Orwell was found murdered, it turned out that her family was close personal friends with the State Senators' family. She had grown up best friends with the Senators' daughter. So with the added political pressure, they had put Luke undercover right away. But now with this second killing, it was doubtful it had anything to do with politics.

Everyone was silent as they watched him. "Well boys, looks like we may have a serial killer on our hands." Luke Manning had never wished he were more wrong. He reached over to the victim and slightly moved the blond wig. The hair beneath was also blond, but a darker shade. The killer must be picky about matching a particular person. He looked over at Blake. "Have you consulted Dr. Hastings yet?" The doctor he referred to was a profiler for the police department. When the detective shook his head no, Luke walked back to the end of the bed. "I'll need you to do that first thing in the morning. I won't have time to while I'm here playing maintenance man."

"Yeah, I can't believe you get to have all the fun while the rest of us have to do all the shit work." A big man entered the room and clapped Luke on the shoulder. The smile left his face as he looked at the bed. "Aw man! What the fuck have we got here? Not much doubt it's the same guy, huh?" Like Luke had before him he noticed all the small gruesome details. Nico Tribiani was Luke's partner and friend. They had graduated the police academy together eight years before.

Since Luke had gone undercover, Nico had been doing extensive background checks on all of the maintenance men that had worked on the property for the past two years, plus some of the residents whose names had popped up with any criminal activity at all. As the photographer went to work, the men moved out of the small bedroom into the living room.

"Have you got a bead on the man that just got fired?" Luke asked.

Nico rolled one shoulder as if to work out a kink. "Hell no. That son of a bitch knows how to go underground. He's still my best bet though. From everything I have found out about him, he is a sick son of a bitch. He has had more than one harassment charge but nothing sticks." He popped a jolly rancher into his mouth. Once again he thought this was not the time to give up cigarettes. It had been three weeks and the craving had not subsided much at all. He had been smoking since he was fifteen though.

The medical examiner arrived and everyone got down to business. It was another hour before Luke could get back to Shannon. As she had predicted, Sam had elected to stay up with her. He sat at the breakfast table with them.

Luke began, "It is almost exactly the same as the last one. The police are going to pull out all the stops on this one. They kept asking me the same questions over and over again. That's what took me so long."

Shannon nodded, "Yeah, I figured that. That's what they did to me last time. Who is it Luke? That's what I'm dreading the most, but I have to know."

Sam reached over and held her hand. "Shannon has worked here for about two years, since the property came out of construction. She knows almost all of the residents."

"Her name was Deborah Sutton, apartment seven oh three," he watched Shannon for reaction hoping she didn't know the girl very well.

She went pale and her lips trembled, telling him his hopes were in vain. "Debbie? Oh my God! She just moved in about six months ago. She was so excited about it because this is her first apartment to live in by herself. She had always had roommates in college. She said she finally felt like a grown up and had so many plans for the rest of her life. I just talked to her and Ephram by the mailboxes this afternoon."

Luke sat up straighter, "This afternoon? Who is Ephram?"

Shannon waved her hand distractedly. "Ephram is just another resident. He's harmless."

Luke made a mental note to check into Ephram later. "Was anyone else around? What time was this, exactly? Tell me everything you can remember." Damn it! He was hoping to keep Shannon a little more removed from this one.

"Slow down, Luke. Give her a minute to think about it." Sam could tell she was trying hard not to cry. "Shannon, will you get me a glass of water?" Gratefully she escaped to the kitchen to try to compose herself. Sam and Luke sat in silence until she returned.

"Luke, I just thought of something." If anything, she looked even more alarmed. The glass of water in her hand was about to spill, so Luke got up to take it from her and give it to Sam.

"Debbie's apartment backs up to Mrs. Martins. Remember she said Ceily was acting strangely this evening? The dog must have heard something. Debbie seemed fine when I talked to her today. It was just before I saw you and Bryan at the playground." Her voice hitched and she sat down heavily in the nearest chair.

"Shannon we'll need to tell all of this to the police. But tomorrow will be soon enough. He could tell she was just getting more and more upset. "Do you have any Excedrin P.M. or anything that will help you sleep? There's nothing more we can do tonight and you won't be able to think clearly in the morning if you don't get some sleep."

"I have some in my room," Sam rolled down the hall to get it for her. Luke knelt down in front of her. Most of her hair had come loose from the braid and he was amazed at how much of it there was. He pushed her hair back over her shoulder so he could clearly see her face."

"Sweetheart, I know this is horrible, but you need to understand there wasn't anything you could do. Get a good nights sleep and I'll be with you tomorrow when you talk to the police. I'll be here for you, Shannon, we'll get through this together." He stood up as he heard Sam returning. The two men shook hands and Luke went out into the night.

*   *   *   *

Back at the crime scene, he wanted to check out an idea he had. With his hands once again encased in gloves, he hit redial on the phone beside the bed. The phone had one of those digital screens for call waiting and number display. Just like he thought, the last number dialed was to the back line of the office. When the killer had talked to Shannon on the phone that evening, he was still here in the apartment. He must have left not long before the police showed up. He used his cell phone to call Nico, "Looks like we have another long night ahead of us partner."

CHAPTER 13

▼

As Nico sat in his car in front of Starbuck's waiting for Luke, he remembered the first time they had met. It was the first day of police academy and Nico was already seated when Luke walked in. The first thing he had thought was what a friggin' pretty boy he was. The boy was positively too good looking for his own good. He looked like he probably sang in the church choir. "I wish I could bet money how long he'll last," he had laughed to himself.

Nico had grown up on the roughest side of Brooklyn and knew how to fight dirty if he had to. His family moved to Dallas when he was twelve and the fighting continued when the other boys gave him a hard time about his strong 'Yankee' accent. Thankfully he had lost much of that accent over the years, but a true Southerner could still pick up on it.

His parents had eventually ended up in Florida, and his only sister, Antoinette, had moved to New Orleans with her husband and had decided to stay there even after her divorce. She had started a private detective agency, if you could call it that. Nico was still pissed off over that one. His little sister ran a company that primarily busted cheating spouses. He just knew one of those angry spouses was going come after her one day. Although, if ever a woman could take care of herself, it was Toni. He had taught her to fight when she was just thirteen, after noticing how many older boys were starting to look at her. As she had grown older, she had continued the training and now possessed a black belt.

He doubted pretty boy had ever seen a fight in his life much less been in one. Later in the day he was taken by surprise when their combat instructor pitted them against each other, Luke had taken him down and pinned him in less than two minutes. Hearing the hoots and calls from the other guys he had quickly jumped up and knocked Luke's feet out from underneath him.

For the next twenty-five minutes or so, the fight was on. The instructor put a stop to it only because it was the end of the day and it didn't look like either man would win anytime soon. They were pretty evenly matched and he was as surprised as everyone else in the room.

Nico was even more surprised when Luke held out his hand and grinned at him from a bloody mouth. "Not bad, man," he panted out, "wanna go get a beer?" They had become the best of friends as the years passed by. Nico knew no one could have a better partner. Hell, he had staked his life on it many times.

As Luke finally pulled up beside him, Nico got out of the car to greet him. "You know the rules, I was here first so you're buying."

He grinned as Luke replied, "I'm here exactly on time, and you just got here early so I'll have to pay. But, hell, I know you'll probably just get a Coke anyway."

"So? I'm still here first. Haven't you learned anything over the years, boy?" Nico had a habit of calling him boy, even though Luke was a few months older then him. In fact Nico did look older than he did, with his dark coloring and thick hair, he had a five o'clock shadow before five everyday. The two of them looked like night and day. Although they were about the same height, Luke looked deceptively laid back and mild, while Nico looked like a dangerous pirate.

They took a cup of coffee and a coke back to Nico's car. He had to laugh at the truck Luke was driving. To suit his undercover persona he was driving an five year old pick up truck. He normally drove a black

Jeep or his prized motorcycle. Nico's car was a cherry red, '58 rag top Corvette. His girlfriend Sherri sometimes complained that she thought he loved the car more than her. Secretly, Luke thought so too.

"I've got a bad feeling about this one, man. That's pretty ballsy to kill two women in the same apartment complex, so close together. After you left, the M.E. discovered something else. This one was sexually assaulted. It wasn't readily apparent because he must have cleaned her up afterwards. There are light bruises around her wrists and inner thighs, only slight vaginal tearing. Almost like he wasn't too brutal. Most rapes have more damage. That's what is bugging me. It's like he hasn't let out his full rage yet."

Luke filled him in on the details Shannon had given him and the fact that the killer had called from the dead girl's phone. "So, if she had just spoken to the girl around four o'clock in the afternoon and talked to the killer on the phone in the office around eight thirty, he didn't waste much time. He may have seen them at the mailboxes. He called Shannon by name on the phone. And that's twice he's done that. Is it just bad timing that she happens to answer the phone each time? Or does he want her somehow involved, personally? That's what scare's the shit out of me." Luke turned his head to stare out into the darkness.

Both men were silent for a few minutes. It occurred to Nico that he had never heard Luke say anything scared him. "So what is this Shannon like? Do you think she's somehow involved?" He watched Luke's face carefully.

"Involved? No! Not with her knowledge. We do need to check out her past though. She has a seven year old son, Bryan." Luke's face softened for a minute as he thought of the precocious kid. "But there's never been any mention of his father. She also lives with her Dad, who, by the way is in a wheel chair. But man, he has a great attitude and sense of humor."

He noticed that Nico was looking at him strangely. "What?" Luke was suddenly aware he must have been letting his feelings show.

"Hey, boy. You're not getting personally involved with this little family are you? Just what does this Shannon chick look like? No one else has mentioned she was hot."

Luke laughed. "Hot? I wouldn't say she's hot, exactly. She ... she's adorable. She always wears her hair back in a long braid. And when she's at work, she wears glasses." He realized he had never seen her wearing them at home. "She's a skinny little thing, she wears her clothes kind of—baggy. Almost no make up"

Now Nico was really curious. That didn't sound like Luke's type at all. "And you want her." It was a statement, not a question. "Dude, you gotta keep your Johnson out of this! You know that's the number one rule you cannot break!" It had been Nico's little joke to have Luke's alias be Johnson. It was a name widely used to talk about a man's most prized possession.

"It's not really like that," Luke became defensive. "She's just kind of sheltered. She shouldn't have to deal with this side of life. We deal with murder and dead bodies all the time. But for someone like Shannon ... she's never dealt with anything like this in her life. It's terrorizing her. And I'm afraid that's what he wants. We've got to check out her ex-husband as soon as possible" Luke's face was grim and determined.

Well, first thing in the morning I have to interview Deborah Sutton's parents. They live in Carrollton. Blake said when he went over there this evening with the Carrollton police to deliver the news; Mrs. Sutton was so hysterical that he said he would send someone over in the morning to talk to them. I'm the lucky someone." Nico shook his head. "You know how much I hate that shit."

Although Luke had sympathy for him he just said, "Yeah, but you're good at that shit. Something about you just has normal citizens open right up to you. Must be that sweet and innocent face of yours." They both laughed at that.

Except the part about the face, it was true. For some reason it seemed hardened criminals came clean quicker with Luke and the general public did exactly what Nico asked of them.

CHAPTER 14

▼

The next morning at the office, everyone was a lot more subdued than normal. Camille didn't even have anything bitchy to say. Shannon's nerves were stretched thin. Even with medication, she hadn't slept well the night before. She had kept thinking of poor little Debbie. The girl had been so full of life it just didn't seem possible that she was really dead. Why was this happening?

The police were questioning each staff member in Heather's office. Heather hadn't even said anything when they had taken over her office. Rita and Ted were on their way out from the corporate office, which usually created excitement among the staff. Today there were more serious thoughts on all their minds. Shannon jumped when the phone next to her rang. She almost answered it until she remembered they had purposefully left it on the answering service. The sign on the front door said they were closed for an office meeting.

Luke came out of the back room and said they were ready to speak to Shannon. As he walked back in with her, Detective Blake looked at him, "You can go now Johnson."

Luke just shook his head, "I promised Shannon last night that I'd be here with her. Plus, maybe the two of us together will help with the details."

Blake just sighed and proceeded with his questions, "Shannon, did you say that Mrs. Martins dog was acting unusual last night?" As the questioning continued, Luke was watching Shannon closely. The early morning sunlight was coming through the window next to her and made her hair look much lighter. On second thought, he realized her hair was looking a bit lighter than usual. That was odd; he didn't think she would be the type to color her hair. Had she had highlights put in it?

He forgot about her hair as he noticed she began to tremble. He snapped his attention back to the conversation at hand. "You don't really think he was calling me on purpose do you?" Her eyes were wide with alarm. "How could anyone know that I'd be at the office at that time of night?" One awful thought was coming on top of another. "You don't think he is watching us do you? Do you think he lives here? I have a son. I have a son to protect!" She sat up straighter in the chair. "That rotten bastard better not go near Bryan!"

Luke was surprised, and oddly happy to see the light of battle in her eyes. He hadn't known she had it in her. And it was much better than seeing her so scared. The detective spoke up,

"Well we really don't know much at this point. I wouldn't really worry about your son though. He seems to be targeting women. As a matter of fact, he'll probably move on to another area. He has to know we're all over this place. It's unusual that he made two kills so close together."

The words sent chills down Shannon's spine, and she seemed to shrink in the chair again. Luke could see that once the thought of protecting her son had been relieved, she once again became almost timid. "You really think he won't be back? Some people from our corporate office are on their way here. We don't know what to tell our residents. I know there is probably already a lot of talk going on. Heather is afraid people might start wanting out of their lease."

A knock sounded at the door and a small red haired woman peeked in. Rita Williams was the vice president of the company. "Excuse me, but I feel like I should be in here with Shannon." She walked over and bent to hug the girl. "Shannon, honey, are you all right?" She was wearing a navy blue business suit and smelled of expensive perfume.

Shannon made the introductions around the room. The other women in the office often acted intimidated around Rita, but Shannon had always found her to be wonderful. She was genuine and to the point. Shannon had thought more than once that she would have loved to have a mother like that. She would have been surprised to know that Rita felt that she would have made a perfect daughter. Rita had two sons and had always secretly longed for a daughter.

After each employee had been questioned, the police left and they all had a company meeting. Ted Maxwell, the President of the company, was there and he lent a comforting presence. Like with Rita, Shannon always felt comfortable around him. He genuinely seemed to care about people. Before they discussed the residents, they wanted to make sure the staff was taking all of this as well as possible.

Ted stood at the head of the table. He was tall and thin. His dark brown hair was curly and almost the same color as his eyes behind the glasses. The mustache he wore suited him perfectly. He spoke gravely, "We have a counselor coming out at one o'clock. I recommend that you all spend some time talking to her. After we decide how to handle the residents, we are considering making her available to some of them as well."

Camille put her hand over her heart," This is unbearable. I've been so upset." She shook her head and closed her eyes dramatically, "I haven't been able to sleep at all since the first girl was killed."

Rita almost rolled her eyes. "At least you didn't find her body. If anyone should be traumatized, it's Shannon." She knew Camille would milk anything to her best advantage.

Amber wanted to put her two cents in on Rita's side, "Yeah, the killer has called Shannon twice. At least you haven't had to talk to him." She shivered and then glanced at Rita to see if she had her attention.

Camille narrowed her eyes and gave Amber a dirty look when she thought no one was looking. Her expression changed immediately when she noticed Luke watching her. The rest of the meeting went fairly smooth. Legally they had to put out notices explaining things the best they could, without causing dramatic alarm. The legal department was working on it. The on-site staff was to refer all calls to them and just act like they didn't have any details at all. If pressed, they were supposed to say they were not allowed to discuss it until the police could finish their investigation.

Heather spoke up as the meeting drew to a close. "I think we should really go all out with our Halloween party to take their minds off of it.

Larry laughed, "Oh, right. Nothing like Halloween to take peoples minds off murder. It's only the spooky holiday." He rubbed his hand over his stubbly chin. "This shit is all we need. I can't wait for things to get back to normal." He was worried because he knew when anything like this happened; they often looked at the maintenance men first. They had even asked him where he had been when both murders had taken place. If his wife found out where he had really been, he'd definitely be in deep shit.

Rita understood where he was coming from, but she agreed with Heather. "I think we do need to act as though it's business as usual. A lot of the residents will take their cue from you. If they think all of you are freaking out, they will too."

CHAPTER 15

▼

Nico took a deep breath as he approached the Sutton house. Once again he thought how much he hated this part of the job, and then put his own emotions aside to deal with what was to come on the other side of the door.

The house was a two story brick, with a covered front porch outlined with white wooden posts. Hell, they even had a couple of rocking chairs facing the front lawn, where an ornate bird feeder was doing a lot of business at the moment. A bird bath nearby had only one fat bird soaking its feathers and looking quite content.

There was a leafy wreath with flowers on the front door and a mat that said Welcome Friends. Nico was glad to see the wording on the mat because of a case that had happened a few years back. An attorney had actually gotten a burglar set free because the people had had a mat at their front door that had just said 'Welcome'. Since then, the mats saying 'Welcome Friends' had become more and more popular. He rang the door bell and waited. It was opened slowly by an older man. His hair was totally white and his shoulders were stooped under the brown sweater he wore. Nico didn't know if this was the Father or the Grandfather.

"Mr. Sutton? I'm Detective Tribiani with the Dallas Police Department. I understand you were told that I would be coming by this morning?"

The man just stared up at him for a moment beneath bushy white eyebrows. Finally he waved the way inside and said, "Yes. We've been expecting you. Please follow me."

He led Nico from the foyer through a paneled den covered with pictures of their daughter at every age, to the back of the house into a brick floored sunroom. The house smelled like cinnamon and apples and the brown wicker furniture had plump cushions covered with flowers and hummingbirds. A woman was slowly rocking back and forth in a matching rocker with her hands folded in her lap. She was just staring out the window and didn't seem to notice them. She was humming what sounded to Nico, like a lullaby. Ivy and ferns dripped lushly from several macramé hanging pots around the room. There was a small fountain in one corner of the room where a baby angel poured water from a bucket.

"Dear? There is a policeman here. Detective, this is my wife Audra. Please have a seat." Mr. Sutton indicated a chair next to the couch, where he took a seat next to his wife.

Mrs. Sutton turned red rimmed eyes to his. "Is it true? Did someone really murder our baby?"

Nico cleared his throat, "Yes ma'am. I'm afraid so. I'm sorry to disturb you so soon, but I want to do everything—anything, necessary to find the person who did this. Do you mind if I ask you a few questions?"

Mrs. Sutton stopped rocking in her chair. "Officer, do you know how old I am? I was forty eight years old when I found out we had finally conceived a child. Debbie was our miracle baby. Our only child. After praying to God for most of our married life, we had just about given up hope. The past twenty four years have been the happiest of our life. Now she has been snatched away. Just like that." Her eyes seemed to blur for a moment. Then she straightened her shoulders and said in a stronger voice, "We'll answer any questions you have, ask us anything at all if it will help you in your investigation. Then you'll answer ours."

After talking and taking notes for over an hour, Nico had to ask the worst question yet. "I really appreciate how helpful you have been. Now this is the hardest part", he admitted to them. "I need you to come downtown with me and make a positive identification."

Mrs. Sutton stood up quickly, "Oh yes, take us to our child. I need to see her again."

Mr. Sutton and Nico also rose to their feet. Mr. Sutton spoke first. "Now Dear, You need to think about this. You don't have to do this. I can go by myself."

"Mrs. Sutton, he's right. You can stay here and return some of those phone calls." The phone had been ringing off and on since Nico had been there and they had just been letting the answering machine take the messages.

She stared down at the floor for a minute, and then took her husbands hand in hers, "We brought her into this world together. We'll do this together as well."

*   *   *   *

Meanwhile, Sam was doing some research. He was worried about the fact that the killer had called Shannon twice, and used her name each time. He called the Austin police department and spoke to the officer that had filed the restraining order against Professor Collins. He told the officer what was going on. "So you can see why I'm concerned. It may just be a coincidence, but I can't afford not to check it out. I would appreciate it if you could find out where this guy is."

Officer Pierce felt like the old guy could use some reassurance. "Sure Mr. Walker, I'll get right on it. If he's anywhere in the state of Texas I'll let you know immediately." As he hung up the phone he thought it was ridiculous to even think a college professor would turn into a serial killer. It was one thing to knock up a student; killing took a whole different personality. Besides it was past lunchtime and he had had people wasting his time all morning.

*   *   *   *

Sam decided to check all the window and doors in the apartment. It wouldn't hurt to be overly cautious. He shook his head when he found all three windows in Bryan's room unlocked. Even the locks they had didn't seem very strong. Maybe he could ask Luke to get some of those extra locks for windows that would hold them more securely.

As he wheeled back into the living room he thought about Shannon and Luke. He had noticed the sparks that passed between them. Nothing would please him more than for Shannon to find the right guy. If it looked like it was heading that way, he could always get his own apartment. Even with his useless legs, there wasn't much he couldn't do. He thanked God everyday that the rest of his body was as strong as it was. He had put every effort into rehabilitation and learning how to do everything he could on his own. He was always on the Internet looking for the latest advancements and gadgets that would make life easier for himself, therefore less of a burden for those he loved.

Speaking of the Internet, maybe he could do some research of his own looking for that Collins bastard. With that in mind, he went to work. After a couple of hours he was sighing with frustration when he heard Bryan come through the front door. He quickly closed down the computer so Bryan wouldn't ask any questions.

"Hey, Grandpa! The kids on the bus say they think there was another murder. Is that true? And how did they know about it before me? Michael wasn't on the bus today. He didn't get killed did he? He's only a little kid, like six or something." Alarm crossed his face as the thought of someone killing a kid felt too close to home.

Before Sam could even began to respond to that onslaught, there was a knock at the door. Bryan threw open the door and was happy to see Luke. He knew Luke would have all the answers. Luke ruffled the hair on top of Bryan's head. "Hey man, I thought I saw you get off the bus. How was school today? Chase any girls?"

"Eeuww! Why would I want to do that? Hey, was there really another murder?"

Luke's expression changed from open to guarded. "What have you heard Bryan?" After the boy repeated everything he had said to his Grandpa, Luke looked at Sam to see if he wanted him to be the one to answer the questions. At Sam's nod Luke began, "Yes Bryan, there was another murder, but it wasn't Michael. It was another young woman. The police were here so fast they probably scared the guy away for good. But just to be on the safe side, why don't you start asking who is at the door before you answer so quickly next time?"

Feeling reassured that it wasn't a kid that was murdered, Bryan promised to be more careful. "I better go finish my homework, I did some of it at school, so it won't take me as long tonight. Maybe Timmy can come over later." He went into his bedroom to get started.

"Luke, I'm glad you came by. I did a window check today and found all of Bryan's windows unlocked. When I went to lock them back, I noticed that the locks they have aren't really that strong. Any way you could get me some of those security locks they have for extra protection now days?" Sam hated to ask for anything, but his family's safety came before his pride.

Luke was glad that Sam had thought of it. "Absolutely, Sam, good thinking. Shannon and Bryan are lucky to have you around. A lot of single mothers never realize how important things like that are. I've seen some bad cases …," he stopped when he realized what he was about to say. It was so easy talking to Sam; he had almost forgotten he was undercover. It made him uncomfortable to know he had to lie to the man.

"Uh …, you know, on T.V.", he finished lamely. "You know what; I'll go to the hardware store right now, before rush hour hits. That way we'll have those windows secured a lot faster. I'll be back soon." As he hurried out the door he told himself he was an idiot. Something about the way that man looks me in the eye is just like my father. I never was any good trying to lie to him either.

When the door closed behind Luke, Sam knew his first instinct had been right. That man was trying to hide something. But if he was any judge of character, he really didn't think it was anything bad. Then it dawned on him. If there hadn't been so much hadn't been going on lately, he would have spotted it sooner. He'd bet his last dollar the man was a cop. It was awfully convenient how soon he had been hired after the first murder. Well, good, he thought. He was glad a cop would be close to his family while this killer was on the loose. He sure as hell wouldn't blow his cover.

CHAPTER 16

―――――――― ▼ ――――――――

*"**Look at the way she is walking home now.**"* He laughed to himself as he saw the way her eyes looked back and forth as she walked. Like she had never seen the place before. *"**Well, I've got your attention now, don't I Shannon?**"* When her eyes swung in his direction, he let the window blind fall back in to place. His hand reached down to ease the uncomfortable throbbing between his legs. He wanted her. Now. Badly. But there was still too much of the game to play.

＊　　　＊　　　＊　　　＊

Shannon was so tired she felt achy all over. She was so grateful to finally be home, she just leaned on the door for a moment. "Hi Dad. Is Bryan still doing his homework?"

Sam noticed how drained she looked. "Yes, he is. He's in his room."

Shannon smiled and tried to muster the strength to move away from the door. "Great, I'm going to go take a hot bath real quick. I'm beat."

"Take your time, Shannon. I'll cook dinner tonight." Sam was so busy all day he hadn't even thought about dinner. "Better yet, let's order in. I think we could all use a break. What'll it be? Pizza or Chinese?"

Shannon was relieved, "That's what I love about you Dad. You always have the brilliant ideas. Let's make Bryan happy and go with pizza."

*   *   *   *

The hot bath felt so good she almost wept. She had used her favorite bath oil and the whole room smelled 'like a botanical garden' according to the bottle. She knew how important it was to pull herself together for Bryan. She didn't want him to worry. Sam had called her at work and told her of Bryan's questions and that Luke had been there to help reassure the boy.

Her muscles began to unknot a little as the warm water help to soothe her tense body. She remembered what her therapist had once said, "You may not be able to control the events around you, but you do have a measure of control about how you react to them." That in itself was very powerful. Her own father was a prime example. She had used it many times in her life to get through difficult times. Like when she found out she was pregnant. She was so humiliated to find out that Doug Collins was a married man with children.

He never wore a wedding ring or spoke of a family at all. A lot of the girls in the class had had a crush on him and Shannon had felt special when he paid her extra attention. She threw the loofa at the faucet and sank down lower into the water. "I'm supposed to be relaxing, not thinking about what a moron I am."

With guilty pleasure she thought about Luke. It seemed he was never very far from her thoughts lately. "How could I not think about him," she wondered. She smiled as she remembered how Mrs. Martin had batted her lashes at him. "Maybe she could teach me some flirting techniques," she mused. She thought about what it would be like to flirt with him, and make him crazy about her. He would look at her with those sexy smoldering, eyes. Kiss her with that unbelievably yummy mouth. Embarrassed at herself, she was mortified to glance down and see her rigid nipples protruding from the bubbles. With a small squeal she ducked her head under the water.

*   *   *   *

Her hair was still curly when it was almost dry, but she was too tired to straighten it. She would just have to braid it tighter in the morning. It felt so good to let it be loose for a change. Looking in the mirror she also noticed the brown color was rapidly fading. Blonde streaks were taking over. She must have washed her hair too much lately. She would have to color it again this weekend. Or—maybe not. She was sick of doing it. Maybe she could just let people think she was getting it lightened. With everything that was going on, no one would probably notice anyway.

She put on an old, faded pink t-shirt she liked to sleep in, and a pair of white leggings, with fluffy pink socks. Bryan always laughed at her when she wore it. He said she looked like a Barbie doll that Timmy's little sister played with. Tonight all she was thinking of was comfort.

She walked out into the living room to hear Bryan laughing. "I know, I know, you think I look like a Barbie doll. Keep it up ..." She trailed off in surprise to see Luke sitting at the table with her Dad and Bryan. Her cheeks flamed as pink as the shirt when she saw the look on his face.

His jaw actually dropped open. Her hair was in long flowing curls almost to her waist. The t-shirt clung to her damp skin slightly less than the white leggings. How had he ever thought she was skinny? The woman had some definite curves! The high color in her cheeks made her surprised eyes seem even bluer. Luke actually felt dizzy. He held on tight to the table for support. What the hell was going on? For a minute he thought there might have been an earthquake. He couldn't feel his heart beating. Then all at once it was beating wildly.

When he noticed everyone looking at him, it was the second time in one day he felt like an idiot. To cover her own embarrassment,

Shannon decided to act nonchalant. She walked to the table and took a seat across from Luke. Bryan's eyes were huge as he took in Luke's reaction. He had never seen anyone look at his Mom like that before. He tried hard not to laugh, but suddenly his shoulders were shaking with mirth. Seeing his grandson struggle to hold in the giggles, Sam couldn't help himself. The look on Luke's face was priceless.

The louder Sam laughed, the harder Bryan laughed. Shannon was looking at the ceiling trying to ignore them. Luke jumped up from the table and held out the box of window locks he had brought. "I ..., I, brought locks," he said gruffly. "I'll just put them on now." He walked stiffly down the hall to Bryan's room.

Shannon jumped up and hissed at the two of them, "Shhh. Come on guys, shut—up!" When they couldn't help themselves, she stalked into the living room and turned on the television. After a few minutes, it calmed down in the dining room.

"Come on Mom, we're sorry." She could still hear the laughter in his wavering voice.

"Come on Honey; come eat some pizza before it gets cold. Bryan was just about to get in the shower, weren't you, Bryan." The boy thought it was a good way to escape before he started laughing again. When you laughed that hard, sometimes it was hard to stop.

"Yes, sir, I'm going right now." He passed Luke in the hallway and thought it was better not to look directly at him.

Sam found he couldn't look at Luke either, without laughing. "You know, I have some reading to do. In my room." he wheeled away quickly.

Luke stood staring at Shannon. He still couldn't believe how different she looked. "I've got some for your room too." He held up the window locks.

Shannon stood up, "Okay, I'll show you the way. She led him into her room and stood by the farthest window. "Look. I'm sorry about them laughing like that. There has just been so much tension lately" ... she trailed off as she looked at his mouth.

That did it. Luke crossed the room to her, raised his hands to each side of her face and kissed her as if he was starving for her. For a brief second, she just stood there, stunned. Then her arms were around him, her hands behind his neck pulling him even closer.

His mouth slanted across hers in a perfect fit. Shannon felt like she was falling, and then realized she couldn't breathe. Weakly she put her hands on Luke's chest to push him away. He stopped abruptly to let her get some air. They stared at each other as he moved his hands deeper in her hair, that glorious hair, as soft as silk, spun with gold. He looked at her mouth; her lips were parted and damp from his own mouth. He kissed her again, once, twice, more softly this time.

It felt like the most natural thing in the world to lead her to the bed; it was like being gut punched to suddenly remember her father and her young son were not far away. With a deep growl of frustration, he caught her close and buried his face in her hair. She could feel the hard evidence of his desire against her belly. Her own body clenched in response. It was as if they were so in tune he could feel it. He jerked against her and groaned.

"I have to leave now, Shannon." His voice was low and gruff. "But we have to talk about this. Tomorrow. I'll see you tomorrow." He kissed her once more and they both knew it took them to a place neither of them had ever been before. Shannon looked as stunned as he felt. As he left the room her knees collapsed and she fell weakly to the bed.

When she could think again, she let out a gasp and put her fingers to her mouth. Her lips felt swollen. And glorious! Oh my God! Didn't they always say, 'Be careful what you ask for'? Now she knew what that meant. She didn't know if she was equipped to handle a man like Luke Johnson. But … oh! It might be worth the risk to find out. She felt dizzy again as she thought of his kisses. She fell asleep without even realizing it.

CHAPTER 17

▼

Luke wasn't as lucky. He went to his temporary apartment with the rented furniture. The only good thing about it was that it was only two buildings away from Shannon's. He was frustrated and pissed off without knowing why at first. How the hell had this happened? He remembered Nico's words the night before, the number one rule about not getting involved. Well, how the hell was he supposed to be prepared for something like this?

When he saw her tonight, she looked like something out of his deepest dreams. He felt like he had been waiting for exactly her all of his life without even realizing it. Like God had made her just for him. No wonder he had never been in love before. He stopped abruptly. "What?"

All of a sudden he remembered that dizzy feeling. He had wondered if they were having an earthquake. No wonder they call it 'falling in love'! "Uh-oh,—whoa man." Don't you have to know someone much better than this to fall in love with her? But he was almost thirty years old. He had had his share of affairs and for the most part, he really cared for most of them. But not on this level. Nothing he had ever felt before was even close to this.

He needed to go talk to Nico. But not tonight. He had some serious thinking to do. There was a killer on the loose. And he might just be after the woman of his dreams. He pictured her again, the way she was tonight. The way the light glinted off the gold shining through her hair. The gold? He pictured her again when he first met her a few weeks ago. He was sure she had been a brunette. When had she started turning blonde? He remembered yesterday, the sunlight was shining through the window and at first he had thought it was the sun making her hair look lighter. Tonight it was even more gold. What was going on here? It was as if the dark color was washing out of her hair.

He thought of the blonde wigs on each of the dead women. Was Shannon a natural blonde? The killer might be doing that as a clue that it's really Shannon he's after. Than why not just go after her? He thought of all the times she walked vacant apartments. There would have been plenty of opportunity.

It looked like he was going to have to talk to go to Nico's tonight after all. He needed to know what the report from Dr. Hastings, the profiler had said. And he needed to know if Nico had found out anything about Bryan's father. If not, he would just have to ask her tomorrow. As a matter of fact, he realized he had a lot of questions for Shannon.

In the meantime he pulled out his cell phone and just punched the number two to call Nico. He answered on the first ring. "Hey man, how'd it go today?"

Nico told him about the Suttons. "It was rough, but for some weird reason I'm glad it was me with them. Nicest old couple you ever met."

"Did you get a chance to talk to Hastings yet?"

"No I didn't, sorry about that. By the time I got around to calling, the good doctor had already left for the day. I'll get on it first thing in the morning. Then I'm going to go to Debbie Sutton's funeral. The first vic was buried in Wisconsin so it's doubtful the perp would have bothered to go all the way up there for it. But something tells me he won't be able to stay away from this one. Parker and Stallings are gonna take pictures from a distance, one on each side of the service, and we'll compare them later with everyone on our suspect list. The Suttons figure on a large turnout."

As the two men continued to discuss the case, the killer was making plans of his own.

CHAPTER 18

▼

That day at work, they were all trying desperately to get things back to normal. The legal department had made flyers reporting the recent deaths on the property. They didn't call it a murder. Larry and Luke were supposed to put the flyers out on each door.

In the office they were busy getting to work on the Halloween parties. They were going with the idea of having one at each clubhouse, one for the adults and one for the kids. Shannon was happy to be in charge of the one for the kids. Due to the recent events, she was going to make it more like a fall festival, than something spooky. They would have haystacks, happy scarecrows and bobbing for apples. She was going to start a contest to see which child could draw and color the best poster for it. Maybe even hire someone to do face painting.

In the midst of all the planning, her mind kept slipping to the night before. She had seen Luke briefly this morning, but with everyone else around, there hadn't been time to talk. When he was sure no one was looking he had slowly winked at her. She opened the top drawer in her desk and there was a note that said, "Let's have dinner tonight." L.

She quickly slipped it into her purse. Dinner? She needed more details than that. Did he mean at her house again? Or out, like a date? She suppressed a nervous giggle. When was the last time she had been out on a date? Then she remembered the uncomfortable night a few months back that her Dad and one of his friends had set her up with son of another friend. The man had been an attorney; all he could talk about was his college days and the people he had been to school with. Shannon had been mortified to admit she had dropped out of college.

The whole night had been pretty miserable, and she had told her Dad to never try to set her up again. But to go out with Luke would be a whole different matter. The phone rang and she answered it with some trepidation. Since the last murder, answering the phone made her anxious. She relaxed when she heard Luke's voice. "Hey, did you get my note?"

"Oh, was that from you?" She teased.

"What?" At first he was worried she had gotten a note from the killer. She laughed and he heard the light note in her voice. "Now she's a kidder," he murmured, half to himself. "Have you ever been to Mazziano's?"

"The Italian restaurant? No, but I've heard of it." She was suddenly uncomfortable.

"Great, how about seven o'clock? I'll pick you up at your place."

"Well, let me talk to Dad and make sure he doesn't have plans so he can stay with Bryan."

"Hey, don't even think about trying to get out of this. We have some talking to do," he half teased.

She noticed Camille watching her from across the room. "Okay, I have to go now. I'll see you later."

Camille just continued to watch her for a minute. Then she got up and walked over to Shannon's desk. Before Shannon realized what she was about to do, she suddenly bent down and pulled the note from Shannon's purse. It only took her a second to read it. "You're dating Luke?" She all but screamed it. Amber stopped talking on her phone to stare at Shannon, waiting for her to answer.

Shannon didn't know what to say. She hadn't thought this far ahead. Then Camille laughed. "That's ridiculous! Why on earth would he go out with you?" Then she took a closer look at Shannon. "Where are your glasses? Have you been dyeing your hair?" She put her hands on her hips. "Well, well, well Shannon. What's going on here? Are you trying to get laid at last?" She was totally pissed to notice how pretty Shannon really was. Why hadn't she ever noticed it before?

Suddenly, Shannon realized she didn't have to try to explain anything. She calmly rose from her desk; she smiled sweetly at Camille, "Bite me, Camille!" She slowly walked from the office into the clubroom, hips swishing on the way for good measure.

At first she heard nothing but thunderous silence behind her. Then she heard Amber laughing her head off. The next thing she heard was the front door slamming as Camille stormed out. Still giggling, Amber came in and gave her a big hug. "That was the greatest thing I've ever seen! Did you see her face? Oh—my—God, that was too funny!" She held her stomach and wiped the tears from her eyes.

"Are you really dating Luke? When did this happen? You know I'm not really surprised. I've seen the way he looks at you. I think the boy is smitten." She grinned teasingly. "So? Tell me. I want details!"

Shannon was almost ashamed of herself. When was the last time she had stood up to someone? "I don't know Amber. Maybe I shouldn't have done that."

"Of course you should have! It's about time. She's just jealous of you. But forget about that. Tell me about you and Luke." Her eyes gleamed in anticipation.

"He just asked me to dinner," she said quietly. "He wants to go to Mazziano's."

"Well, girlfriend, why don't you seem more excited?" Amber knew even Camille would have been thrilled to go out with Luke.

Shannon was embarrassed to answer. Saying it out loud would sound so stupid. She let out a deep sigh. "I don't—have anything to wear," she half wailed.

Amber's eye's widened, and then she cracked up again. When she finally calmed down, she put her arm around Shannon. "Don't you worry about that. Come to my apartment for lunch we'll find you something. You're not as skinny as me, but it'll be good for you to wear something tight for a change."

Shannon agreed, with some trepidation. But she was touched that Amber wanted to help her. And she really didn't have anything to wear to a restaurant like that. She touched Amber on the arm. "Thanks so much, that's really sweet of you."

Amber snorted, "Oh hell, if I can't go out with Luke, at least my dress can!" Both girls were laughing as Luke came in. He was startled to see them looking so chummy. "Just another question I'll have for Shannon later," he thought.

CHAPTER 19

▼

That night, Shannon was afraid her knees would start shaking any minute. Amber had browbeaten her into wearing a little black dress. 'Little' being the operative word in Shannon's opinion. It had spaghetti straps and even showed some cleavage. At least it did almost reach her knees—in case they really did start to shake. Amber had also loaned her strappy black sandals with high heals and talked her into wearing her hair down.

She had even come over to Shannon's apartment to help her do her make up and get ready. She had just left after proclaiming Shannon her masterpiece, and Shannon was glad to have a few minutes alone. Bryan was spending the night with Timmy and her Dad had gone to visit a friend.

She looked in the mirror and almost wanted to call the whole thing off. There was a part of her that felt ridiculously embarrassed, but another part of her felt thrillingly decadent. "No, she said out loud, "I can't do this." Just as she was about to take the dress back off, the doorbell rang. Her hand stopped half way to the zipper. "Oh well, I guess its fate. I can't open the door naked." With trembling bravado she went to answer the door, and only faltered once in the high heels.

Luke had prepared himself in case she had her hair down. This time he promised himself he wouldn't act thunderstruck or jump on her like a wild animal. He was in total control of himself.

Until she opened the door.

He thought he might swallow his tongue.

He just stared at her silently for a minute. Then he managed to croak, "What are you trying to do to me?"

Nothing could have pleased her more. A little inexperienced she might be, but she was still woman enough to know what that meant.

He took her to a little red sports car and opened the door. When he saw her surprise, he answered her unspoken question. "It belongs to a friend of mine." No way was he taking her out in that pick up truck.

At the restaurant, Luke ordered wine and they placed their dinner orders. They had a table on the patio and the umbrella over the table had twinkling white lights in them, as did the nearby trees. There was low, romantic music coming out of hidden speakers from close by. As beautiful as the setting was, they couldn't quit staring at each other.

Shannon thought Luke looked beautiful in a black suit with a matching French blue shirt and tie. She like the monochromatic look. He reached over and took her hand. "Shannon, you are the most gorgeous woman I've ever seen." He said it quietly and sincerely. No one had ever said that to her before.

"Now I need to tell you a few things. I'm not a real fan of one-night stands. If we decide to take this to the next level, I'll want to have a relationship with you. I already have strong enough feelings for you that I'm half scared to death."

When she said nothing and just continued to stare at him, he continued, "I'm telling you this because when I'm in a relationship with someone, I want complete honesty. On both sides. So I'll go first." he took a deep breath, knowing he was not supposed to do this. Nico was going to kill him.

"My last name is not really Johnson. And I'm not really a maintenance man. I'm an undercover detective for the Dallas Police

Department and I'm working on the recent murders at Sherwood Village." He was quiet for a minute to give her the chance to absorb the impact of his words.

Shannon blinked twice and continued to sit quietly for a minute more. "You're a cop? And you want to have a relationship with me?" Suddenly the fun innocent night seemed far different than what she had imagined. "Luke ... is Luke your real name?" When he simply nodded she went on. "This is all a little overwhelming for me."

A frown appeared between her eyes. "I have my father and son to think about. I can't just jump into relationships. That's why I don't date much."

"Is that also why you dye you hair and sometimes wear glasses you don't need?" Luke wanted to give her time to adjust to all he had said. But he also wanted answers to his questions.

Shannon was nonplussed at first, and then gave a dry chuckle. "Well I guess you really are a detective. But let's start with you first, Luke. Who are you really? Tell me about yourself.

They had to pause as their dinner arrived. Shannon realized the waiter had also poured her a second glass of wine.

"I'm a middle child. I have two sisters, one older and one younger. I grew up around a lot of women and I am thankful for that. I was always good at sports because I was the only one interested in playing ball with my Dad when I was little. I have a wonderful family and I know they will love you. And Bryan, and Sam." He squeezed her hand. "I know you come as a package deal, and I respect that."

Shannon felt near tears as those words poured so easily from him. He always seemed so at ease with everything. Which was only one of the reason she didn't think he would understand her. She realized he was waiting for her to speak. It was her turn.

"Well, I'm an only child. My mother ... "If she was having a hard time telling him about her mother, how could she ever tell him the other parts of her life? She tried again. "My mother left us when I was really young. She didn't die or anything like that, she just—left. Dad has had to raise me pretty much on his own." When she didn't see the expected pity in his eyes she went on. "You want to know about Bryan, don't you?" She almost whispered this last part.

Luke filled both of their glasses again and waited patiently for her to continue. Shannon drew a deep breath to fortify herself. When her breasts swelled above her neckline, Luke almost called for the check. "Down boy," he warned himself. He knew the wait would be worth it.

"I met Bryan's father in college," She dropped her eyes to their clasped hands. She didn't want to look him in the eyes for the next part. "He was my professor." Bryan was glad she had dropped her eyes so she didn't see him wince. "It was only later I found out he was married and already had two children." She looked him straight in the eyes then, waiting to see the revulsion on his face. It never came. "We only spent one night together. I had just turned nineteen." She could feel her cheeks grow warm and was grateful for the low lighting.

Luke sighed, "That's the kind of man that gives us all a bad name. What did he do when you told him about the baby?"

Again Shannon dropped her eyes, "He told me I was a fool and that he was already married. He told me to get rid of it. Just like that. Get rid of it."

After a moment of contemplation, Luke thought he was starting to understand a lot of things. Like why she went so far to downplay her looks. When he saw tears swimming in her eyes he knew it was time to stop. He didn't want their evening completely ruined. There was just one more question he had to ask.

"Do you know where he is now Shannon?" At the sound in his voice, Shannon looked at him sharply.

"Is this the cop wanting to know?" Then it dawned on her. "You don't think he could be involved in these murders do you? Luke, that's ludicrous. He was probably glad when I quietly moved away. I'm sure he is still in Austin."

Luke took a small notepad out of his jacket. "I need his first and last name, Shannon." Suddenly he did seem all cop. She realized there must be two different sides to this man. She went ahead and gave him the name and a description, even though she felt there would be nothing to come of it.

"Shannon, is there anything else you should tell me?"

The flame from the candle in the middle of the table flickered a little bit, and despite the fact that the breeze was getting cooler, Shannon was feeling very warm. It could be the wine, she thought, but more than likely it was the man. She looked at Luke with speculation. "Luke, are you in danger all the time? Do you deal with murder and death on a daily basis?"

The wind was blowing through her hair, lifting the long strands as if the very air itself wanted to dance with her to the softly playing music. Luke was more enchanted by the minute and never noticed that she had avoided his last question. He shifted in his chair and tried to keep his mind on the subject at hand.

"Well, yeah, I do deal with it on a regular basis, but thank God there isn't always dead bodies everyday. As for the danger part, it's not very often. We usually arrive after the murder has taken place. It's usually domestic or drugs. Serial killers are rare, despite what you see in the movies. I have a partner, named Nico. We watch each other's back." He linked his fingers with hers. "He wants to meet you, by the way."

He continued, "I have a house on Lewisville Lake. I'd like to show it to you. Do you need to be home any specific time tonight?" His slightly rough fingers gently rubbed the middle of her palm and up her wrist. He could feel her pulse speed up. He noticed she had an unconscious habit of biting her full lower lip when she looked at his mouth. When his eyes dropped to her neckline, he could feel his own heart rate increase.

Shannon smiled, despite the unexpected turn the evening had taken she was feeling more relaxed than usual. "Are you kidding? Dad and Bryan were thrilled we were going out. They would probably be disappointed if I got home very early. I thought if the date was a bust I would go hang out at Starbucks or something."

That was one thing Luke really loved about her. She had the ability to joke when he least expected it. Never taking his eyes off of her, he raised his hand for the check.

They drove up Dallas Toll way and then West on the 190 turnpike. Luke had a Bryan Adams CD on the stereo and when the song, "Have you ever loved a Woman?" came on, he thought it finally had meaning for him. Shannon thought it was the most romantic song she had ever heard. When it was over, Luke simply pushed a button and the song began again. He took her hand in his as they drove through the night.

CHAPTER 20

▼

When they pulled up to an electronic gate, Shannon was surprised. The long country rode they had been on didn't seem to lend itself to electronic gates. The asphalt drive way curved around to a large a-frame cabin in the woods. She could see the lake sparkling in the moonlight behind it.

When they got out of the car, she was delighted to notice a rose garden with a white gazebo off to the left side of the house. When she looked at him with her eyebrows raised, he grinned and shrugged. "This place was built by my grandfather for my grandmother. She used to love to sit in that swinging chair in the gazebo, surrounded by her roses, and watch while my grandfather taught us to water ski." He could see the chair swaying back and forth.

"As much in love as they are, I imagine the place was used for more than that though when they were younger," he said somewhat ruefully. "Anyway, she used to come out in the boat with us sometimes until her legs got bad. She has Phlebitis and has to spend some of her time in a wheel chair. They live in Louisiana now and when they put the place up for sale five years ago, I knew I wanted it. I spent the best summers of my life out here. So I bought it from them."

Shannon was already captivated by the place. She smiled and put her hand to his cheek. "I don't blame you. This place feels magical."

Luke looked down at her and felt like he was indeed under a spell, "It's never felt more magical than tonight." He kissed her slowly, tenderly. His tongue tasted the wine on her lips and tilted her head back further to deepen the kiss.

Finally he took her by the hand and led her through the wide front door. The back wall was made up of large windows that overlooked the lake. There was a gigantic limestone fireplace on the left, with the stones rising all the way up to the second floor. On the right was a bar, with the kitchen on the other side. "There are also two bedrooms down here. Mine is a loft upstairs." He motioned to the low white sofa that faced the windows. "Have a seat and I'll get us a drink."

Feeling a little nervous now that they were here, she was glad he wasn't trying to rush things. She walked over to a stereo by the fireplace while he went to the bar. She pushed a button and jumped back as Mick Jagger's voice belted out into the room. She loved classic Rolling Stones but hadn't been prepared for it. As she found the volume control, she heard Luke laughing. "I'm sorry; I tend to like it loud when I'm alone. There's an assortment of music in the cabinet below. Why don't you pick something out?"

She was delighted to find another Bryan Adams CD. She put it in and turned around to see Luke walking towards her with a glass in each hand. He smiled slowly when he heard her choice of music and handed her a glass. He had removed his shoes and tie, and opened the top buttons of his shirt. The animal magnetism of the man had her taking a quick swallow of her drink to cover another attack of nerves.

She almost choked as she realized it wasn't wine. The fire of the sherry hit her stomach hard at first, and then quickly spread warmth through her entire system. "Are you trying to get me drunk, Luke?" she gasped.

He laughed again, "I'm sorry, I should have warned you, I just don't want you to be nervous. I want you so badly, I'm afraid I'll scare you," he admitted.

She placed the glass on the shelf behind her. She didn't know if it was the sherry or his admission of wanting her, but suddenly she wasn't nervous at all. She surprised him by putting her arms around his neck and whispering, "Don't you know that I want you too?" She lightly, playfully, bit his ear lobe, causing him to groan and sweep her up in his arms. He carried her up the curving staircase that led to his loft.

Setting her down beside his bed, he put his hands in her hair and looked deeply into her eyes. He was relieved to see that she didn't look scared at all. She reached up and lightly traced his lips with her tongue. With a stab of desire, he knew that she did want him as much as he wanted her, if that were possible. He pulled her head back and rained kisses along her neck, just above her shoulder. She smelled and tasted so good, he sucked lightly on her soft skin.

Shannon felt her knees go weak and a hot liquid seep into her belly. She moaned and tilted her head to give him even more access. Gently he stepped back from her to allow her dress to slip to the floor. She hadn't even known he had unzipped it. She stood before him in nothing but black lacy panties and those strappy high heels. Her hair flowed around her in long and silken curls. His breath caught in his throat.

"My God! You're beautiful." Her breasts were heavier than he had expected, with honey tipped nipples that pointed up, they seemed to be begging for his mouth. She had a tiny, nipped in waist and yet wonderfully rounded hips. When he saw that her cheeks were turning pink, he began to kiss her again.

He felt her shyly unbuttoning his shirt. She felt rock hard muscles beneath, lightly covered with hair. She lost her shyness in the fascination of exploring his chest. He removed his clothes and laid her back on the bed. He lifted her leg and bent to unstrap her shoes. When the first shoe fell to the floor, he kissed the inside of her ankle and moved to remove the other one.

She kept her eyes on him, feeling like she was in a dream. She had thought him beautiful before and now realized she hadn't known the half of it. His shoulders were broad, his chest and stomach strongly muscled. Her eyes roamed his body down to slim hips. It was her turn to loose her breath when she saw the hard proof of his desire for her. She felt a moment of uncertainty that he would even fit inside of her.

He kissed his way up her legs, taking his time to caress every inch of her. He kissed the top of her black panties and breathed in deeply the intoxicating scent that was all Shannon. With one swift move he pulled the black lace down her legs. Looking up he couldn't resist her breasts any longer.

As he drew her into his warm mouth, it was electrifying. She arched her back and dug her fingers into the hair on the nape of his neck. She moaned and moved her hips restlessly. He couldn't take anymore and used his knee to spread her legs. She was so small he had to work his way slowly inside of her. The little noises she made in the back of her throat almost drove him over the edge.

Gritting his teeth, he vowed to take it slowly. He didn't want to hurt her. She put both hands on each side of his face and looked him in the eyes. When she saw how much he was trying to stay in control, she kissed him deeply and suddenly raised her hips up hard. The need in her was strong and she didn't care if there was a little pain. When he was buried to the hilt, she continued to move her hips. He couldn't resist any longer and plunged with her to a shattering climax.

CHAPTER 21

▼

When he came to his senses, she was breathing as hard as he was. He was stunned at the amount of passion in this small woman. When he looked at her face he saw that her eyes were closed and yet there was a smile on her face. Would she never cease to amaze him? She opened her eyes as if she felt him staring at her. Her smile turned a bit sheepish.

"What?" She asked as he just continued to stare at her.

When he opened his mouth, he was not prepared for the words that came out. "I'm totally in love with you."

She sat up quickly and tried to reach for the nearest thing to cover herself with. She gave up when she realized there wasn't so much as a pillow left on the bed.

"Luke, I told you, I couldn't rush into anything. God, I have more feelings for you than I know what to do with. But this is all so new to me. I ... I guess I need to take it slower than you." When she saw some of the light go out of his beautiful eyes, her heart felt like it cracked a little. Still feeling weak and a little foggy, she was afraid she would never find the right words.

"There has just been so much going on lately. I was never expecting something like this. I would rather take it slow so that we don't make any mistakes." She sighed, "I'd tell you that you were the best I ever had, but it probably doesn't sound like much when there was only that one other time."

Luke's head came back up. "Seriously? There was only one other time? You have lived your whole life with only that one other time?" He couldn't believe it. Even trying to disguise her looks, he had still been powerfully attracted to her. Were all the other men in the world insane? "Do you never go out on dates?" he asked.

"Well, I have been out on a few. But I just never wanted to sleep with any of them. Would you feel better to know, I've even had a few fantasies about you?" She smiled seductively. Boy did she learn how to play the game fast, he thought. He couldn't help but laugh. He loved being with her.

"Well, sweetheart," he rolled on his back and dragged her down on top of him, "Let's make up for lost time!" And they did.

CHAPTER 22

▼

Shannon woke up and stretched, at first she was taken by surprise as she felt the soreness in body. She was extremely sore, and yet she had never felt better in her life. She had never been happier in her life. She looked over and saw Luke watching her. A part of her was shocked that she didn't feel acute embarrassment. Then she thought back over the night they had just spent together and thought, what would be the point?

In one short night, he had taught her things she had never even thought of. Actually, she wouldn't have thought much of it was possible. As one particular memory came back to her, she did feel her face began to grow warm. She smiled and lowered her eyes; her long lashes fanned her bright pink cheeks.

Luke knew that if he weren't already in love with her, he would have fallen in that moment. He loved the fact that she could still blush after all they had done with each other just a couple of hours ago. Maybe she was kind of new at this, but the girl was a fast learner. "You're amazing," he said quietly.

"I was just thinking the same thing about you. So, what is your last name? I can't believe I slept with someone and didn't even know his last name!" At that moment her stomach growled loudly. They both had to laugh. "Luke placed his hand over her belly. "Well, I was planning on jumping you again, but it sounds like you body has other ideas."

She looked at him solemnly, "My body definitely has other ideas. I'm not sure I'll ever be able to walk again." She said it so seriously; he couldn't help the totally smug, totally male smile that took over his face. Screaming in outrage, she threw a pillow at him. "If you dare laugh at me, I'll never talk to you again." Wrapping the sheet around herself she tried to stalk to the bathroom, she couldn't help it that it was ruined completely when she had to limp a little bit.

"Manning," he called to her. "My last name is Manning."

CHAPTER 23

▼

Nico sighed as he was driving to Debbie Sutton's funeral. He usually tried to avoid going to funerals if he could help it, but he had a feeling the perp might want to be there. The first girl Kimberly Orwell was buried out of state and Nico knew that a lot of times, killers couldn't resist the high it gave them to go to the funeral. Even if they just watched from a distance. Kind of like an arsonist sticking around to enjoy watching all the chaos he's caused.

They had agreed for just that reason to keep Shannon away. Luke had talked to Rita about keeping everyone from the office from attending just to keep the perp from getting any more kicks, although, Rita and Ted would be there to pay their respects for the company.

Even though he was arriving early, the parking lot was full of cars and people were streaming into the funeral parlor. Because he was driving his own car, he had to find an open parking place just like everyone else. Finally he had to park down the road and walk. He was surprised at the amount of people, and not a little frustrated. How would he ever spot a potential killer in this throng?

He saw Mr. and Mrs. Sutton standing by the doorway. Mr. Sutton was shaking hands with a man about his same age, but Mrs. Sutton had her arms crossed in front of her body as if she were just trying to hold on to herself. Just trying to hold on period, probably, Nico thought.

When she saw Nico, the dullness left her eyes for a second, replaced with alarm.

"I'm surprised to see you here Detective. For a moment it scared me, as if you had something else horrible to tell us. Then I realized there couldn't be anything more horrible than this." The dullness returned to her eyes as she looked around.

"I came to pay my respects ma'am. I didn't expect such a crowd."

"Oh, well, I did. Debbie was loved by everyone. These are people from our church, people she went to college with. Some of these people are ones she went to elementary school with. Plus a lot of our family has flown in. A lot of her neighbors from the apartments are here, she glanced at a group that included Ephram Peters." She trailed off as she looked around. It just seemed so odd to her that it was such a beautiful day. She felt like there should be clouds pouring rain from the heavens, as sad as she felt herself. Thunder and lightning ripping across the sky to show the unbelievable anger at what had happened to their baby girl. At the thought of that she gasped and her hand flew to her throat.

Nico was alarmed, but Mr. Sutton was there to quickly wrap his arm around his wife. "Come on dear, lets go inside and sit down, I know your exhausted. And I am too." His soothing manner seemed to calm her immediately. As he led her into the church, he looked over her head at Nico for understanding.

The power of the sheer grief and incredible sadness in his eyes had a lump forming in Nico's own throat. He stood there in the warm sunshine and felt a shudder run up his spine. Turning suddenly, he scanned the crowd. Everyone was milling around, talking in hushed voices. He was looking for anyone that seemed out of place, or stood out from the crowd. For a split second he saw a man standing alone staring straight at him and then the crowd shifted as crowds do and he was gone. Nico quickly moved in that direction, the hunt was on.

*   *   *   *

Later at the burial grounds, Nico was once again studying the throng of people. The casket was open and he could see pretty little Debbie laying there like a princess waiting for a prince to awaken her. A young woman that was about the dead girls own age walked up to the casket with Mrs. Sutton by her side, together they lifted her slim hand and placed a small butterfly ring on her finger.

Nico heard the girl say, "She always loved this ring. My Mom said the butterfly represents eternal life." Her voice broke and she buried her face in her hands. Mrs. Sutton wrapped her arms around her and they swayed back and forth.

In a watery voice, the grieving mother replied, "Now she'll always be our angel."

Looking away Nico spotted the two cops with cameras in the distance. He was especially glad they were there today, because he kept getting caught up in the personal grief hanging so heavy around him. He mentally shook himself. He had been to his share of funerals, but this one was just overwhelming.

He couldn't believe his own eyes as they were lowering the coffin into the grave and a beautiful cloud of golden butterflies flew right through the tent that was covering the site.

CHAPTER 24

▼

Later that same day, Shannon was glad to get a rest. It was past lunchtime and they had been busy showing apartments without a break. Saturdays were usually busy, but not this busy. Some people were saying they didn't need an apartment until next spring and that they just wanted to look. "What they really meant was that they were morbid curiosity seekers," she thought to herself.

After she had shown one man the model apartment, she had found out that he was really a reporter from a Houston newspaper.

Sitting at her desk, she was filing her guest cards when she noticed something sticking out of her purse. Thinking it was another note from Luke, she smiled as she opened the envelope. When the pictures fell onto her desk, she just stared at them numbly for a minute.

There was a picture of her at the Cowboy game, another one showed Kimberly Orwell talking to some friends out by the pool. The second picture showed Kim lying on her bed with terror in her eyes. There were more pictures of Debbie and Shannon by the mailboxes. Then—Debbie just before she must have been killed. But the picture that caused Shannon to jump up from her desk, screaming, was the picture of Bryan. He was smiling up at the camera, as the large shadow of the person taking the picture seemed to loom over him.

With her hand covering her mouth to prevent another scream, she looked around the office to see who might have put the pictures in her purse, but Amber was still out showing an apartment and no one else was there. Heather and Camille were off for the weekend. The she remembered Luke was on call. Quickly she flipped through the Rolodex to find his cell phone number, she also had the number in her purse, but couldn't stand the thought of touching it yet.

Just as she was about to dial the number, Luke walked in the door. "Hey sweetheart, I couldn't stay away ..." His voice trailed off as he got closer to her and saw the look on her face. She was still standing behind her desk, her face was white and her eyes looked wild. "Shannon, what is it? What's wrong?" His eyes followed hers to the pictures on her desk. The first one he saw was of Kimberly Orwell with her mouth gagged and large pleading eyes looking at the camera.

He went around the desk to take Shannon's arm and lead her to sit in one of the chairs in front of her desk. She was shaking so hard, her knees just collapsed beneath her. Tell me where you got these pictures." He went back behind the desk to see them as they had dropped, he didn't want to touch them. When he saw the one of Bryan he understood the wild look in Shannon's eyes. Quickly he called Detective Blake, then immediately called to check on Sam and Bryan. After bring reassured that they were both all right, he told Sam to make sure all the windows and doors were locked and he would explain more later. He took a pair of gloves out of his pocket and carefully looked at each picture.

He no longer had any doubt that Shannon was at the root of all this. Or that she was a target.

Shannon jumped up, "I'm going home now. I have to be with Bryan." As she tried to pass Luke he caught her arm. "Shannon you just heard me talk to Sam. They're fine. We have to wait here to talk to the police. The more information we can give them, the faster we can catch this guy." Seeing that she had no choice, she called her Dad herself and talked to him until the police arrived.

They took the pictures and the purse for evidence and fingerprints. They also dusted Shannon's desk and drawer handles. They questioned Shannon and Amber closely about the people they showed apartments to, and wanted the names and apartment numbers of any of the residents that had come in to the office that day.

Shannon called Heather and told her what happened, "Oh shit! Are yall okay?"

"Yeah ...," taking a deep breath, Shannon tried to steady herself. "Yeah, we're alright."

"Okay, put a sign on the door saying that the office will be closed for the weekend. I'll call Rita and Ted. And Shannon, thanks for calling—and take care of yourselves."

After everyone had left, Luke and Shannon wasted no time getting to Sam and Bryan.

CHAPTER 25

▼

Sam was waiting for them and had Bryan involved in playing video games. Bryan jumped up to hug his mother. He had gotten home from Timmy's that morning after she had already gone to work. The police had agreed that Luke would be the best one to question the boy. "Hey slugger, did you have fun at Timmy's?"

Bryan could sense that the grown ups were upset about something. "Sure, we always have fun. Yesterday we played a game of hide and seek, until it was almost dark. Then Timmy's Mom made us come inside. We got to eat hot dogs and chips for dinner." He looked guiltily at his mother, "I even got to drink a coke at nighttime."

"Bryan, was there someone around taking pictures while you were out playing?" Luke asked the question as carefully as possible. Bryan just shrugged his shoulder, "Yeah, just that 'vestor guy. He's been around before. You know the one that's thinking about buying this place."

Shannon unconsciously put her hand to her throat, "Do you mean an investor?" When Bryan nodded his head she remembered, just last month, when a group of investors had come out to inspect the property. More than one of them had had cameras. Bryan had seen them while he was out playing and she had told him that properties were bought and sold all the time, but her company would probably still manage it.

Luke put his hand on Bryan's shoulder, the boy felt so slim and small, it made Luke feel even more protective. "Can you tell me what this guy looked like? We want to make sure he's with the same group of guys."

Bryan folded his lips and turned his eyes up to the right to give it some thought. "You know what? I don't really remember if he was with that first group of guys or not. But when I asked him if he was a in-vestor, he said yes."

"You said he has been around before, are you sure it was the same guy? What did he look like?" Luke knew it was important to keep this as casual as possible.

"Well, he's tall with short black hair and light black skin. He wasn't wearing a suit, but his camera was around his neck, just like the last 'vestors. Timmy was kinda mad 'cause the guy only took pictures of me."

"You said he wasn't wearing a suit. Do you remember what he was wearing?" Luke was taking notes as Bryan gave the description.

Bryan nodded his head, "Yeah, he was just wearing jeans and a shirt. He seemed pretty cool. Can I play my game now? It's the bottom of the eighth with one out, I think I'm fixin to win!" He looked at his Mom for permission.

"Sure, honey, go ahead." Shannon was glad he had something to hold his attention so they could talk. She knew as soon as he finished this game, he would ask to play it again. The adults moved into the dining room and sat around the table.

Luke asked Shannon, "Did you see anyone in the office today with light black skin?"

"No", she shook her head, "Not that I recall." She paused, "I can't believe my son was talking to a killer. What does all this mean? Is he after us? Why would anyone be after us?"

Sam was watching Luke too, waiting for an answer. Luke sighed and knew he had to be straight with them. Hoping they would be straight with him too. "As a matter of fact, I do think he may be after you. Maybe it is someone from your past, or maybe he got fixated on you after the first murder. How many people know you're a natural blonde?" Since the night before he knew for sure that she was indeed a natural blonde.

She blushed and lowered her eyes. She definitely didn't want to look at her Dad, when she answered the question. "Not many people know. I've been coloring my hair for years. This is the lightest I've let it get since I first started dyeing it." She thought for a minute, "Hey wait a minute, a couple of months ago, Mike was in my bathroom repairing a condensation leak, when I walked in he was looking at the box of hair color I use. I was mad because he didn't have any reason to be under my sink, the leak was above the tub. That was just the day before he was fired. Do you think he thought I got him fired? I never even told Heather or anyone else about it."

Luke sighed, "Well, he doesn't fit the description of the man taking the pictures. I saw a picture of Mike, after I replaced him. But I can think of someone else that would know." Sam looked surprised when Luke said quietly, "Doug Collins would know. What did he look like?"

Sam cleared his throat and leaned forward in his chair. "Um, I've been doing some checking of my own on the Internet. I can't find a record of Professor Collins anywhere in Austin, or at any of the university's in Texas." he looked uncomfortable for a minute. "There's something you should know Shannon. After you quit school, I raised quite a bit of stink, and they fired the man. It turns out there had been other incidents they had been able to keep quiet. I convinced them that I wouldn't keep quiet about this. Not only did he loose his job, when his wife found out, she left him."

Shannon was dumbfounded. "Dad, I can't believe you did that. How did you do all of that without my even knowing about it?"

Sam's face hardened, "Shannon, you wouldn't come out of your room for weeks at first. I wasn't only worried about you, I was angry. Do you think I would let anyone mess with my little girl like that and not do something about it?" When she still looked upset about it, he added firmly, "I may be in a wheelchair, but I'm still a man, and a father."

She reached over and covered his hand with hers. "Oh Dad, I know that. I'm just surprised that you never told me." She smiled a little, "I guess I'm glad that he had to pay for it a little bit. Maybe he won't ever do that to another girl." She thought for a moment, "But it couldn't be him. He isn't a light skinned black man either. Doug's of English descent, with very light skin and hair"

Luke decided to share some other information, "The police profiler thought he would be a white man, age twenty five to thirty five. She thinks he wipes their make up off to try to make them appear more pure and innocent." He noticed Sam looking at him speculatively.

Then Sam grinned, "You are a cop, aren't you? That's what I figured."

Now it was Luke's turn to be dumbfounded. "How did you know that?" Then he remembered the slip up when he was talking to Sam about the window locks, which, combined the profiler information must have given it away to a perceptive man like Sam. Knowing he was busted, he confessed, "Yes sir, I am. I've been undercover on this case. I told Shannon about it last night."

Since Luke had known even the name of Doug Collins, Sam thought it must have been a night of confessions. That meant the two of them must have been getting very close, which pleased him greatly. Luke's next words confirmed that too. "I'm in love with your daughter, sir."

Before Shannon could say anything, Bryan let out a loud whoop. "Did you just say you're in love with my mother? Did I just hear you say that? I told you she was great. Are yall gonna get married?" He had just finished his game and was going to ask if he could play another one, as his mother had known he would.

Shannon jumped up to try to take control of the situation. "Now wait a minute guys. We are not going to rush in to anything. We need to get to know each other better first. All of us do." She turned to Luke accusingly, "Didn't I tell you that I needed some time?"

Luke just grinned at her. "See? I had to tell them so they can help me convince you. We could be married by Christmas. Heck, we could do it sooner than that, but my mother would kill me." He looked at Bryan, "You know how women are, and they like to make a big fuss about weddings."

"What? What!" Shannon couldn't seem to find any more words. How had this all gotten so out of control? She thrust her jaw forward and squinted her eyes; walking over to Luke she poked him in the chest. "Look, you. I won't be rushed into anything." She looked over at the other two. "By any of yall!" With that she stalked into her bedroom and slammed the door. She didn't know why, but she felt close to tears.

For a minute there was complete silence in the room. Finally Bryan said in amazement, "Did you see that? I've never seen my Mom like that. She has a temper!" He looked at Luke, "You must make her feel like that. Remember Grandpa, she kinda fused at us when we couldn't stop laughing at Luke the other night."

Luke grinned, "Yeah, I guess I do bring it out in her." He looked pleased with himself.

Sam was grinning too. "Listen Bryan, maybe you can go and play another game. Knowing your mother, she'll probably take a long hot bath to calm down. By the way, she used to have quite a bit of temper when she was little." When Bryan went to the other room, the two men got serious. There was still a killer out there.

"Listen, Sam, I need to go into the station for a while and see if anything new has come up. Will yall be okay here? I know you've already checked all the windows. Don't let Bryan answer the door at all. I also want to stop and get some extra locks for the doors. For some reason, this guy does seem to have an interest in Shannon. I have to figure out why."

*   *   *   *

The man was pissed off. "Why in the hell is that guy hanging around so much? Shannon has never dated much before, why now?" He had purposely left the pictures for her, thinking she would be so upset that she wouldn't even think of going on another date. He saw Mrs. Martin walking her stupid dog and thought of how much fondness Shannon seemed to have for the old lady, "I guess I'll have to step things up a little to get her attention."

*   *   *   *

As Mrs. Martin inserted the key in her front door, Ceily started growling and barking madly. "Ceily, darling, whatever is the matter with you?" Just as she started to turn around and try to control her precious dog, she was hit sharply in the back of the head. Ceily broke free and attacked the man who had hit her beloved mistress. It gave Mrs. Martin just enough time to get in her door and lock it. She was dizzy and fighting the pain as she dialed nine one one. She passed out just as she heard Ceily howl in pain.

When the police arrived, they found Ceily just outside the door. She was lying there, panting heavily with blood coming from her mouth. There were bloody streaks on the concrete, from her body to about three feet away. She must have dragged herself to the door after she had been hurt. The police knocked on the door twice, before they heard a weak call from inside. They could hear someone trying to unlock the door. They had guns drawn as Mrs. Martin finally got it open and collapsed at their feet.

CHAPTER 26

▼

Luke was at the police station, in the war room with Nico and Blake. He had already told them of the description Bryan had given him. "Well if Shannon didn't recognize the description, it must be that the killer fixated on her after the first murder. I still think he was in that apartment when she found the first girl dead. Remember, she heard a noise while she was in there." Nico had said this theory before.

We've been researching wigs. Do you know how many places sell wigs in this metroplex? Hundreds! There are even kiosks in the malls that sell them now. Plus, both wigs had the tags cut out of them. We don't even know who the manufacturer is. These are a pretty high quality though, so that will help to narrow it down some.

There were pictures of both dead girls up on a large white board on the wall. The men stared at them trying to see any missing pieces. As Blake started to say something else a young female police officer entered the room. "Hey, guys, I thought you might want to know, there's trouble again out at Sherwood Village."

Luke jumped to his feet, "Another murder?" he asked, with fear hitting hard in his stomach.

The girl shook her head. "No, some old lady got hit in the head. The mean bastard even hurt her dog." She looked outraged. "Nico, I finally found some information on that Professor you were looking for."

It was decided that Luke and Blake would got to the apartments while Nico followed up on the professor. Even though he didn't fit the description, they couldn't afford to leave any stones unturned. Luke put the portable flashing light on the dashboard of his car until he was a block away from the complex. He was thinking about an old lady and her dog. Somehow he knew it was Mrs. Martin.

His cell phone rang as he pulled into the gates of the community. He saw by the caller I.D. that it was Shannon's house. "Shannon?"

"No. No, Luke its Sam. We heard sirens and Shannon left to see what happened. Has there been another murder?"

"No, Sam. Someone was hit over the head. Did you say Shannon left the apartment?"

"Yeah, I told her to stay here, but she said she needed to go. It looks like her headstrong ways are coming back along with her temper."

"Well, I'm here now Sam; I'll let you know something as soon as I check it out. I'll get Shannon home too."

He put the phone down as he pulled up to the building where there were already two police cars and an ambulance. They were just loading the woman into it. He saw Shannon standing there holding Ceily's leash and knew he had been right about it being Mrs. Martin. He rushed up to the ambulance, only to be told that the woman was unconscious. They said they didn't know if she would ever wake up again.

Standing not far behind him, Shannon covered her mouth with her hand and tried not to scream. Large silent tears were pouring down her face. Ephram Peters was right beside her looking helpless. Several groups of residents were standing around, trying to stay back out of respect. A couple of policemen were questioning some of them. Another police car had left earlier with Ceily trying to take her to the Veterinarian and hopefully save her life.

With nothing left to do at the moment, Luke put his arm around Shannon and walked her home. "Shannon, I think we need to talk about moving you and your family out of here. I don't know if this was the same guy or not, but it's hitting too close. That picture of Bryan says he's trying to shake you up. He's trying to terrorize you."

Shannon stopped walking and straightened her spine, "Why would that son of a bitch hurt Mrs. Martin and Ceily? Maybe somebody was just trying to mug her, and it doesn't have anything to do with the murders." As horrible as it was, she didn't want to think of that killer touching Mrs. Martin.

Luke put both hands on her shoulders and looked her in the eyes. "Shannon," he said quietly, "There was a picture of you and Debbie at the mailboxes, just before she was killed. He must be watching you and know of your fondness for Mrs. Martin. I don't want to scare you any more than you already are, but we need to get Bryan out of here at least."

With a lump in her throat, Shannon shook her head, "There's no where for him to go, Luke. I told you about my mother. My father was an only child and his parents died in a car accident before I was even born. And I can't leave here right now either. If this does have something to do with me, I need to help put a stop to it."

They were silent as the resumed walking. Finally Luke stopped walking again. They were almost to her apartment. "Bryan and Sam could stay at my house. I could even have someone stay out there with them and I can stay with you at your apartment."

"Luke, that wouldn't work, Dad has special needs because of his wheelchair."

"Shannon, I know we left in a hurry this morning and you didn't really get much of a chance to look around last night, but don't you remember me telling you about my grandmother being in a wheel chair? The whole house has been customized for her. Especially the kitchen, but even one of the downstairs bedrooms and bathrooms has been converted. The doorways are wider and there are rails like those in Sam's bathroom."

When she didn't say anything for a minute, he pressed on. "Shannon, trust me on this. We need to get Bryan out of here. Somehow I knew as soon as I heard that an old lady had gotten hurt out here, that it was Mrs. Martin. It's not hard to see how the killer is thinking. He's trying to hurt you."

Shannon took a deep breath; "Let's go talk to Dad." When they walked into the apartment, Luke was relieved to know that Bryan had already gone to bed. It was unusual on a Saturday night, but he and Timmy had stayed up so late the night before, he was more tired than usual.

When they told Sam everything that was going on and the idea of going to Luke's house, Sam was quiet for a while thinking it over. He agreed about getting Bryan safely away, but didn't want to leave Shannon. "I think Shannon needs to go too."

Shannon shook her head, "I can't Dad. I have to try to stand up to the maniac, or we'll have to worry about him following us wherever we go. This has to stop. Now." She tilted her chin up in defiance.

Sam felt his heart squeeze as he thought that she had had that same look on her face quite often when she was a little girl. He felt like for the first time since he had been shot, he was finally seeing the real Shannon again. Even though he was worried, he was proud of her. "How would we explain all this to Bryan? He won't want to miss school."

Luke spoke up, "I think you should pretty much tell him the truth. He's a pretty smart kid. When he wakes up in the morning, we'll just say we're going out to my house. Shannon can pack his bag. When we get out there, he's going to love it. We'll ask him if he wants to stay there with you, while we catch the bad man. He's likely to think of it as an adventure."

When Sam still looked doubtful, Luke knew needed reassurance in another area. "Sam, like I said before, I'm in love with your daughter; I'm not going to let anything happen to her."

After that they all worked on the details for the next day. Luke was going to leave tonight; the others would leave in the morning as if for a family outing. An unmarked car would discreetly follow them to make sure no one else was following. Even with that they would take an alternate route to Luke's place.

As Luke stood to leave, he made one more decision, "I have to leave, but I'm just going to my apartment here on property. I won't be far away if yall need me. Plus there are several undercover officers around."

Sam shook Luke's hand and thanked him for all his help. Then he left the room to give the couple a few minutes alone.

Luke took Shannon in his arms and held her tight for a minute. He put his face in her hair and breathed deeply, she always smelled like flowers. It shook him how fast he had come to care so much for her. Nothing in his life had ever felt this important. "I hate to leave you, but we don't know that he somehow watches your apartment. I don't want him to have any idea that anything is changing until we get Bryan and Sam out of here. If my guess is right, when he realizes that I'm staying with you, things are going to escalate. We have to be prepared."

Shannon looked deeply into his eyes. She could hardly believe this awesome man kept saying he was in love with her. "Luke, thank you so much—for everything. I don't know how I can ever repay …"

Luke cut her off abruptly. "You better stop before you offend me," He was only halfway joking. "It's not your gratitude I want, sweetheart." His mouth swooped down on hers.

CHAPTER 27

▼

Shannon couldn't sleep. Something was nagging at her, but she couldn't put her finger on it. Her thoughts kept swinging back and forth between the danger they were in and the sweet moments with Luke. She also kept thinking she heard a noise and had checked on Bryan at least ten times.

She remembered that when Luke had left earlier that day, he had said he was going to the police station to see if they had anything new to go on. Although it was late, she called him on his cell phone. When he didn't answer, it went into his voice mail. She thought that was weird because he had said he would keep it near him in case there was trouble. Getting worried, she decided to go over there. It was only a couple of buildings away and no one would be expecting her to leave her apartment.

As she left, she made sure to lock the door carefully behind her. She looked right and left. What moon there was, was behind the clouds. It was a dark night, but every few feet there were old-fashioned looking street lamps. Because of the recent changes in temperature, fog was rolling in. "Just great," she thought as she crept along, "nothing like conjuring up Jack the friggin' Ripper or a scary movie. All we need now is organ music."

She jumped at a loud noise off to her right. A big black cat ran across the sidewalk in front of her. She looked up at the swiftly moving clouds, thinking it was a good night for cats to get into mischief. Looking behind her to make sure no one was following; she didn't even notice the man in front of her until he was right on top of her.

As she started to scream, he quickly put his hand over her mouth. "Shhh, if you scream, you're going to scare everybody." The man seemed huge, just his shoulders blocked out the building behind him. He had coal black hair and a closely cropped beard, with a small gold hoop in one ear.

Shannon fought him fiercely, with every ounce of strength she had. She was using nails, teeth and finally slammed her knee between his legs as hard as she could. When he grunted and bent over, she did it again. He had no choice but to let her go. "You son of a bitch!" She doubled her fist and slammed into his mouth.

She didn't wait around to see what would happen next. She ran to Luke's apartment. Just as she got there he opened the door and caught her in his arms. "Luke get your gun, hurry get your gun, I just ran into a madman and he may still be out there!" She was panting and half hysterical. When he just stood there, she tried to shake him, "What's the matter with you? Get your gun! Luke?"

Luke was trying hard not to smile. "Shannon, you just beat up my partner." At that time, the partner in question was limping up the stairs behind her, bleeding mouth and all. She squealed and jumped behind Luke. "Shannon, meet Nico. Nico, this is Shannon."

Shannon peaked out from behind Luke. "Oh." The rest of her body followed her head, to come out and stand beside him. Standing stiffly, she kept her eye on the big man. She realized he was about the same height as Luke, but whereas Luke was sleekly muscled, this man was bulging.

She cleared her throat and primly held out her hand to him. "Hel— hello, Nico." Gingerly he shook hands with her. "I'm sorry I hurt you, but you scared me to death."

Nico was torn between embarrassment and feeling proud of her. He knew she was beginning to mean lot to his friend. He grinned and wiped at the blood on his mouth. As a matter if fact he was bleeding in quite a few places, "I would say it's nice to meet you, Shannon," he put his hands in front of his crotch, "but the jury's still out.

Nico's voice was strained and Luke could tell he was having a hard time standing up straight. He couldn't help it and laughed loudly as he ushered the two of them inside. "I could hardly believe my eyes when I looked out my window and saw her whaling on you." He looked at Shannon. "Looks like I've got a berserker on my hands."

Shannon noticed Luke's wet hair and assumed he had just gotten out of the shower. That would explain why he hadn't answered her call. As if he read her thoughts, he said, "I was just in the shower for two minutes, by time I answered the phone you had hung up. I was going to wait a couple of minutes for you to call again, and if you didn't, I was going to go to your house. Nico was supposed to be here any minute, that's why I looked out the window." He let out a breath and shook his head, "I wish I had my video camera, the guys at the station would pay big money to see that."

Then he narrowed his eyes and looked at Shannon. "What in the hell are you doing out by yourself at night?" When Shannon started to protest, Luke wouldn't hear it. "I know you did a pretty good job on Nico, but don't you realize it was because he was trying 'not' to hurt you?"

Shannon looked again at the size of the man and knew Luke was right. "I couldn't sleep. I wanted to ask you what you had found out at the police station, before Mrs. Martin got hurt. When you didn't answer, I was worried about you. I didn't have a choice but to come check on you."

Luke looked amazed. "You were going to check on me? What? You were going to—save me?" He was incredulous.

"Well, you said yourself he wanted to hurt the people I care about. I care about you, Luke," she said more quietly. She looked shyly at Nico. He just grinned at her.

Her comments took the wind out of his sails, as Luke realized she had put herself in danger thinking she would try to save him. A shiver traveled up his spine and his heart felt like it turned over in his chest. God, he loved this woman.

Shannon looked at the two men, "Well ... anything new?"

Nico looked at Luke; he wasn't sure how much he could say in front of her. Luke smiled in understanding. "Go ahead Nico, Shannon and I don't have any more secrets from each other. He took her hand and held it close. He also explained his theory about Mrs. Martin and their current plan to move Sam and Bryan to Luke's house by the lake. Nico agreed it probably was a good idea.

Then Nico looked uncomfortable for a minute. He wasn't used to discussing a case in front of a civilian, especially one involved in it. "Well, I did find out that Doug Collins now lives in Mesquite, about twenty minutes from here."

Shannon sat forward in her chair. She hadn't wanted to believe Doug could have anything to do with this. He was her son's father. Then she remembered Bryan saying the man that took his picture was a light skinned black man. She didn't think Doug could ever bring that off, even to a child.

"He's a waiter at a restaurant." He looked at Shannon waiting for her response.

"A waiter? Really?" she asked in disbelief, remembering the prestige he had enjoyed at the college. "But anyway, didn't Luke tell you the description of the man that took Bryan's picture? Doug doesn't come any where near to that.

"Shannon, he could have had someone else take the picture. He could have paid someone to do it while he waited nearby. If that's the case, this guy is smarter than we thought he was." Luke paused, "Maybe it is the professor."

Nico held up his hand. "Wait a minute yall, there's more. We found a glass at the last crime scene. It has the ex-maintenance mans fingerprints on it." Shannon found that more believable. Even more, she knew she didn't want Bryan's real father to be a killer.

"But why would he focus on me? He paid more attention to Camille and Amber than he ever did to me. Unless he really thinks it was me that got him fired?" She sat back to think about it.

As the two men continued to theorize, Shannon looked around the apartment. What a difference from Luke's house. The apartment was pretty like the other ones at the community, but the furniture looked cheap. There were no personal photos or knick-knacks at all. There was a picture above the couch; it looked like it must have been from the same furniture rental company. The recent adrenaline was wearing off and she suddenly felt tired.

"Luke, do you mind if I make us all some coffee?"

"Oh no, that's alright, I'll get it. Besides, Nico likes a special brand." She was surprised a few minutes later when he came back from the kitchen and threw Nico a coke.

Nico just grinned and saluted her with it after he twisted off the top. "This is my favorite kind of caffeine."

Shannon enjoyed the easy camaraderie between the two men and realized their friendship really ran deep. They were so different in looks, one dark, and one light. But she could tell their minds ran on the same wavelength. As she listened to them do most of the talking, it struck her again that there were two sides of Luke and that being a cop was a huge part of him.

They talked over different scenarios for a while, until Luke noticed the shadows under Shannon's eyes. It was almost two o'clock in the morning when he walked her home.

CHAPTER 28

▼

The next morning Bryan was excited to get to go to Luke's. They were up and on the road by eight thirty. Luke had described the car that was supposed to be following them. It wasn't even a police car at all; it was a red Porsche Boxter that was driven by a swat team member that was a friend of Luke's. They drove around Dallas for a while until the man in the Porsche called them and said there was a green light to go to Luke's. They passed the Galleria Mall and then went west on 635, LBJ freeway then headed north on Interstate 35.

Bryan was playing his Gameboy Advance in the backseat and it was a while before he noticed how long it was taking them. "Man, where does he live anyway? In Oklahoma?" I need to go to the bathroom, Mom."

Just hold on honey, it won't be long now. You're going to love his place. His grandparents used to live there when Luke was little and it was his favorite place to go. The house sits right on Lewisville Lake."

Bryan did think that was pretty neat. "Does he have a boat?" Just like a kid, Shannon thought, right to the details. "You know I'm not sure, but I'll bet he does. He said he Granddad used to take him out on a boat when he was a kid. He taught him to water-ski."

As Bryan and Sam discussed the joy of water sports, Shannon was looking in the rearview mirror for the Porsche. It was a beautiful day, the temperature was supposed to get back in the eighties today. It seemed surreal to think there could be a murderer out to get them. Finally she saw the red car again and felt reassured. Boy that guy really stayed far behind. Then she noticed it wasn't the same red car. This looked different. She called Luke on his cell phone and told him about the cars.

"That's okay, sweetheart. Nico is on his way out too. He called the other boys off and took over. It was Nico's car we went out in the other night. He's bringing his girlfriend out too. I thought we could bar-b-que out by the gazebo. Then maybe go out in the boat. The water is perfect today."

Shannon smiled, "Bryan will be thrilled. He just asked me if you had a boat."

Bryan spoke up from the back seat. "Is that Luke? Can I talk to him?" Luke heard him and said he wanted to talk to him too. They stayed on the phone all the way there.

When they arrived at the electronic gate, Luke told her the code to punch in. He was waiting on the front porch when they pulled up. Bryan jumped out of the van almost before it was stopped. He ran to Luke and Luke picked the boy up and lifted him high in the air. They were so obviously happy to see each other; Shannon didn't have the heart to scold him for getting out of the van like he did. Especially when she thought about not seeing him for a while, at least not until they caught the killer.

Nico and his girlfriend, Sherri pulled up in the driveway. They got out of the car and introductions were made all around. Sam had no trouble with his wheel chair. In the light of day it was easier for Shannon to see the renovations that had been made to accommodate Luke's grandmother. Sam easily made it through the wide front door. The inside of the house had gorgeous hardwood floors. Luke had taken up all of the thicker rugs that Shannon remembered from the other night. As Luke showed them around, it was easy to see that his grandfather had thought of everything that could be done to make things as comfortable as possible for someone is a wheelchair. He had even had the original cabinets; counters and sink replaced with lower ones in the kitchen.

Bryan had opened the back French doors and was standing out on the deck. He saw the boat docked, rocking in the sunlit water. A big fat frog jumped right on top of his shoe. He laughed with glee, and looking around, felt like he had come home. He knew he would love this magical place.

Out by the gazebo was a huge built in bar-b-que pit. Luke had already started smoking the meat and the rich smell was mouth watering. Bryan ran to investigate and was then distracted by the porch swing. As he sat to swing on it, he was delighted to see a swarm of Monarch butterflies descend around him. They had just learned in school that week about the migrating butterflies and how they flew across Texas this time of year.

The adults were watching him out of the windows. Luke smiled a little smugly at Shannon and Sam. "I told you he would love this place. I remember what it was like to be a boy around here. I never wanted to go home."

The day passed quickly as Luke and Nico decided to take Bryan out in the boat, before the meat was done. They knew it was torture on the boy to wait. Sam took charge of cooking the meat, and Shannon and Sherri went in to the kitchen to make potato salad and corn on the cob. The two women got to know each other better as the sat around the table peeling potatoes and snapping green beans

"So, I hear Luke's really got a thing for you," Sherri had a gleam in her brown eyes. "I'll be happy for him to settle down. I'm always afraid that Nico will get restless because Luke makes it look like so much fun to be single. I swear that man has a new knock out looking girl each week, the women just about swarm all over him. He's even dated more than one Dallas Cowboy cheerleader." When she noticed the look on

Shannon's face she stopped abruptly. "Oh, honey, I'm not saying I don't think he's ready to settle down. He was just waiting for the right woman." Sherri's glossy brown mop of curls bounced as she nodded her head. Her hair was cut short, and even with the curls it looked like the latest fashion. She was wearing a red and white-checkered blouse that tied above her belly button, and very short blue jean shorts that sat low on her hips. She looked so wholesome; Shannon was surprised to see a small rose tattoo on her ankle.

Suddenly Shannon felt dowdy and couldn't help but think of all the girls Luke was used to. Probably 'Dallas Dollies' as they were called, all with French manicures and four hundred dollars purses. Girls more like Heather, Camille and Amber. Not for the first time, she wondered why Luke hadn't gone for one of them.

As if to answer her question, Sherri went on, "We thought he might have met his match once before, but the girl turned out to be a big ole' liar. It seemed she couldn't tell the truth about anything. When Luke opens up to somebody, he expects total honesty. No holding back. When he found out all sorts of things about her, he felt betrayed. Turned out she had even been married before and had like, three or four abortions. Now I'm all about freedom of choice, but for God's sake practice birth control!"

Shannon was glad to see the boat heading back in. Sherri was rapidly taking the fun out of the day. She had never been into 'girlfriend gossip.'

"But, honey, he's so into you, he's even ready to take on a ready made family." She laughed, "I never thought I'd see the day. Wonder what his Momma thinks about that. Well here they come; I'm going to go powder my nose before they come in."

Trying not to think too much about everything Sherri had said, Shannon took a good long look around the big country kitchen. All the appliances and cabinets were white on white, which complemented the dark wooded floors beautifully. The stove had a pot rack above it with several copper pots hanging from it, along with some dried flowers woven into the chains. There was a window box above the sink that just cried out for fresh flowers and herbs. She could tell there hadn't been a woman's touch around for quite a while.

"A ready made family." The words came back to haunt her. She knew a lot of men's egos couldn't take that. She resolved even more to not rush into anything with Luke. How long could he be happy with a plain girl like her when he was used to the kind Sherri had described? She looked down at the knee length khaki shorts and almost prim white cotton blouse. Maybe she could get some 'girlfriend' type clothes.

As Luke came in the door he was enchanted to see Shannon sitting at his kitchen table, cutting up potatoes. The sun was shining on her bright hair and she looked lost in thought. He hoped he would have the opportunity to see her sitting there like that for the rest of their lives.

✳   ✳   ✳   ✳

By the end of the day, as he had predicted, Bryan was more than happy to get to stay there. As for the bad man, he had just said to hurry up and catch him. Sam assured them that everything was perfect for him too. "I think I'm as in love with this place as Bryan is," he grinned. "We don't really need Roberts to stay here with us."

He was talking about the cop that had arrived earlier. Shannon covered his hand with hers. "I know Dad, but I would just feel so much better. It'll be over with soon, I just know it." She smiled even though her eyes were starting to swim with tears. She hated the thought of going off and leaving the two of them. They had rarely been separated.

As Luke and Shannon drove off through the night in a rented Yukon with darkly tinted windows, he thought he understood her mood. Not only were they going to be separated from her family for a while, but also the danger they were facing was very real. He had to figure out the mind of the killer and anticipate his next move. He admitted to himself that he was worried about missing something because he had never been this personally involved in a case before. Something about finding the glass with fingerprints at the last crime scene just didn't fit. Was the killer getting careless, or was he just trying to show his superiority over them?

CHAPTER 29

▼

"How could I have missed them this morning?" He was furious when he had realized they had left for the day. The big blue van had been missing from its assigned space since he got there at nine o'clock that morning. Now it was ten thirty at night and they were still not home. When he saw a dark SUV with darkly tinted windows pull up in front of her building. He almost didn't pay attention at first. Then he saw her *get out of the vehicle. He watched as she met Luke at the other side and they walked hand in hand into her apartment.*

"What in the hell was going on? Where are the old man and the boy?" This couldn't be happening, he had plans for them. "Fuck! First the old lady and her dumb ass dog, now this." It dawned on him that they were trying to outsmart him. Out maneuver him. Well, they just didn't realize how long he had been planning this. He could always go to plan B.

They next morning Luke and Shannon decided to not disclose to anyone at work the steps they had been taking. The less people involved the better. Luke left her apartment early to go to is own and get changed. He put in another call to the hospital and found out that Mrs. Martin was still in a coma. Ceily had a few broken ribs and a punctured lung from a vicious kick or two. The Veterinarian had agreed to keep her for a while, in light of the situation.

When he got to the maintenance office, Larry was in a foul mood. "Those fuckin' cops can't stay out of my business. Next thing I know they'll be asking me to take a polygraph or something." He looked at Luke, "You're lucky you didn't start to work here until after the first killing. They probably don't bother you much at all do they?" He stuck some Copenhagen in is bottom lip and moved it around with his tongue.

He leaned towards Luke and lowered his voice conspiratorially, "To tell you the truth man, I was making a little visit to Vicky in apartment twenty two fifteen. Her husband was out of town and she called me over just as brazen as could be. I'm telling you, she was all over me. How's a man supposed to resist something like that? You know what I'm talking about. I've seen the way women come on to you too." He winked like they were in some kind of club together.

Luke just nodded his head, "Yeah, I know what you mean." The man was scum. "Why don't you just tell the cops that?"

"You kiddin' me man? If my wife ever found out, she'd skin my balls. We just had another baby five months ago." He pulled his jeans up on his skinny hips. "Yeah, we got a great marriage. I'm not lettin' nothing come between that." It was all Luke could do not to roll his eyes. He knew the first chance he got he would check it out to see if that girls husband had really been out of town.

Meanwhile in the inner office, Shannon was having to deal with problems of her own. Amber had told Camille all about helping her get ready for the date with Luke. Camille was pissed and didn't care who knew about it. She was actually slamming things around, like it was some kind of personal insult to her. Amber regretted ever telling her, but it had been just too much fun to resist.

Finally Shannon had had enough. "Grow up Camille. Don't you think we have more important things to worry about? Mrs. Martin is still in a coma. Even her poor little dog almost died."

Camille snorted, "Who gives a shit about that damn dog?" She narrowed her eyes at Shannon. "You know, you sure have gotten a lot mouthier since a man has shown some interest in you. Well, don't get too big of a head, honey, you're just a novelty to a man like Luke. Hell, he probably had a bet with Larry to see who could get in your pants first." She smiled meanly. Shannon moved to walk past Camille. She knew she had to get away from her.

Not ready to give up the fight, Camille had one more thing to say, "Does Bryan know he has a slut for a mother?"

Shannon whirled around, before she could stop herself, her fist connected with Camille's mouth. With a shrill scream the girl fell backwards to the ground, with blood streaming from her lips. For a minute there was complete silence.

Camille removed her hand from her mouth and stared at the blood on her fingers. She ran her tongue over her teeth. "You fuckin' bitch!" she screeched. "My front tooth is loose. I'm going to kill you!" She jumped up and launched herself at Shannon.

Luke had been watching from the doorway and, having anticipated Camille's wrath, got to the girls before anymore harm was done. He grabbed Camille around the waist and had to wrestle with her as she continued to kick and scream.

"What in the hell is going on out here?" Heather had rushed into the outer office as soon as she heard the screams. She couldn't believe her eyes. Camille calmed down and proceeded to cry pitifully, as Shannon rubbed her bruised knuckles.

"Did you *hit* her?" She asked in disbelief. "What is wrong with you girls? Now I have to fill out an incident report." With a sigh she looked at the sobbing girl as blood continued to drip onto her blouse. "Well, damn it. I guess I better take you to the doctor first. Anytime there's blood involved, I'm required to get the person medical attention." She gave Shannon a dirty look. "I'll deal with you later."

After the two women left, Luke, Shannon and Amber just stood there looking at each other. Finally Amber let out a whoop, "Oh— my—God, Shannon, you totally knocked her on her ass! That was the coolest thing I've ever seen!" Shannon was still so shocked at what she had done, she was speechless.

Luke couldn't erase the grin from his face. He went into the clubroom kitchen and wrapped some ice in a cloth. Coming back into the office he was glad to see that Shannon had finally sat down. He took her hand and placed the ice on her knuckles. Neither of them had said a word. Amber was on the phone telling one of her friends about it. She was still laughing as she related the story.

The smile left Luke's face as he saw how upset Shannon was. "I don't know what's gotten into me lately. That's the second time in a week that I've attacked somebody. And made them bleed." She looked up at Luke. "I made her bleed, Luke." Tears swam into her eyes.

"Sweetheart, I heard some of the things she was saying to you. She was way out of line." When she looked at him doubtfully, he nodded his head, "Seriously, she had it coming. You have to stand up for yourself in this world."

CHAPTER 30

▼

Later that night, they decided to go to Joe's Crab shack for a casual dinner. The seafood was great, but the margaritas were what Shannon needed at the moment. After her second one she was feeling much better. The festive mood of the restaurant made the earlier troubles of the day seemed to fade away. Except for the cut on her knuckle from where it had connected with Camille's tooth.

Luke wanted Shannon to relax. He didn't want to talk about the case or Camille. He put his glass down and linked his fingers with Shannon's. "You know I think you have a great family."

She nodded her head and smiled. She loved the fact that he cared about her family. Still his next words were a bit of a shock. "I want you to meet mine. Well at least some of mine. My mother and sisters are coming into town to go shopping next weekend. I thought we could have another bar-b-que. My sister Sarah is pregnant again and she said she couldn't seem to get enough to eat. This is her third child in five years."

Shannon's eyes widened in disbelief. "Three in five years?" She looked thoughtful for a minute trying to imagine it. "I felt like I was pregnant with Bryan forever. She must really feel like she'll be pregnant forever." She shook her head, amazed by the idea. Luke smiled as he pictured Shannon pregnant with his baby. Somehow he knew it would happen someday. He remembered the line from that Bryan Adams song that had been playing in his car on their first date. 'You can see your unborn children in her eyes.'

Shannon sighed. "It's hard to make plans for the weekend until this guy is caught." She looked over at the corner table where an undercover couple sat. The police felt another move would come soon, as Shannon and Luke was seen dating. Like didn't want to think about what his chief would do if he knew that it was for real.

His cell phone rang and he spoke into it quietly. His eyes met Shannon's and suddenly his were alight with pleasure. He took her hand in his again. "Guess what, sweetheart? Mrs. Martin is out of the coma and she is going to be fine. She's fully alert and remembers everything."

Shannon closed her eyes for a moment. "Thank you God! Oh, Luke you don't know how happy that makes me." She was beaming at him. Luke was struck again at how beautiful she was and wondered how she had managed to hide it for so long. She was almost bouncing in her seat in excitement. "Let's go to the hospital. I can't wait to see her." She grabbed her purse ready to slide out of the booth.

Luke shook his head. "Not tonight sweetheart. The doctor said she is resting and they have some more tests to do as soon as she is up to it. We'll go tomorrow, okay?" Shannon was just so happy that the dear old lady was recuperating, she readily agreed.

Before they left the restaurant, Shannon had one more margarita. Luke was amused when he had to hold her steady on the way out. Although the starry night was crystal clear, the ride home was a blur to Shannon. When they walked into the apartment, she abruptly decided she wanted a bath. Still standing in the living room, with a slightly confused look on her face, she began to take off her blouse.

With his arms crossed over his chest, Luke watched from across the room. When she almost fell over trying to take her jeans off, he went to help. He picked her up and carried her half clad body into her bedroom to lay her on the bed. "How about I go draw the bath for you, while you just rest here for a minute?"

Bleary eyed she peered up at him. "You'll draw my bath? Wow, thas the nicest thing anybody's ever done for me." She giggled as she looked up at him through half closed lids and raised her arms above her head to stretch luxuriously. Her breasts swelled above her bra. Completely happy for the moment, she sighed in contentment.

Luke turned to walk into the bathroom a little stiffly, the front of his jeans straining tightly. He knew she had no idea of what a little sex kitten she was at the moment. Thinking to distract himself for a moment, he looked around the bathroom. Spying an assortment of what looked like bath oils and bath salts, he started to fill the tub with steamy water while he decided which one to use. When the first bottle didn't produce any bubbles, he added some powder from a box. The rich botanical smells blended beautifully as they filled the small room.

Hearing a noise he turned around to see a shyly smiling Shannon watching him. "Thanks, Luke. You really are a wonderful man." Her voice was a little husky from the tequila. She turned to start pinning up her long spiraling curls. He was relieved to see that she seemed to have lost some of the buzz. He knew he had to get out of the room before she slid into the bubbles or she would never have the time to bathe. Before he left though, he took the time to nab a clear plastic bottle to take with him.

When Shannon came out of the bath room a little while later, she couldn't believe her eyes. He must have found every scented candle in the apartment. Her room was aglow with flickering lights as music played softly from the living room. For some reason, though, he had made a pallet of beach towels on the floor at the foot of her bed, with pillows at one end. With one brow quirked, she raised her eyes from the pallet to look at him inquiringly. When he produced the bottle of baby oil from behind his back she was even more confused.

Luke sat the plastic bottle down and walked over to her. With one hand behind her neck, he cupped the back of her head. Looking deeply into her eyes, he whispered, "Trust me." He kissed her softly and then took her hand to lead her to the pallet.

He removed her towel and lowered her to the floor to lie on her stomach. Saying nothing, she watched him over her shoulder as he took the bottle and poured the oil into his hands. He straddled her hips and began at the base of her naked spine as he took his thumbs and massaged slowly all the way up. As he finally reached the top, a low moan escaped her lips.

"Luke," she whispered weakly, "have I died and gone to heaven?"

He chuckled deeply, sexily, "Just you wait, sweetheart." He continued to rub every inch of her until her skin was glowing in the candlelight. As the music continued to play softly, she almost felt like she was floating. The scent of the candles filled the room as he turned her over to start on the front of her body. He lifted one long leg and slowly, deeply, massaged her foot working his way up her leg to her knee. He repeated this decadent delight with her other long shapely leg. As he smoothed the oil in circular motions up her thighs, she thought she might faint from expectation.

He just smiled and took the bottle to dribble the oil across her breasts and down the valley between her ribs. Letting the oil run as it may, he smoothed his hands up the outer sides of her body. Slowly, up. Slowly down again. Up again. Down again. As more of the oil reached his hands, the contrast of the slick oil and his rough, calloused fingers caused her sensitive skin to quiver as he repeated this over and over.

By the time he began to caress her taunt breasts, she was starting to tremble with need. Her skin was hot and slick as he ran his hands all over her. Their tongues met as he kissed her passionately. She slanted her mouth and grabbed the back of his hair to deepen the kiss. She had never felt a need like this. Never knew it existed. As he leaned over her to lay his lithe body next to hers, she rolled even more until she was lying on top of him. She sensuously rubbed her heated, oiled body up and down his until he was as slick as she was. She sat up and straddled his hips. Reaching back she took the pins from her hair, letting the curls free to swirl around her waist. She looked him straight in the eyes as she took him inside her inch by inch.

CHAPTER 31

▼

It was much later when Shannon woke up. She didn't remember how they managed to wind up sleeping in the bed. Moving slowly so as not to waken him, she rose on one elbow to watch him sleep. My god, the man was truly gorgeous. Even his wide smooth forehead was beautiful. She wished she were an artist so she could draw him, or paint his portrait. "Oh, God, is he too good to be true?" She wondered.

She realized that was one thing holding her back. When he whispered during the long night, that he loved her, she still had not said it back.

This magnificent man said he loved her. Could it possibly be true? She had no doubt that he believed it. But she had to worry that his feelings were mixed up due to the case and his feelings of protection, for her and her family. How could a man that looked like this be such a great person? A part of her felt unworthy.

Her eyes roamed the length of his body. To her disappointment, the sheet covered his midsection, and then her eyes stopped in disbelief. At the end of the bed, his feet were sticking out of the sheets. His feet were … she felt a giggle well up inside her chest. His feet were positively ugly. They had to be at least a size thirteen and his hairy toes seemed to bend in different directions. She had the urge to pull the sheets back to see if these unsightly feet could possibly belong to him.

Knowing she couldn't hold back the hilarity a second longer, she grabbed a pillow and turned over to try to stifle her laughter with it.

Luke woke up to see Shannon laying there with her back to him. He was instantly concerned to see her shoulders shaking. "Shannon, honey, don't cry! What's wrong, sweetheart?" When her shoulders just shook even harder, he rolled her over to try to console her. It was only then he realized it was laughter causing her to shake. Thoroughly confused, he just cocked his head and stared at her.

Seeing the look on his face, she threw back her head and erupted with laughter. Tears were streaming down her face and she started to hick-up, making the uncontrollable laughter begin to hurt her stomach. Luke was really worried. Maybe all the stress was starting to get to her. He sat up and tried to take her in his arms. Her eyes widened and she held one hand to her heart and one hand out to hold him away. He backed away to give her some room; she seemed to be having trouble catching her breath. Her hair was tangled and wild around her flushed face. He truly didn't know what to do as she struggled to contain herself.

Luke got out of bed and walked naked around to the other side. The sight of his strong, hard body help to take her mind off his feet and she managed to calm down a little. As he stood beside the bed, she tried desperately not to look down at his feet. Instead she looked up into his clear blue eyes that were watching her with such concern. She rose to her knees in the bed, letting the sheet fall away to expose her own nakedness. She reached up to put her hands on either side of his face and draw him down for a kiss. "Oh Luke, I love you so much!" She sat back on the bed and wiped the tears from her checks.

"What?" Luke was mystified. "You're laughing like this because you love me?

Realizing what she had said did the trick of sobering her up completely. Her fingers flew to her mouth, as she knew the words were true. Her eyes were round with the wonder of it. Not taking her eyes from his, she nodded her head. "Oh. I do. I truly do!" She laughed again from the sheer joy of it. "I feel free! Somehow, today, I feel like a new person. I feel truly free to be myself." She wrapped her arms around her waist and squeezed her eyes shut to savor the moment. When she opened them, Luke was standing there, proudly letting her see how her declaration was affecting him. The evidence of is desire seemed to be reaching out for her.

"Well," he said in a fake western drawl, "I was pretty good last night." Pretending indifference he curved his hand to study his nails. When he peeked over at her, he was relieved to see her smiling at him, with no trace of the madness he had witnessed earlier. He dived on the bed and began to kiss her face. "So," he said between kisses, "You realize you love me." He kissed her cheeks, her forehead, and her nose and, lastly, her softly parted lips. Then he drew back and looked at her quizzically. "What was it Shannon? What finally made you realize it?"

When she covered her mouth with her hand and looked up at the ceiling, he thought she was embarrassed to admit it was sex. He grinned a bit smugly. "Come on, admit it. You love my ..."

"Feet!" She declared.

He drew back and stared down at her with a stunned expression on is face. "What?"

Keeping her hand firmly over her mouth, she pointed at his feet.

"My feet? You love me because of my ugly feet?"

She nodded her head again.

Luke cleared his throat and sat up. "Okay. Shannon," He took her hand in his. "Could you please explain?"

Shannon laid her free hand on his cheek and smiled into his eyes. "I do love you, Luke. So much." She sighed and rested her hand in her lap as she tried to find the words to explain. "I've always thought you were wonderful. But you were so perfect. I was afraid I could never measure up, or ... or be good enough for you. I was scared that you were too good to be true ... and then." She looked at his feet.

"You fell in love with my feet?"

She threw a pillow at him. "No, you idiot. I've never seen feet that ugly in my life. But somehow,—somehow they made me see how ridiculous I was being. I knew that even if your face looked like that, I would still love you. And, that you weren't too perfect. You're just a really good man."

Luke put his hand behind her head and drew her to him. He touched his lips to hers. "That's the best compliment I've ever had. I love you Shannon. I really love you." He laid her back on the bed, his intention pressing hard against her belly. Shannon's moan of pleasure turned into a groan as they heard his beeper go off. Luke was instantly alert as he checked the number. "Damn, it's the station. A nine one one" He looked at her apologetically. "I'm sorry, sweetheart. I have to go."

As Luke dressed Shannon noticed how brightly the sun was starting to shine through the window. Looking at the clock she knew she had to start getting ready for work too. Still, watching Luke move around her bedroom, she took the time to just lie there and savor the moment. Too quickly, he was pulling her up to crush her body tightly to his and kiss her goodbye.

It wasn't until after he left that her mind shifted enough to wonder what the emergency was. After she called to check on her Dad and Bryan, she showered and dressed quickly. Even with worry beginning to nag at her, she felt like she was glowing inside. On the walk to the office she thought the flowers looked brighter. The birds were singing more than usual. She thought being in love with Luke made the whole world a better place.

*   *   *   *

He watched her walk to work. The bitch actually had a smile on her face. He rubbed the scratches on his chest from the struggle the night before. An evil smile crossed his face, as he knew her world was about to be rocked again. *"I'm getting closer, dear Shannon."* He sneered.

"Soon it'll be our turn. Soon!" He slammed his fist into his open palm.

CHAPTER 32

▼

For once, Shannon wasn't the first to arrive. Amber looked at her with a huge smile and raised eyebrows. "Hey, hey, hey! It looks like love," she sang out the last word. Shannon stopped in mid stride and looked at her in amazement. Finally she dropped her eyes shyly. Amber screamed and ran across the room to hug her. "I knew it! I can spot love at first glance." She hugged her again. "I'm so happy for you. And Luke. You two just fit." Then she cocked her head as a new thought occurred. "You know what? I should be a matchmaker. A match maker," she said again, almost reverently as the idea took hold. "Don't you think I'd be a good one? I knew from the beginning that none of the rest of us had a chance with him. There's something kinda different about him. You know, like you."

Shannon didn't really know exactly what she was talking about, but she liked to think she and Luke were on the same wavelength. As Amber rambled on Shannon moved to sit at her desk. Both girls had been working steadily on paperwork and chatting when they realized it was almost nine thirty. "That's weird," Amber commented. "We haven't even heard from Heather. Usually when she's going to be late, she at least calls and gives us a list of things to do. And Camille's late again too, although now that I think about it, she's probably going to have the day off because of her tooth." she grinned and shook her head.

"Man, I still can't believe you did that. I hope the dentist could fix it somehow, or else she's gonna kill you." They both turned to see who was coming in the front door.

It was Heather, and as she got closer they could see her face was swollen from crying. She was shaking and pale. A policeman walked in behind her, then stopped as though to guard the front door. Heather dropped into a chair in front of Amber's desk. She looked over at Shannon.

"Come over here and sit with us honey."

Shannon walked across the room on wooden legs as dread filled her stomach. Her feet were already frozen. She looked at Amber and saw that tears were filling her eyes. They both knew. Before Heather even opened her mouth again, they both knew. Heather reached out and took each of their hands in hers.

"Girls," she began, and then she stopped and took a deep breath, "Camille was murdered. They think it was the same guy. But I heard one of the cops say … he said that this was much more violent." She started sobbing again. Amber came around her desk and put her arms around the other two. The three of them just huddled together and cried for a while.

Shannon was not only horrified to know that Camille had died a violent death; she was overcome with guilt as she thought of their last moments together. She had actually hit the girl on the day she died. Suddenly she couldn't breathe. She backed away from the other two gasping for air. Heather knew immediately what was happening. "Amber, go get a paper bag out of the top drawer of my credenza."

Amber ran to get the bag as Heather held onto Shannon's hand. When she returned, Shannon put the empty bag to her mouth to try to breathe in and out. As she slowly regained her breath, Heather started to talk to her. "Shannon, I know what you're thinking. When you and Camille had that fight yesterday, you had no way of knowing she didn't have long to live. Don't even let yourself go there," she said sternly.

Shannon looked at Heather in surprise and Amber's eyes filled with tears again. Heather looked at the two of them. "What? You think I never have feelings or something? I am human you know." Then she grinned a little humbly, "Why do you think I have those paper bags in my office? I have anxiety sometimes. I may not do a lot of the work around here, but I am responsible for it."

"Well," she stood up briskly and smoothed out her skirt. "I have to go call the corporate office. I'm afraid they might close us down." She walked a little unsteadily to her office.

✳   ✳   ✳   ✳

Camille's apartment was on the front corner of the property. Luke was still inside with the police. Camille's body had been draped with a sheet, as they were getting ready to move her. The apartment was torn up. Either she had put up a hell of a fight, or the killer's rage was getting out of control. Her body was pretty beat up, except for her face. The only cut on it was the one from Shannon's fist. Luke would have to explain that to the medical examiner later. At this time, cause of death looked to be strangulation.

Nico sighed as he was making notes. "Did you notice how he put the wig on her head? Kind of like he just half ass did it. Remember in the beginning how precise everything was? I think he's losing it man. He didn't even wipe all of her make up off. And there's no doubt of sexual assault this time." He shook his head as he thought of the vicious marks on the body. "Yeah, he's losing it. There's blood and maybe some skin under her fingernails. Hell, he even left bite marks."

Luke looked around the apartment. "Or, something's made him mad." he said quietly. They had thought his dating Shannon would induce the killer to make a move, and they had thought they had been ready. Extra patrols had driven the property all night. An unmarked van with two officers inside had been sitting in the shadows just down the parking lot from Shannon's apartment.

Nico slapped Luke on the shoulder. "Well boy, looks like its back to the drawing board.

*   *   *   *

Heather came out of the office to find the Shannon and Amber just sitting there, each lost in her own thoughts. "I just got off the phone with Rita. We are going to keep the office open for the residents only. We're not going to lease any more apartments for a while, but we'll still be open for work orders and resident activities."

"Resident activities? You mean like the Halloween parties?" Amber was skeptical.

"Yeah, but now we'll just keep it simple and have one party for the kids, here in this clubhouse. We're to all stay together as much as possible. They don't even want us to walk the property alone. And we're going to have a community meeting to answer all the residents' questions. Rita and Ted will be here as well as Detective Blake and some of the other officers."

Shannon was relieved they wouldn't have to field all the questions by themselves. "When is the meeting?"

"This evening at six o'clock."

"Who is going to call Camille's family?"

Heather took a deep breath. "I think the police have already notified them. I'm going to go confirm that and then call them myself." She braced her shoulders and went back into her office.

"Wow. I always thought being the Manager was the easy job. I wouldn't want the job right now. And you know what? I think I might really look into working in a different field. What about you, Shannon? Aren't you kinda scared to work here?"

Shannon nodded her head, but the truth was, she didn't know if she would be any safer anywhere else. They hadn't told anyone that Shannon might be the ultimate target.

CHAPTER 33

▼

At the police station Luke was in a meeting with several of the others that were involved in the case. Detective Blake had just informed them of the meeting with the residents to be held that evening. Many of the officers were not looking forward to it. Blake sought to alleviate their concerns.

"They're not going to riot on us or anything, but they are justifiably afraid. The chief said we have received almost a hundred phone calls so far. And most of you will just be there to show a definitive presence. The chief will be answering most of the questions. Plus there will be some people from the corporate office that own the property."

One officer sneered, "Yeah, they'll just point the finger at us and say it's our fault for not already catching the guy."

Blake nodded, "You may be right, and we have to be prepared for that. After all …" He took a moment to look each man in the eyes, "It is our job to keep this city safe. And this guy is making us look bad, men. Real bad."

After most of the men had filed out, Luke, Nico and Blake had a private meeting of their own. Blake turned to Luke. "You know, maybe he's turning his focus away from Shannon. He didn't contact her in any way after this murder."

Luke sighed, "Yeah, that thought has occurred to me and I'm hoping you're right. But my gut tells me otherwise."

Nico spoke up, "I've run a check on any and all the residents that have been evicted since the property opened. None of them have any serious criminal records. We've spoken to most of them and checked their alibis for the specific times of the murders, but there are still three of them we can't locate. Just like that last maintenance man. There is one guy I'm kinda looking at. His name is Ephram Peters and he seems to think a lot of Shannon. He has a pretty bad stutter, but the more he talked about Shannon, he stuttered a little less. I've got Mallory pulling his background."

"And I did get to talk to the professor. He says he doesn't bear Shannon any ill will at all, if you can believe that, which I sure as hell don't. He acted like he didn't even know where she was living now."

"Well I have to ask Nico, you didn't tell him did you?"

"I'm going to pretend you didn't ask me that. Do I look green to you?"

Blake wanted them to get back to the subject, "Well, do you like this guy for it?"

Nico leaned his chair on its back two legs while he thought carefully before answering, "Truth to tell, I was convinced it was that maintenance man, I mean we did find that glass with his finger prints on it at that one crime scene. But I'll tell you; now that I've met the professor ... well, he is a slimy son of a bitch. You can tell he thinks he is a real ladies man. But he doesn't have any respect for women at all. I think it bears investigating his childhood."

"What did he say about Shannon and Bryan?" Luke had a lot of curiosity about this man.

"He said he was real sorry. Said he wished she had never come on to him so strongly and he never could be sure the kid was even his. It was like he thought he was the victim and wanted me to be sorry for him. I just left it like that, man."

Luke nodded, "Let's get a tail on him immediately. And put a team together to do nothing but track that former maintenance man down." He looked at his watch. "I've got to get back out there."

Each man closed their notebooks and agreed to meet at five o'clock so they could once again compare notes before the meeting with the residents.

Luke called Shannon on his way back to the property. "Hey, sweetheart, how're you doing?"

"I'm okay, Luke. Are you on your way here?"

"Yeah. I've been tied up or I would have called you sooner. How is everyone taking it about Camille?"

"Well, it's been kinda strange of course. It's had a huge effect on Heather. She's been—nice, all day."

"Sometimes things like this can really put it in perspective for some people. How's Amber?"

"She's holding up. She's talking about changing jobs. You know, it's like the three of here in the office have kind of bonded today. It's weird." She paused, "Is it true that … that this time it was even more violent?"

The chaotic scene from this morning flashed through Luke's mind. "Hey, you know what? I'll be there in a few minutes. We'll talk then okay?"

As Shannon hung up the phone, she knew Luke was avoiding her question. That meant it must have been really bad.

CHAPTER 34

▼

So many residents had called about coming to the meeting that they had to set up a site outside behind the pool. The police department had sent out a podium platform, a microphone with speakers and two hundred and fifty chairs. Even with that many chairs, there were a lot of people standing around the edges and in the back. The media had shown up and Shannon was surprised to see there would even be national coverage.

The police chief wasn't surprised, he was dismayed. "Shit, I should have had the mayor here. Why the hell didn't somebody tell me the media would be here?" The man was about five feet ten inches tall with snow white hair. His droopy dark brown eyes and the jowls along his jaw line gave him a hound dog look

Luke thought the man had been in the business long enough that he should have figured it out for himself. His eyes scanned the crowd looking for Shannon. When he saw her awkwardly trying to field questions from a group of residents, he went to take her hand and tell her the meeting was about to start. They sat on the front row with the people from the corporate office.

Undercover agents were mingled in with the crowd. Nico was standing on the platform with several other officers, although he was still in plain clothes. With his arms folded across his massive chest, the muscles in his arms were bulging. He had on sunglasses and looked to be staring straight ahead. Shannon thought he looked formidable and was glad he was on their side.

Rita was the first speaker. She tapped the microphone to check the sound. The crowd immediately fell silent. With complete grace and composure she began. "Ladies and gentlemen, my name is Rita Williams. I am the Vice President of Kingsway Properties. We asked you all here tonight to address the tragic events of the past month. We will answer as many questions as we can, but please be aware that this is an ongoing investigation and you may very well expect to hear 'No comment' to some of your questions."

As several dozen hands rose in the air she held up her hand to stop the flood of questions.

"First we are going to let Chief Conway give us what information he can, then he'll accept your questions. I just want to say that we offer our sincere condolences to those of you that have lost friends and neighbors. Our hearts are broken, along with yours." With somber dignity she turned the podium over to the chief and took her seat.

"Good evening," the chief began rather stiffly. "We at the Dallas Police Department understand the concerns many of you must have at this time. I, myself have spoken to some of you on the telephone." His eyes scanned the rows of faces before him. "Let me assure you that we have put every available man to work on this case. We have even called in the Texas Rangers. This was news to Luke, and he decided he didn't mind at all. Lives were at stake here.

Nationally, Luke knew that most people thought of the Texas Rangers as a baseball team. But in law-enforcement The Texas Rangers are the oldest law enforcement agency in North America with statewide jurisdiction. They are even sometimes compared to other world-famous agencies such as the FBI, the Royal Canadian Police, and Scotland Yard. The Texas Ranger Division performs an assorted range of criminal investigations including murder.

After giving out as few details as possible, the chief concluded, "One final thing before taking your questions, we strongly recommend you each return home tonight to check your door locks and your window locks. In an unprecedented move, the owner is allowing you the right to add extra locks of your own, even on your doors, until the suspect is apprehended."

"Do not walk alone at night, and be very aware of your surroundings at all times. Awareness is the key. Please report any unusual activities, noises or persons at once. Do not hesitate to call 911. Now let's be practical with the order of asking these questions. I will accept one question from every other row. We'll start with the front row and work our way to the last. At this time, I will not accept questions from the media. I am here tonight for the residents of this community."

Every hand on the front row raised in the air, except for those of the people that worked for Kingsway. The chief selected a plump man of about forty years old. He stood up importantly as he was singled out.

"Chief Conway, are these murders completely at random, or do you think he knows the victims?"

"At this time, there is no way to tell."

The man tried to ask another question but Conway waved him down. "One question per person please." He pointed to a lady in the third row.

"Did the attack on Mrs. Martin have anything to do with this?"

"It does not appear to be connected."

The questions went on for almost forty minutes. At the end the residents didn't really feel anymore reassured, but they did feel unified. Many of them agreed to start building watches. Their new attitude was that of taking care of their own and helping to protect each other.

*   *   *   *

"Yeah, right. Like these assholes have a chance of ever catching me." He was right there in the middle of everybody. He gave a nod to the lady staring at him. Just look how she had smiled at him. He looked at her skin and wondered how she would taste.

He carefully kept just the right expression on his face. It wouldn't do to let them see how much fun this was. He was glad that he had taken the time to participate in this before he had to go out of town to pick up the—package.

CHAPTER 35

▼

Shannon woke with a feeling of dread in the pit of her stomach. Today they would bury Camille. Tears immediately filled her eyes. Sensing her need, Luke rolled over and took her into his arms. He tucked her head under his chin and just let her cry for a while, listening to the rain pound at the windows.

*   *   *   *

Nico arrived late at the funeral home. He glanced at the clock in his car again to make sure. Where were all the cars? Thunder rolled in the sky as rain continued to fall in sheets. Although it was close to one o'clock in the afternoon, it was almost dark as night outside. Maybe the storm was making everyone else late too. He spotted Luke and Shannon as they hurried through the front doors. Pulling his collar up at the back of his neck he made a dash to catch up with them.

He could hear the organ music playing softly as soon as he opened the heavy wooden door. Shannon walked over and took his hand. "I'm glad you could come, Nico. It doesn't look like too many others are here yet." She shivered and stepped back closer to Luke for warmth.

Putting his arm around her, the three of them moved to the doorway that led into the chapel. The room was done in all whites and very light ice blues. In stark contrast, the black coffin was displayed in front of the white wooden pews. There was one display of soft white lilies on the left side.

Shannon glanced at her watch, the service was supposed to begin in ten minutes and yet there were only seven people seated so far. Heather was sitting next to Rita and Ted. Hearing a commotion behind her she turned and saw that Luke was helping Amber with her rain coat.

Walking towards the casket, Shannon's knees felt weak. As she bent down to lay the flowers she brought she felt a little light headed. Gratefully she felt Luke's hand at her elbow. Turning she saw a dark headed woman that strongly resembled Camille seated in the front pew and knew it must be Camille's Mother. She was talking on her cell phone. Her black suite looked expensive. However the way she had her legs crossed, it rode high up her legs. She had on a large black hat with some kind of feather sticking out of it. Shannon thought she looked kind of like Joan Collins in a scene from Dynasty.

"Should we go offer our condolences?" Shannon looked up at Luke.

"Sure." Tucking her arm through his, they went over to where a man was seated next to the woman. He had been watching them rather intently.

"Hello." Shannon held out her hand. 'Are you Camille's Father?"

"Oh, ah …" He gave a self depreciating chuckle; his face turned an alarming shade of red all the way down to both of his double chins. The wisp of hair on top of his head swayed from side to side as he shook his head. "No. No. Actually, I'm husband number six. Camille's Dad was husband number two. He, ah … couldn't make it here today."

Next to him the woman slammed her cell phone shut. "Well why should he be bothered? He hasn't seen her in five years anyway." She said sarcastically. I'm Nora, I'm her Mother." She nodded towards the coffin.

Luke cleared his throat. "We're very sorry for you loss ma'am."

She shrugged her shoulders. "I always knew this would happen. I always knew she would come to a bad end. Bad girls come to a bad end. I've told her that since she was little." She glanced at her watch. "How long is this supposed to last? Can't we get started?" She turned around in her seat to look around. "Paul, go tell them to go ahead with it." She pulled a compact out of her purse to apply more red lipstick.

Shannon gasped, this was Camille's mother? She didn't look like she had even shed a tear. "A bad end? What do you mean? Camille didn't bring this on herself. She was …"

Luke clamped down on her arm and began to pull her away. "Nice meeting you, we'll just take our seats."

"Luke! She …"

"I know, I know. Listen. Let's discuss this later."

Shannon could feel tears threatening again as she sat in a pew next to Amber, behind Rita, Ted and Heather. Amber reached over to hold her hand as the music changed and the service began.

Luke and Nico exchanged looks. Nico shook his head and spoke in a low voice to Luke, "Now this is sad. I thought Debbie Sutton's funeral was sad, but I guess there is sad and then there's sad."

Grimly, Luke nodded his head, understanding just what he meant.

✳   ✳   ✳   ✳

The actual burial took place inside a mausoleum. Once again everything was white, except for the small ficus tree in the corner near the window at the end of the hallway. Shannon couldn't believe no one else had shown up for the service. It was a small somber group that watched in silence as two men slid the coffin into place and quietly shut the small door. Amber cried quietly into a handkerchief.

This was the second funeral Nico had been to that was connected to this killer. The difference in the two was like night and day. He had only met Camille once, but he thought everyone deserved better than this. He looked into her mothers eyes and finally saw a quite desperation and sadness. Maybe she had just realized her own passing would be just as bleak. It was a bad time to realize that actions have consequences and if you go through life being a bitch to everyone, you wouldn't have many friends or loved ones along the way.

CHAPTER 36

▼

As the week went by the days were long, and the nights were short as Luke and Shannon spent each one in each other's arms. They constantly called Sam and Bryan, until Sam made them agree to set specific times to call. "We feel like we're on vacation out here, except for the damn phone ringing all the time."

On Friday night, Luke and Shannon were eating Chinese food they had had delivered. "So, my Mother and sisters are coming in tomorrow."

At Shannon's surprised look, Luke reminded her, "I told you they were coming. They can't wait to meet you. And Bryan and Sam. They want to meet us at my house in the morning." When Shannon looked agreeable, if not a little shy, he went on. "As a matter of fact, they thought it might be fun if you'd go shopping with them while I take Sam and Bryan out on the lake. We'll use the same method as last time driving out there to make sure we're not followed."

"But Luke, if I am somehow a target to this killer, couldn't it be putting your family in danger too?"

"Since he didn't contact you at all after killing Camille, we're hoping you're not his intended target at this point. But as I said, we'll be extremely careful going out there. Plus, I don't think he'd be looking for you at the Galleria Mall." He didn't add that he would have people tailing them because he wanted her to feel more relaxed.

Whenever they were out he'd noticed how she tensed up and kept glancing at the undercover agents when she knew who they were.

With her eyes lowered, she had to ask, "What if they don't like me?"

"Who?"

"Your family!"

"Shannon." Luke took her hand in his. "How could they not love you? The women in my family are great, like you. Mom's been trying to get me to settle down for years. And my sisters will just be happy to keep me away from their friends."

"Why don't they want you to date their friends?"

Luke looked uncomfortable, "Well, uh, I tried that a couple of times and it didn't work out." He looked around for something to change the subject. Shannon thought he must have left a trail of broken hearts behind and it made her more than a little uncomfortable.

*   *   *   *

When they arrived at Luke's house the next morning, Bryan ran out to greet them. Even in the October sun he had spent so much time outdoors that his face was tan. He was talking as fast as he could, trying to tell them everything at once. Shannon looked around and was glad they had arrived before Luke's family. Just the thought of meeting them had the butterflies returning to her stomach.

Sam was waiting just inside the door. "Hi Dad." His face also showed signs of being in the sun. "I'll have to remember to buy yall some sun block today." She bent to give him a hug and felt comfort in his familiar embrace. This week was one of the longest periods of times they had ever been apart. Even when he was in the hospital, she had visited him regularly.

Before they had much time to catch up, they saw a beautiful pearly white Lexus driving up to them. Luke had a big smile on his face and put his arm around Bryan. "We're about to be surrounded by women for a while, but I promise as soon as they go shopping, we'll have some manly time. I thought we'd take the boat out again today. Are you up for it?"

Bryan gave Luke a big hug, "You bet I am!" He turned to see three women get out of the car. One of them looked like she was going to have a baby, one of them was skinny and the other one—she was smiling at him, and it looked like she had tears in her eyes.

Nanette Manning had seen the obvious love and affection between her son and the little boy. The sight of them together made her grandmotherly heart swell. But her heart was the only grandmotherly thing about her. She was a tall slender woman in her mid-fifties. Her softly blonde hair was caught up in a clip behind her head and she had fluffy bangs above lively light blue eyes. Bryan thought she looked like an angel. She even had on pale gold slacks with a matching sweater set.

When she bent down in front of him, Bryan felt unaccountably shy. "You must be Bryan."

Even her voice seemed soft and angelic to Bryan. Without realizing it, Bryan took a step closer to her.

"Yes, mam. I am Bryan." He swallowed hard. "You look just like an angel!"

With a tinkling laugh, Nanette knelt down and took him into her arms. "Well, aren't you just the sweetest thing! My name is Nannette, but you may call me Nannie, if you'd like." Bryan thought she smelled like heaven too. He was glad that when she stood up, she kept her arm around him. He thought he might be in love.

Luke had been greeting his sisters, but had not missed the exchange between his mother and Bryan. It looked like love at first sight, he thought with a lump in his throat.

"Mom, I see you've met Bryan. This is Sam and Shannon."

He turned to Sam and Shannon, "This is my mother Nannette, and my sisters, Sarah and Rachel."

Everyone shook hands and made small talk while they went inside. As they were seated around the living room, Nannette and Bryan stayed close together. Shannon agreed with her son. She thought Luke's mother looked like an angel too. It was hard not to stare at her, the woman was really beautiful. And she had obviously passed it on to her children, she noticed as she looked around the room. Sarah had light brown hair, cut shoulder length and her mother's light blue eyes. Rachael's long straight hair was medium blonde like Luke's, and she had bright blonde streaks placed strategically throughout. She was also tall and thin, but very curvaceous. The tight jeans and loose blue sweater she wore showed off her figure beautifully yet tastefully. Suddenly Shannon wished she had not just worn her hair back in a braid and that her clothes were a bit more updated.

Watching her, Luke took her hand in his, causing her to blush at the open display of affection in front of their families. He knew how shy she was and he felt a little sorry for her. His mother and sisters as a group often intimidated other women. Shannon didn't realize she had nothing to feel uncomfortable about. She was every bit as beautiful as the women in his family.

Sarah smiled as she pressed a hand to her swollen belly. "Hey Bryan, have you ever felt an unborn baby kick?"

With his eye's wide Bryan shook his head. He could actually see her hand move as the baby beneath it was kicking.

"Come on over here and you can feel it." Sarah patted the seat beside her.

Bryan walked slowly over to her. As she took his hand and placed it on the spot where the baby moved, he laughed out loud. "Wow, there really is someone in there! That's the coolest thing ever!"

Everyone laughed and some of the tension in the room dissipated. After an hour or so of conversation, Rachel pressed the women to go shopping. "Come on, yall. That's one of the main reason's we came. And by the time we get back, Luke can have the bar-b-que ready."

Nannette had grown even more enchanted with Bryan. She took his hand," Would you like to go shopping with us, honey?"

Bryan actually considered it for a moment. Then he remembered Luke's promise of the boat. "No ma'am, I'd rather stay with the men. But you'll come back, won't you?"

"Well of course I will." She winked at him, "How about I bring you back a little surprise?"

*   *   *   *

When the women had all piled into Nannette's car, the men waved them off. Suddenly it was a lot quieter. Bryan shook his head, "Wow, I never knew girls were so noisy." He took Luke's hand. "I love your mother. And your sister's are nice too."

"Well, that make's it convenient because I love your mother too. Hey, why don't you go change clothes and we'll take the boat out." Luke wanted a few minutes alone with Sam. The two men discussed in detail all the latest news about the case.

"So Shannon doesn't know you'll have people tailing them all day?"

"No, she tends to be more nervous and she can't help looking for them. If someone were watching her, they would figure it out. But my mother and Rachel know. If there is trouble they only have to look for someone wearing bright yellow of some kind, like a yellow tie, a yellow purse or shirt. But, honestly, I think they'll be completely safe today. I wouldn't stay out here otherwise."

CHAPTER 37

▼

The four women walking through the Galleria mall did cause heads to turn, even though the mall was full of beautiful Texas women. The enormous building was several stories high and had all the best stores, national chains and smaller specialty shops. In the middle of it all was a large ice-skating rink, surrounded by delicious smelling, bistro restaurants. Shannon knew that in less than thirty days, there would be a gigantic Christmas tree in the center of it. Bryan loved to come here during the holidays and see all the elaborate decorations. It was tradition for them to come every year. Shannon had taught him to ice skate when he was just four years old.

She was telling Nannette about it when she noticed Rachel looking at her intently. She broke off what she had been about to say and cocked her head, "What?" She raised her hand to her braid to see if it was coming undone.

Rachel cleared her throat. "Shannon, I'm a very blunt person, and I just want to say, I really like you."

Clearly surprised, Shannon felt a little embarrassed. "Well, thank you. I think you are all wonderful. Luke has told me a lot about yall, but getting to know you is even better." She smiled warmly at all three of them. She truly had felt comfortable with them all day.

When Sarah put her hand on Rachel's arm in warning, Rachel impatiently brushed her aside. "Good. Then you won't mind if I'm completely honest with you?"

Now a little weary, Shannon just nodded her head. Uh oh. Here it comes. They don't think I'm good enough for Luke. With her heart sinking she braced herself for what was surely to come next. She didn't realize she was holding her breath until she let it out in a rush when she heard what Rachel had to say.

"I think you're pretty, but I think you could use a more modern look. Can I be in charge of giving you a makeover?" She said it in a rush because she had been holding it in for hours.

Sarah slapped her on the shoulder. "Rachel! For God's sake. Leave her alone. Luke loves her just the way she is. Didn't you see the way he was looking at her? I've never seen him look at anything or anyone that way. Have you?"

Rachael smirked, "Yeah. Mom's fudge." She looked at Shannon. "Nobody, and I mean nobody makes better fudge than our mother." She thought for a minute, and then nodded her head, "Yeah, that *is* how Luke looks at you. Kinda like he just wants to eat you up."

Shannon felt herself blush up to the roots of her hair. She folded her lips together tightly to avoid laughing inappropriately. Finally they all laughed together. It felt so good to be with the group of them. She felt young and carefree for the first time in a long while.

"As a matter of fact, I have been wanting a new wardrobe, since I started dating Luke. For our first date, I had to borrow a dress from a girl I work with. She even put my makeup on for me. I've been so caught up in just being Bryan's mom for so long, I just didn't pay any attention to how I looked." She smiled shyly, "Until I met Luke. All of a sudden it seems more important."

Rachel jumped up and gave her a great big hug. "I knew it. You're so feminine; I knew you'd like a make over. I love 'em. This is gonna be so much fun!" She all but squealed in her excitement.

Nannette was relieved that her daughter hadn't hurt this lovely young girls feelings. She knew it wouldn't take long for her to become a part of their family. She couldn't wait to tell her husband, Alan. Knowing what a whirlwind Rachel could be she took Sarah's hand. "Why don't we go find that baby shop your friend told you about? We can shop for your layette while the girls have their make over." She looked around and was reassured to see a man with a yellow tie standing at a jewelry stand not far away. He wasn't looking at the jewelry or at them, rather at the people around them. A woman in a bright yellow skirt passed them with an assessing glance.

Sarah was relieved to go off with her mother. As much as she couldn't wait to see the transformation, she was afraid she'd never be able to keep up in her condition. It was agreed they would all meet back by the ice rink at four o'clock.

CHAPTER 38

▼

During the shopping marathon that followed, Rachel took complete control. First they went to a make up artist and had her make up professionally done. Shannon was relieved that the man, Rah', agreed that natural colors suited her best, but when he was finished she doubted she could ever achieve the same results. Rah' spent an extra twenty minutes teaching her each technique.

Next came the piles and piles of clothes. Rachael commandeered the biggest dressing room. She had a stylish personal shopper named Chantal, start bringing in even more clothes than they had already picked out, in Shannon's size and best colors. She sat in a chair in the corner and had gasped when she saw Shannon in only her bra and panties. "Good lord! You've been hiding a body like that under all those baggy clothes?" Then she laughed and rolled her eyes. "Trust my brother to hone in on the best body in Dallas, even if it was hidden."

Time flew swiftly as Shannon tried on dresses, skirts, blouses, shirts, sweaters and pants. Rachel had even had matching shoes and boots brought in. When they had finally agreed on which outfit Shannon would wear home, it was time to take her hair down and see what they had to work with. When she shook it out, Rachel just gaped at her. Then she gave an unlady-like snort. "Hell, I've been wrong all day."

Shannon was alarmed, all that work and it was wrong? "What? I'll cut it if you want me to. I just never have time for it so I just pull it back. I know straight hair is in fashion. Can't we put a straightener on it or something?" She started to pull the offending hair back when Rachel stopped her.

"Shannon, I really did think you were pretty before. But you are … stunning. Luke was right." She just kept staring at this girl who could become her sister-in-law. "Woo-hoo! I can't wait for him to see you like this." Rachel left the room to tell to the sales girl that Shannon would wear this outfit home.

Staring at herself in the mirror, Shannon had to admit she was thrilled. The way Rah' had darkened her eyebrows a little and lined her lips, made her feel, well, sexy. Yet it was so subtle it wasn't sluttish. And while the slacks and sweater fit her curves closely, they weren't too tight. She looked—wealthy, like most of the other women who frequented this store. Speaking of wealthy, how was she going to explain to Rachel that she would only be able to get this one outfit? She had almost had a heart attack at the cost of the make up alone.

Chantal came in to remove the tags on the clothes she was wearing. The ankle high leather boots didn't have a tag so Shannon started to take them off.

"Oh, don't worry about that, we've taken care of it." Chantal beamed at her.

Shannon thought the sales lady seemed as excited as she felt. The camel colored boots fit her like a glove and were the exact same color as the slacks. Her hair flowed over the cream-colored cashmere sweater. She decided it was going to be worth the hit to her bank account.

She went out to meet with Rachel and was horrified to see her standing at the counter checking out with *all* of the clothes they had liked. With her hand on her heart she rushed over to her. Not wanting to embarrass her she took her hand and pulled her over to the side.

"Rachel," she said desperately, "there's no way I can afford all of this at one time. I'm just going to get this one outfit today. I'm sorry I didn't explain that to you. You just go wait for me over there and I'll explain to the sales ladies."

Rachel laughed, "What ever are you talking about? You said I could give you a make over." She looked expectantly into Shannon's eyes to see if she got it. "'Give' being the operative word. I only let you pay for the makeup because I had wandered off to look at the jewelry."

"Are you crazy?" Shannon looked over to where three sales women were putting plastic bags over several sets of clothes. "This one outfit is over $300.00!" Shannon felt dizzy and looked for a place to sit down.

Not quite understanding, Rachel led her over to a nearby seat by the dressing room. "Please tell me you're not going to insult me by not accepting my gifts. I thought you understood I was giving it to you. You've let me have so much fun dressing you up and everything." She considered for a minute.

"Luke did tell you who we are didn't he? I know he's been undercover, but he has told you his real last name, hasn't he?" Rachel's brows were drawn low over her eyes, as she was prepared to get mad at her brother.

"Manning. Of course he told me his name is Manning." Shannon almost stammered the words as it was starting to occur to her. "Manning! Not 'The Manning's?'" When Rachel just nodded her head, Shannon was glad she was sitting down. "You mean like the Louisiana oil well Manning's?" She asked weakly.

Rachel just looked at her fingernails, "Well, oil is one of our businesses; I guess it is the one that got us started." She called over to the sales people. "We'll bring the car around shortly to pick that up." She put her arm around Shannon's shoulders as she led the shocked girl out of the store. "Come on now, we have to hurry if we're gonna meet Momma and Sarah at the ice skating rink on time. "Wait until you see the jewelry I've picked out to go with the clothes and shoes."

*   *   *   *

On the ride back to Luke's house, Shannon was quiet and subdued, so Rachel talked almost non-stop. She told Shannon of the times Luke had dated some of her friends and when things didn't work out the girls had gotten their feelings hurt and she had lost three or four friends because of Luke. "That's why we're so happy he has found you. This is the first time he has ever said he's been in love with someone. Heck, I've been in love at least five times already, and I'm two years younger than he is. Sarah was in love at least twice before she married Gabe. Are you gonna let Luke keep being a cop after yall are married? You'd be Daddy's best friend if you could talk him out of it. He just thought it was a rebellious phase when Luke started at the academy. He never thought he'd really make a career of it."

Sarah spoke up from the front seat. "I think Daddy's kinda proud of Luke. Although he does expect him to take over the business someday."

CHAPTER 39

▼

Shannon was extremely relieved when they arrived back at Luke's. They could smell the brisket being cooked as soon as they opened the car doors. Bryan came running up to them with a huge smile on his face.

"Mom, wait until you see the fish I caught. It's so big that Luke had to help me." He stopped in his tracks and stared at his mother. "Mom? Wow! You look great! I better not give you your hug until I clean up a little bit." He ran off to do that as Luke and Nico came around to the front of the house.

They both stopped short as they looked at Shannon. Then Luke grinned and came up to kiss her. "It looks like Rachel got a hold of you. I hope you didn't mind, she just loves to doll people up. You do look great, sweetheart. Thank God she didn't mess with your hair." He couldn't resist stroking the silky mane.

Nico was making the rounds hugging and kissing all the women. When he got to Shannon, he put his arm around her shoulder and squeezed. "This is one of the main reasons I'm friends with this boy, just look at the women in his life."

Rachael sauntered up to Nico, "Hey Nico, how's the Goddess?" She was referring to Nico's sister. She always called her the Goddess because of her looks. It would be easy to picture her as some famous Greek Goddess that legends were made from.

"Toni is just fine. Probably getting herself in trouble exposing all those lying—cheating spouses. When's the last time you spoke to her? She probably tells you things she hides from me." He raised his eyebrows waiting for an answer. Rachael just smirked and walked away from him, with a coy look over her shoulder.

He moved off to say something to Nannette as the group walked away and Luke came back to Shannon's side. "What is it sweetheart? You look kinda shell shocked."

Shannon just pointed to the trunk of the car. "Open it."

Luke went to the driver's side of the car and pushed a button. The trunk sprang open to reveal mounds of bags, boxes and clothes. "What?" He asked her. "This is what it always looks like when they go shopping."

"Luke, most of that is for me. Rachel bought all of that for me. She said I gave her permission when I said she could 'give' me a makeover. And that's not even all of it. They're going to send us the rest!" She looked at him accusingly. "You're Lucas Manning."

"Well … I told you that." He was uncomfortable knowing that she hadn't really understood at the time.

"You said your last name was Manning. I knew your first name was Luke. You know I never put it together to be *The* Lucas Manning!" She crossed her arms over her chest and looked away from him.

"I told you I was from a great family."

"Well I think my family is great too. You should have said a GREAT family. As in millions of dollars."

"Actually, it's billions, sweetheart."

Shannon thought she was about to have a panic attack. "You just sent me off with them today. For a while there I actually thought I could fit in with them. I really liked them."

"What? You don't like us now because we have money?"

"Luke! How can I, or my Dad and Bryan ever fit in with yall? We're from two different worlds!"

"Now wait a minute. Have I ever seemed like a snob to you? Does the rest of my family seem like snobs?" He demanded with a dangerous look on his face.

"Well, no. But be a little realistic, Luke."

"I think it's realistic as hell the way my heart speeds up just to be near you. Hell, it even speeds up when I talk to you on the phone. Nothing has changed Shannon. I'm in love with you. And you're in love with me!" He grabbed her and crushed his mouth to hers.

Shannon felt her knees go weak and had to cling to him. She wrapped her arms around his neck and kissed him back with a passion that always shocked her. "Luke, I do love you, but I'm scared of so many things right now."

He held her close and stroked her silky hair. "I love you more than words can say, Shannon. You're everything I've ever dreamed of. And I love Bryan too. We had so much fun today. You should have seen his face when he caught that fish."

They were laughing when Bryan came back out of the house. "Come on yall, let's go eat, I'm hungry!"

He took each of their hands in his and walked between them to the gazebo. When Nannette and Sam saw the three of them coming, they smiled at each other the way parents do when they're happy for their children.

*   *   *   *

He couldn't believe he had seen her at the mall. Even in that outfit, there was no doubt it was her. No one else had hair like that. When he heard the other girl with her tell the salesclerk the address to send the extra purchases to, he had walked away and written it down.

He had to wonder if that's where the boy was. No wonder he hadn't seen him around the apartments. Tucking the address in his pocket, he had to hurry to get to work on time.

CHAPTER 40

The next day, all the guys decided to go out on the boat, while the women stayed to help Nanette make shrimp gumbo. As the spicy aroma filled the house, Rachel asked Shannon if she wanted to look at some old family photo albums.

They all sat around the kitchen table to be near the simmering food. The sunshine was pouring through the open windows and Sarah had put on a Van Morrison CD. Shannon knew it was a time she would always remember. Looking at the happy women surrounding her, she marveled that Luke wanted her to be a part of this family. Sisters, she would have sisters.

"Hey look at this one!" Rachael held up a picture of a smiling, drooling baby. "Does this look familiar Shannon? Just like he drools over you." Laughingly she passed the photo.

Shannon was mesmerized. She could actually see Luke in those baby eyes. Her own eyes felt misty for a minute, until she noticed that it had gotten so quite around the table. She looked up to see Rachel watching her as Nanette and Sarah shared a secret smile. Blinking rapidly, she offered a smile of her own, "He still has that kinda crooked smile."

"Look at this one," Rachel held up one of a little boy dressed as a mummy. "This is Luke at Halloween. How old was he here, Mom? About six? Oh, look Sarah this is you!"

They looked at one page after another, one photo album after another. Sharing all their favorite memories. Their stories were so vivid Shannon felt like she had been there. She held up one with a look of delight on her face. "Is this really Luke?"

Sarah and Rachel howled with laughter. "Oh, he's gonna kill us now. He hates that picture."

Shannon looked at it closer, he looked to be about six years old and was standing there with ragged tennis shoes on and very skinned up knees. The funny part was the red polka dot dress he was wearing, along with a curly red haired wig. He was missing his two front teeth. The look in his eyes was acute embarrassment, although he was grinning widely.

"Was it Halloween again?"

That caused the women to laugh even harder.

"No … no. He lost a bet with Sarah. He …"

She broke off and jumped guiltily as the subject of their laughter opened the kitchen door and walked into the room. Everyone got suddenly very quiet as Rachel tried to slip the picture under one of the cuter ones.

She wasn't fast enough.

Luke reached out and grabbed her wrist with lightning speed. When he saw the one she held in her hand, he just sighed and walked over to Shannon. "Have they been making you sit here and listen to childhood stories?"

She smiled up at him and smiled hugely. "Yes, and I've loved every minute of it!"

The sparkle in her eyes meant more to him than any embarrassing picture. "Do you still love me?"

Her eyes widened as she tried not to look at those surrounding them. At her barely perceptible nod, the room erupted in shouts and laughter once more.

*　　　*　　　*　　　*

Later the house was quiet, Sarah was taking a nap, and the others had gone out for a nature walk. Shannon was just standing in the open back doorway staring out at the lake as the sun was about to set. The wind was blowing her hair and she looked lost in thought. Luke walked up behind her and, wrapping his arms around her waist, he brushed the hair away from her neck to place kisses all along her jaw line. Her head tilted to give him more access and with a sigh she just leaned back into him.

"Am I dreaming Luke?"

"If you are I am too." He softly kissed her lips. "But we're not. This is as real as it gets, honey." His voice was low and soft.

"Mmmm," She turned and threw her arms tightly around his neck. "I'm just so happy and content I'm almost frightened with it. But I'm not gonna let myself be. For once I'm going to just—just go with the flow and drift away." Her voice was soft and dreamy as she laid her head on his chest; inhaling his scent she knew she was lost in love with this man.

Their bodies started swaying together and it was the most natural thing in the world to slow dance right there in the kitchen, to music only they could hear.

About to walk into the kitchen, Sarah stopped short and silently watched them for a moment. With misty eyes, she turned away and, placing her hand on her stomach she felt the baby kick inside her. With a tear slipping down her cheek, she smiled. "You're gonna have a cousin soon if I don't miss my guess. My little brother has found love at last."

*   *   *   *

The weekend had passed with so much fun and laughter that it was a jolt to know it was already over and they had to get ready for the workweek ahead. The Manning family was so down to earth; it was hard to feel any different around them even knowing how wealthy they were. It didn't seem to bother Nico and Sherri at all. And when Shannon had told Sam, he said he had already figured it out. They were all so good to Bryan that he positively glowed from all the attention. It had been decided that they would all spend Thanksgiving in Louisiana at the Manning family home.

CHAPTER 41

▼

As Shannon dressed for work on Monday morning she found she was looking forward to talking to Amber, although she couldn't exactly tell her who Luke was. He was still undercover. The weekend had been quiet at the apartment community, not so much as loud stereo was reported.

Shannon wanted to see if she could take a long lunch to go visit Mrs. Martin at the hospital. The reports Luke had gotten were much better than anyone expected. Thank God for her indomitable spirit. Shannon knew she would always be grateful that Mrs. Martin wasn't hurt any worse than she had been. She could still see in her mind how white and still the little lady had looked as they loaded her into the ambulance.

It felt funny walking to work without Luke. He had left earlier saying he had business to take care of at the police station. Shannon noted that the community had a closed up look that was far different from usual. Every window had the blinds closed and there were no little children at the playground. "Please God; let them catch that maniac soon." She was still silently praying as she noticed Amber sitting in her car.

As soon as Amber saw her she got out of her car with a wry expression on her face. "Hi Shannon. I—uh, well I just didn't want to get out of the car and go into the office by myself." She giggled nervously. "To tell you the truth, I wouldn't have come back at all if you and Heather weren't still here. My parents said I should move back home and find another job. I thought about it for a while. But when I told them about my idea to be a matchmaker, my Dad just rolled his eyes and my Mom laughed at me. That's when I knew I could never move back in with them."

Shannon smiled and walked into the office with her as she continued to chatter in a way that was uniquely Amber. They both paused as they stood looking over at Camille's desk. The office had a strangely deserted feel to it. It was so unusual to be closed down for an entire weekend, it was as if the space and furniture itself felt the difference.

Amber swallowed audibly. In the sunlight drifting through the windows the dust motes seemed to be dancing eerily. Shannon tried to shake it off and moved swiftly to turn on the lights. "Hey Amber, why don't you turn the stereo on?" She jumped as the phone rang shrilly next to her.

Both girls froze before Amber finally picked it up. At first she looked confused when no one was there, then laughed nervously as she realized the line was still connected to the answering service.

"I guess I better check the messages. Where are Heather and Larry? Plus I thought they said they were gonna post another cop at the front door."

Just as she said that, the door slowly creaked open and they saw a shadow looming in the foyer.

CHAPTER 42

▼

Luke was at the police station arguing with Nico. The six story building was still pretty new. Only about two years old. They were in one of the "war" rooms, a room that was designated for the Sherwood Village murders. There was a pair of pictures for each victim. One, a happy smiling face, the other as they looked as they were found dead. The bare, florescent lights glared down on each face. There was also a site-map of the community with a red X marked on each of the victim's apartments. The smell of coffee permeated the air. "I don't give a shit if you think it's a good idea or not. I'm going."

Nico sat on the edge of Luke's desk holding his habitual can of morning Coke. "You're just asking for trouble, boy. You know I've already checked the guy out. Plus the Rangers have had a tail on him twenty four/seven. You just wanna get a look at him because he was Shannon's first and Bryan's father."

Rolling his stiff shoulder Luke huffed out a long sigh. "Well, yeah, I guess that is part of it. I need to see him for myself." He held up his hand as Nico started to protest again. "Nico, I just need to do this."

The look in his eyes convinced Nico to let it go. But he didn't have to like it. He jumped up and began to pace, Luke wondered how many cans of Coke he already drank that morning.

"I tell you, it has to be that maintenance man, Mike. His finger prints were on the glass found in Sutton's apartment." His thumb jerked back towards the photo board. "What more do you want? A signed confession?" He ran his hand through his hair in frustration.

Luke continued to sit still at the table as he watched his friend continue to pace. It was always like this with them. When one of them was keyed up, the other settled down. Luke figured it must be some kind of checks and balance kind of thing.

"Well think about that for a minute, Nico. As careful as this guy has been, why would he just leave that glass there in plain view? It was like someone left it there on purpose. How convenient is it that Doug Collins is a waiter? It wouldn't have been too hard for him to get someone's fingerprints on a glass. When I'm there today, I plan to get a good look at the type of glasses they serve in that restaurant."

Nodding his head slowly, Nico made a decision. "Okay, but I'm going with you." He grabbed his jacket off the chair he had thrown it across earlier. As he headed for the door, he looked back expecting Luke to follow. When he saw him still seated behind the table, he cocked his head and raised his brows in question.

"You can't come with me. You've already met the asshole. I'm just gonna have lunch and watch him for a while." The gleam of anticipation in his eyes didn't help Nico to settle down at all.

"Well, I'll just park across the street and wait for you then. Come on, let's get this over with."

Luke just laughed and shook his head. "Look at the clock, man. We've still got a couple of hours before lunchtime. I want it to be busy in there so he'll have less time to pay attention to me. Plus why don't you check in with the Texas Rangers that are tracking down your man Mike. Surely they've gotten some kind of lead by now."

"Well, fuck it." Nico kicked back the chair and slammed his big body into it. "You need someone to watch your back." As he continued to glower, Luke picked up the phone to check in on Shannon. On the fourth ring he was about hang up and rush out there just as Amber answered the phone.

"What took you so long to get to the phone, Amber? Is everything alright out there?" Hearing the concern in his voice made Amber wistful.

"I'm sorry, Luke we just have a lot of residents in here right now. Everybody wants an update and a few of them think they saw something or someone strange this weekend. Seems like everyone has a theory now." She gave a short laugh, trying to make light out of the situation, but Luke could sense the stress. "Shannon has the patience of a saint. She has been talking to Ephram Peters for about ten minutes now. You know the guy that stutters so badly? I think he has a crush on our Shannon 'cause she always takes the time to be so nice to him." Amber was curious to see if Luke had a jealous side.

She was a little disappointed when he seemed to ignore the reference. "Is there an officer posted there again today?"

"Yeah, he was a little late, but he did get here just before all the residents started coming in."

"He was late? Is it the same guy that was there last week? Gomez wasn't it?"

"No, this time it's that young guy. He's been here before," she hastened to reassure him.

"Okay, tell Shannon I'll check in with her later, will you?" He swore as he hung up the phone. What the hell is the matter with the Captain? He's got that rookie back out there."

Nico's brows rose, "You're kiddin. The one that always looks kinda scared? Hell, he'd probably piss all over himself if anything did go down." He suppressed his amusement when he noticed Luke didn't think it was funny.

*　　　*　　　*　　　*

"Ju ... Ju Just try to b ... b ... be careful, Sh ... Shannon." Ephram cocked his head and studied her for a minute." I l ... like you ... your new ha ... hair color. It ... it ... suits yo ... you." Seeing that she looked a little uncomfortable and embarrassed he decided to take his leave. But first, surprising himself with his own boldness, he covered her hand with his own. "I ... I'm gonna watch out for you." He stammered seriously, almost perfectly.

Shannon sighed as Ephram finally left the office. He was such a sweet guy. A little younger than she was, he had the kind of complexion girls would die for. His cheeks were always pinkened as if he wore blush, but Shannon didn't doubt it was natural. He was so shy it was almost painful to watch him around other people, but he seemed to come out of his shell a little around her. She guessed it was because she let him take his time, instead of trying to finish his sentences for him like so many others did.

She knew what it felt like to feel shy and awkward around people. She wondered what his childhood had been like. He had moved in about six months ago, but she had never seen him with anyone else. No friends—no family. Poor guy.

She glanced over at Amber, "I'm sorry. I know you had to handle twice as many people as I did. But I just can't hurt his feelings by trying to hurry him up. Plus he thinks he saw a guy sitting in a car watching my apartment on Saturday night." The vague description he had given her sounded a little like Doug Collins, but she didn't mention that to Amber. That would just open up a whole different can of worms and she didn't want to go there. She could barely acknowledge it to herself.

"He said it was weird because the guy had just sat in his car for quite a while before he went up and knocked on my door. Then when no one answered, he just went back and sat in his car again. Like he was waiting. Ephram said he was just about to call the cops when the guy finally left."

"Shannon, he probably totally made all that up just to get your attention and show you how protective he can be. You know he has a huge crush on you. Plus, he is kinda cute." she teased. When Shannon lowered her eyes and blushed Amber laughed and relaxed for the first time all day. Now that felt like old times. A shadow crossed over her face as she slanted a look over at Camille's desk and knew deep down inside that nothing would ever be the same again. She stood up abruptly, "I'm gonna go tell Heather she can come out of her office now and quit hiding." She leaned towards Shannon and whispered conspiratorially, "I don't know why she bothers, most of the residents don't even know who she is anyway 'cause she's always "running errands" or hiding out in her office."

As she left, Shannon also looked over at Camille's desk. She hadn't missed the brief sadness on Amber's face and thought it was awfully tactful of her not to bring it up to her. She knew she would always feel horrible about how things had ended between the two of them. She still couldn't believe she had actually hit Camille and busted her lip on the very day she had been murdered. "I guess I'm lucky I'm not a murder suspect too," she muttered. And once more her thoughts turned to Doug Collins.

CHAPTER 43

▼

The very subject of her thoughts was busy handling the lunch crowd. Even in the midst of it all, as he was courteous to most of the clientele and even a little flirtatious with a few, he was laughing at the cops on the inside. Those idiots thought he didn't know he was being watched. He was even pretty sure that guy studying the menu at table seven was an undercover cop. He would dearly love it to show them how much smarter he was than they were. But he knew the time wasn't right. And wasn't timing everything? He smiled into the eyes of a dreamy young girl about the same age Shannon had been when he had met her. The girl giggled and preened under his attention.

Luke thought he might be sick. Watching the girl delight in the advances of that pervert was disgusting. He had to admit the man was aging well. As he took the time to get a really good look at the guy, his height, build and his blond hair, he hoped to God that Shannon didn't think the two of them resembled each other.

Suddenly the man turned and stared directly into Luke's eyes. He maintained eye contact as he crossed the room and came to his table. "Good afternoon, sir. Have you made your selection?" His voice was low and smooth.

Luke stared directly into his eyes. He'd be damned if he was going to be the first to look away. As if he was very aware of the power struggle, Collins smirked and glanced down at the menu. He felt he didn't have anything to prove. He was plainly this mans superior in everyway. He thought of his smoothly shaved face and perfectly groomed looks. Looking at the stubble on Luke's face, he thought it was stupid to try to cover his pretty boy looks. He was the type that probably resented that phrase. Idiot.

As Luke waited for his order, he took a good look around the restaurant. He noted that the glasses being used had a totally different look than the one found with the maintenance mans fingerprints on it. Damn, there went that theory. The white tablecloths were pristine; each table had a small vase with an exotic looking flower in it. The noise of the lunch crowd was rising steadily as the place filled to capacity. Dishes were clinking and all the normal sounds of a busy restaurant were in the back of Luke's mind as he tried not to think of Shannon with that man. Maybe Nico was right. He shouldn't have come here. But he knew one thing for sure. The man wasn't a simpleton. Luke knew the man made him to be a cop and thought it was funny. "Well, we'll just see who laughs last buddy" he muttered to himself.

*　　　*　　　*　　　*

Later, Luke was sitting in his truck, making a few notes, when he noticed the ex-professor leave the restaurant. The man looked right and left before hurrying up the street. He had on a long black trench coat and sunglasses. With an oath, Luke threw down the notepad to follow after the man.

He had to hurry to catch sight of the guy, turning the corner just in time to see him enter a parking garage. He disappeared behind a large concrete column and didn't come out on the other side. Then Luke saw him peak around it, confirming that he knew he was being followed. He turned and started running up the ramp to the next level.

Pulling out his gun, Luke yelled, "Freeze,—police," then started in pursuit as the man didn't stop. Rounding the corner, he quickly gained ground and finally tackled the man as he began trying to run up another ramp. He turned him over and felt the joy of punching him in the face just once as the man yelled out.

"You've got the wrong guy! Stop! You've got the wrong guy." Looking at him up close, Luke could see he was right.

"Well, fuck! Who the hell are you?" He jumped to his feet, pulling the man up with him. The guy was about the same height and coloring as Collins. Looking down Luke noticed he was even wearing the same black pants with a black satin strip down each side. "Who put you up to this?" He had the man grasped at the collar and shook him roughly.

The guy spit blood over to the side and sneered, "I don't have to tell you anything. But what I am going to do is file police brutality." He spit again, "Shit, you broke my fuckin tooth." To demonstrate he took his front tooth between two fingers and wiggled it back and forth. "My attorney is going to have a field day with your ass, man."

Feeling like he had been played for a fool, Luke wasn't in the mood to be concerned by his threats. He shook him again. "Listen, you son of a bitch, you tell me who put you up to this, or I'll break your fuckin nose this time." He pulled his fist back again, ready to make good on his words. Even after that run, he wasn't even breathing hard. The look in his eyes must have reflected his mood, as the guy backed down.

"Okay, okay, it's not worth bleeding over. I'm an actor. I eat at the restaurant a lot. This guy that works there asked me if I thought I could portray him with any believability. He said he'd pay me extra if I noticed anyone following me and ran for it. He even told me which way to go."

"And you didn't find all that a little weird? This guy, are you talking about one of the waiters?"

"Yeah man, Doug. The tall dude."

"You know his name?"

The guy cast his eyes to the ground. "I told you, I've been in there a lot." He suddenly looked nervous.

"Look, I don't want any trouble. I'm just an actor and right now I gotta make money any way I can."

Luke picked up on the sudden nerves and guessed the reason. He let go of the guy's shirt.

"Let's see some I. D. you asshole."

Getting more nervous by the minute, the man pulled out his wallet slowly and held it up for Luke to read. "Well, Tommy, how is it you're on first name bases with the waiter. You're so close, you do whatever he asks?"

"No man. Not whatever he asks. I told you …"

"Yeah, yeah, yeah, you go in there a lot. What else do you do to make extra money, Tommy? Sell a little blow on the side?" When Tommy's eyes looked away quickly, Luke knew he was right.

"Ever sell any to Doug Collins, Tommy?" He asked softly.

When Tommy didn't volunteer anything, Luke patted the pocket on the front of the guys' shirt. He could feel the tightly folded foil packet inside the pocket. "Well, well, what have we got here, Tom?" He just pulled it out and held it in front of the guys face. When Tommy's face turned white, Luke shook him again. "Look, I don't have time to run a two bit hustler like you in right now. Just tell me what you know about Douggie, and I'll let you go. This time."

Heaving a big sigh, Tommy sank to the ground and put his head between his knees for a minute. When he looked back up a Luke, there were tears in his eyes. "I didn't mean to cause you any trouble. I really don't know him all that well. I have sold him some blow from time to time, but lately he has just paid me to impersonate him."

Luke straightened. "What? Are you saying you've done this before?" Tommy just nodded his head.

"When?" he grabbed the back of his hair and pulled his head back, "You tell me how many other times and when. You tell me right now

Tommy, and I won't run you downtown. You make me take you in and you're gonna wish you never got out of bed today."

After Tommy told him everything he knew, Luke jerked him up and roughly handcuffed him behind his back.

"Hey, wait a minute man! I thought you said you weren't gonna take me in! Tommy wailed.

"I lied," was all Luke had to say.

CHAPTER 44

▼

Shannon took her lunch hour to visit Mrs. Martin at Medical City Hospital. She was happy to find a gift shop on the first floor. She bought a huge bouquet of exotic looking flowers and a happy face balloon with a band-aid on its head.

Mrs. Martin was sitting up in her hospital bed. The television was on, but she was gazing towards the window. She looked small and fragile, but Shannon was glad to see color in her cheeks.

"Surprise!" Shannon walked over to the bed and bent to kiss her on the cheek.

"Oh, honey! You didn't have to come way over here just to see me. I'll be home in no time. Oh what beautiful flowers! I've always loved orchids." Then she laughed and pointed across the room to another happy face balloon with a band-aid on it. "Look, Luke brought me one just like it." She giggled like a school girl, "Looks like the two of you are of a like mind." She patted the bed for Shannon to sit down next to her. "So, tell me all about your romance."

Shannon could feel her cheeks getting hot and quickly tried to change the subject. "That can wait Mrs. Martin. Tell me how you're doing. Luke said you were doing great, but I wanted to come and see for myself. I snuck off at lunchtime. No one even knows I'm here. Amber let me borrow her car to run some errands."

"Oh, I'm fine, I told that doctor I could go home already, but he insists on keeping me here. Either my insurance is better than I thought it was or that old man has a crush on me. Why, he's almost as old as I am," she sniffed indignantly, but Shannon could tell she thought it was funny. "I get bored in here, and I want to go home and get Ceily." A shadow of sadness passed over her face for a moment.

"Well, guess what? I called the veterinarian before I left the office and she said that she has fallen in love with Ceily and will be happy to keep her until you go home. She said Ceily has recovered nicely but she can tell she misses you."

"You know she saved my life don't you? There I was not paying attention, I was in a hurry to get in the house and see my television shows. When Ceily first started to growl, I just thought she saw a bug or something—you know how girlie she is." She shook her head. "I really don't remember much after that. To think that man would hurt my little girl. I can't wait to get out of here and go kick his ass after I track him down." Shannon had to laugh at that. "But seriously dear, do you really think you should have come here alone? The police are saying that my attack was probably just a random mugging, and not in connection to those murders. But I'm telling you, a man that would attack a little old lady and her little dog has to be a monster. And it's a monster that's killing those poor girls. I never got to see the man that attacked me, but I could feel him. I could feel pure evil."

CHAPTER 45

▼

Luke was watching through a one way mirror as Nico interrogated Tommy, the wanna-be actor. He had admitted to everything and pretty much repeated everything he had told Luke. Nico wasn't finished with him though. Not by a long shot.

"Want some more coffee Tom?"

"No, no sir. But I do need to go to the bathroom."

"Oh, you need to go to the bathroom? Well let me go check on that for you. It's not common practice to let suspects leave the interrogation room."

"Suspects! I'm a suspect? But I'm tellin' you everything I know. I swear Detective Tribiani. I just really need to go to the bathroom."

"Like I said, Tom, let me go check on that for you."

Nico left the room and ordered a uniformed officer to stand guard. He walked around the corner and entered the small room that Luke occupied.

"So, what do you think?"

Luke snorted out a laugh. "What do I think? I think he's about to shit his pants, that's what I think. How many cups of coffee did he drink?"

"Four. Let's let him stew a little while longer."

The subject of their discussion laid his head down on his arms crossed over the table in front of him and tried not to cry.

Finally, Nico went back into the room. The commander says I can't let you go to the bathroom until you give up any and all information you have. Think hard, Tommy, think real hard. There must be something else that could help us."

The young man sniffed and rubbed his nose. "Well I did remember one thing. One time, the first time Doug asked me to act like him?" Nico nodded and motioned for him to go on.

"Well he said if I agreed to it, they would be very grateful. He said they. You know? Like it wasn't just him. Like he had a partner or something. I thought that was pretty weird, but then he showed me the cash and I kinda forgot about it. Money's money man." His eyes shifted guiltily to the right.

Nico stood up abruptly and went to the door. "Officer, please escort this man to the facilities, and then bring him back here."

Luke was waiting for him. "A partner? Do you think he's talking about the man that took pictures of Bryan?"

"That's the first thing I thought of. But he could have just been trying to intimidate this guy. My gut tells me that the guy that took the pictures of Bryan was probably another flunky, paid to do a quick little job, just like Tommy boy here."

Luke looked thoughtful. Two different people could explain why it's sometimes more violent."

Nico shook his head, "It's not sometimes more violent. It is getting progressively more violent each time. Plus this perp is an expert at not leaving any type of DNA behind at all. Not a finger print, not even a friggin' pubic hair. Plus with everything going on, he somehow manages to get into these girls apartments without breaking in—like they just open the door right up to him or something."

"Except the glass with Mike Reynolds finger print on it. He could be using a key to get in." Luke sighed in frustration.

"No, the more I think about it, you were right about the glass with the print on it. It was too obvious. Planted. Just because the glasses they used at the restaurant today didn't look like that one, doesn't mean that the professor/waiter didn't use that one specially just to get his finger prints on it."

Blake poked his head in the door. Just wanted to let you know, the professor is gone—just left in the middle of his shift. We got a warrant to search his apartment and it looks like he was in a hurry to leave. There was an empty suitcase open on the bed, but you could see where another, larger one had been sitting next to it. The closet and dresser looked ransacked, like he just grabbed what he thought he would need and took off."

"Fuck! That's just great." Luke bowed his head for a minute. "His bank account. Freeze his bank account as fast as you can. See what credit cards he has in his name and freeze those too."

Without a word, Blake turned around to hurry back into his office to get it taken care of.

Seeing that Tommy had returned back to the interrogation room, Nico went back in to talk to him.

"Listen, Tommy. We're gonna keep you in lock up tonight."

Tommy started to jump up and protest when Nico waved him down.

"Tommy it's for your own safety. You're in over your head in this and I really don't think you have a clue about what's really going on. Plus if something else does happen, you'll be in the clear because we'll know you were in here."

Tommy hung his head. "Man! How the hell did I get myself into this?"

*   *   *   *

That evening, the sun was hanging heavily over Lewisville Lake as Sam watched Bryan try to skip rocks over the water. When one actually skipped three times before sinking into the dark blue water he threw his hands in the air in celebration, with a loud "woo hoo"!

The man in the boat could just hear his shout of triumph as he watched through his binoculars. The kids' laughter drifted out across the way as his grandfather turned his head toward the house. The man noticed another, younger guy was holding up a phone. Looking once more at the boy, he thought the kid must be the picture of health. Shannon must be so proud. It was just too damn bad she would never get to see him finish growing up. He laughed in excited delight as he turned the boat towards the opposite shore.

CHAPTER 46

▼

Later that night, Shannon, Luke, and Nico were sitting in her apartment catching up on the events of the day and eating take-out Chinese food. Shannon had confessed about her trip to see Mrs. Martin at the hospital and was telling them how elated she was at how well she was doing. "I couldn't believe my eyes! She said she wants to hurry and get out of the hospital so she can help catch the guy and kick his ass." She paused and said sadly, "She almost seems to blame herself for not being more alert and letting him sneak up on her."

Luke had gone by the hospital too. He didn't want to tell Shannon that the doctor was keeping the older lady for a few more days because he was concerned about her heart. He also decided not to tell her about his run in with the professor until later.

Like's voice was deceptively mild," Shannon, did it ever occur to you to tell us that you were going?"

"I know, I know. But I also know how busy yall have been and I was very careful. I took Amber's car, and I kept looking in the rearview mirror to make sure no one was following me. I parked right by the door of the hospital and when I came out; I looked carefully around before approaching the car. I even looked in the backseat before I got in." Seeing the look in Luke's eyes she hastened to add. "Luke, I would never have forgiven myself if I didn't go to see her in the hospital."

Nico spoke up to change the subject, "I hate to say this, but the guys trying to find Mike Reynolds haven't come up with anything."

Luke swore and jumped up to pace. "Maybe we should find somebody else to put on it that really gives a shit. How could these guys not find anything at all and still call themselves Texas Rangers?"

"Well, they have interviewed just about anybody they could find that ever spoke to the guy. They tried to call the references he had listed on his resume, but it's missing from his file. He must have taken it before he left.

"Maybe we should call in the F.B.I.?" Shannon asked innocently.

Both men turned to stare at her as if she had just delivered the most horrendous insult.

Luke replied stiffly, "The F.B.I.—works on Federal crimes."

"Besides," joined in Nico, "Those guys couldn't find their own ass with both hands if they had an itch."

Stifling a giggle, Shannon murmured, "O-Kay ..."

Luke continued to pace in his frustration, just as Nico had earlier that day. Now it was Nico that was calmly sitting there watching Luke. He stopped pacing suddenly and crossed his arms over his chest. "I just don't think so. Something's not right here." He once again thought of Collins. They had put out an APB on him by two o'clock that afternoon.

Wearily Shannon laid her head back on the couch. She closed her eyes for just a minute and fell asleep as the two men continued to discuss various subjects.

It was much later that Luke carried her into the bedroom. Suddenly she was wide awake as they undressed each other and fell into bed. It was much later that they found sleep together.

CHAPTER 47

▼

She knew she was getting drunk. Things had just been so stressful lately. This felt like an escape. She wasn't going to think about the murders tonight. She swayed as she let the thrumming music take over. The swirling lights continued to dance around the dim nightclub, the smell of cigarettes and alcohol hung heavily in the air. She was lifting a glass to her lips again just as the cute bartender sat another one down in front of her.

She smiled at him sexily, "Why Kyle, I haven't even ordered another one yet. Are you tryin' to get me drunk?" The idea kind of excited her. She had been in this bar many times before and had always had a thing for Kyle. Some of her friends thought he might be gay because he never did take any of them up on their invitations. But she didn't. She just thought he must have a girlfriend. She tried to discreetly tug the top of her tight white blouse down even lower.

"Not me sweetie." He jerked his chin over his left shoulder, "That dude over there sent it to you." He used his small white towel to dry up a spill on the bar, and then hurried over to respond to one of the other patrons. The place was really hopping for a Monday night. It was almost time to turn on Monday night football.

Squinting across the bar, the girl tried to see which man he was talking about. The drinks she had already had, combined with the smoke, and dancing lights made it difficult for her to see that far. Shrugging her shoulders, she continued to swing her hips to the beat of the music. Suddenly a red rose appeared in front of her.

*   *   *   *

Almost an hour later she couldn't believe her luck. This guy must be loaded. She had never been in a car like this before. She didn't even know what kind of car it was, some kind of foreign job. She was a little disappointed they were just going to her apartment. She thought, if his car was this cool his house must be awesome.

She was thrilled as he kept his arm tightly around her as they took the stairs up to her place. He nuzzled her neck all the way up. "You smell so good; I just can't seem to get enough." He inhaled deeply. She giggled as she opened the door. He looked around as she flipped on a light. Everything was neat as a pin, decorated to the hilt. "You must have lived here for a while, huh?"

She smiled proudly, "Yeah, since the place first opened, I'm the only one that has ever lived in this apartment." She shrugged away the memory of the six-week mistake called Greg. Turned out he was just looking for free rent. Feeling like she was starting to loose her buzz, she crossed over to the little bar by the kitchen. "Can I get you something to drink?"

He was still standing by the front door. "Since the place first opened, huh? You must know Shannon, then."

She thought he seemed different since entering her place. She suddenly felt uncomfortable. "Shannon? At the office?" When he quirked a brow and just nodded, she said, "Yeah, she's great."

"I was hoping you'd say that." His smile was radiant as he flipped open the gleaming knife.

Looking into the face of death, her heart slamming into her ribs, she knew she had just made the worst mistake of her life.

CHAPTER 48

▼

The next morning Shannon had been at her desk for about an hour trying to return all the messages. She paused for a minute to shift uncomfortably in her chair. She blushed suddenly as she realized all that sex was taking its toll. She took a deep breath as she remembered some of the things Luke had done and said to her the night before. She was so in love with him she guessed she was lucky her eyes weren't crossed with it.

She was lost in thought as a shadow fell over her desk. A young woman smiled at her tentatively. "Um, hi. I need some help"

Shannon jumped guiltily to her feet. "Oh sure! I'm so sorry; I didn't hear you come in. What can I do for you?"

"Well, I feel kinda silly. I work just up the street at the Nocona office building. Our manager hasn't come in yet today, and we haven't heard from her, which is really unusual. And, well, she does live here ..." she trailed off and looked hopefully at Shannon.

Shannon understood perfectly, as a cold finger of dread worked its way up her spine.

"Oh. Oh, yeah, I guess I know what you mean. Who is your manager?"

The girl smiled in relief at Shannon's understanding, "Katherine. Katherine Ball. You might know her. She said once that she has lived here for a while. She even referred Pam Nichols here."

"Yes, I do know Kat. I'll tell you what, why don't you have a seat in the clubroom, and we'll send someone over to her apartment to check on her. You can watch T.V. while you wait, and there is coffee and pastries on the bar. Please, help yourself."

Once she had the girl settled she went to the back of the office to radio Luke. Heather and Amber were just quietly watching her. Amber had heard the girl and informed Heather while Shannon had taken her into the clubroom. The three of them stayed unusually quiet until Luke arrived.

Seeing the look on their faces, he knew immediately that something was wrong. Shannon explained in hushed tones, knowing the girl in the clubroom could walk around the corner any minute.

Luke tried to not to look too concerned for their sake. "Sure, I'll get Officer Gomez and we'll run up there and take a look. Probably nothing to worry about though, there were undercover agents around all night and no one reported anything unusual. Right Heather?"

Something about his tone reassured her and Heather smiled in relief. "That's right. There must be twenty men patrolling this property at night. I don't see how anything bad could have happened. Plus I know Katherine; she's a smart girl. She wouldn't take any dumb chances."

"See, I'll be right back." Luke tried to smile reassuringly as he walked off. He hoped his smile didn't look as wooden as it felt.

*   *   *   *

Officer Gomez followed Luke through the door and into the apartment. "Holy shit! Looks like a tornado hit this place." Plants had been uprooted from their pots, some pictures were hanging askew on the walls, and some of them were ripped and torn, thrown on the floor. The coffee table was turned upside down.

Luke didn't say anything, just walked straight back into the bedroom. She was lying posed on her back, nude, and her hands crossed over her chest like the others. Just as with Camille the wig on her head was placed haphazardly. The make up was smudged all over her face instead of completely wiped off. The strains of Pink Floyd drifted mournfully into the room.

Just as he pulled out his cell phone to call it in, Luke noticed something under the bed. He put on a pair of latex gloves and carefully picked up the item on one edge. The embroidered nametag said Mike. A nametag such as one a maintenance man would wear.

CHAPTER 49

▼

Once again the office closed down. A virtual troop of officers were questioning residents. Brinker, the lead State Trooper was questioning the ones that had been patrolling last night. He was absolutely furious that this had happened on his watch.

"Right under your fucking noses! How in the hell did you let this happen?" He took a deep breath, trying to calm down.

"Okay, let's start with the basics. Did any of you guys see anything out of the ordinary last night? Alvarez, what about you?" He pointed his beefy finger at the hapless man nearest to him. The man sat up straighter, if that were possible. He actually turned a little green around the mouth.

"Yes sir, I think I did see the victim come home last night." He lowered his head for a brief second before bracing his shoulders and looking Brinker straight in the eyes. "With the killer."

Brinker sat heavily on the corner of the table behind him. "What?"

When the man started to repeat himself, Brinker held up his hand to stop him. He closed his eyes and breathed in and out of his pinched nose for a few minutes. No one dared make a sound. Finally, letting out a long disgusted sigh, Brinker indicated that he was ready to hear the details.

"I was posted in the apartment diagonally across from the victim's."
He pulled a small notepad from his breast pocket. "At exactly nine
thirty six p.m. I noticed a fancy car pull up in front of the building. A
man got out and went around the other side to help a young woman
out. It seemed as if she might have had too much to drink, the way she
was leaning heavily into him, and giggling. He had his head all but
buried against her neck all the way up the stairs, so ... I ..." The agent
audibly swallowed. "I didn't get a real good look at the man. The way
they were bent into each other, I'm not even sure as to height." This
last part was almost a whisper.

Brinker almost felt sorry for the man. "Let me guess, because you
were looking at a happy little couple, the idea of one of them being the
murderer never crossed your mind." The eyes of the nearby agents
shifted back and forth as if silently asking each other if they would have
done the same.

One of them spoke up. "Sir, I think we were all thinking of a single
suspect. Not a couple that apparently lived here." At that the group
erupted into arguments.

Luke walked away, having heard enough. He learned later that the
man had been wearing a long coat, so the agent didn't know if he could
have been wearing a maintenance uniform or not. But just like the
glass with fingerprints on it, Luke thought it was just a little too
convenient. Or did the guy just think he needed to give obvious clues
to his inferiors? Luke walked up to Nico to discuss it with him, and
found him having an argument of his own on his cell phone. Trying to
wait patiently, Luke could hear that he was talking with Sherri. Finally
Nico slammed his phone shut with a resounding click.

He shook his head and turned to his friend, "Man! Can you believe
that? I'm knee deep in all this shit, and she doesn't think I'm paying
her enough attention. I'm telling you, boy, sometimes it just ain't
worth it."

Luke informed him about what he had just overheard. They both
shook their heads over the incompetence and agreed to meet back at

the police station to compare notes with the other cops. At this point, they didn't feel it would do any good to hang around here. Shannon had left earlier when Rita Williams had come out in a limo with heavily tinted windows to take the staff back to the corporate office in downtown Dallas. They were going to have a video conference call with Ted, who was currently in London. She had agreed to call him before they left the office building to return home. Brinker had gone with them.

*   *   *   *

"Oh man, this is great! Look at the shock and awe on their faces. When are they going to learn that I'm unstoppable? There isn't a Ranger or a cop alive that can stop me now."

With each killing he felt himself growing stronger. He couldn't believe they couldn't see it. After all he was right there in front of them. He remembered the thrill of walking right past them last night. He knew they wouldn't recognize him. All he had had to do was keep his face buried in her neck like he knew he was about to get lucky. The thrill was so intense, he just had to see what he could get by with next. "But don't worry Shannon, the others don't mean a thing, it's you I'm really coming for."

*   *   *   *

Back at the police station, the group was once again in the war room. Luke solemnly marked a red X on the site-map just over Katherine Balls' apartment. The topic of discussion at the moment was the news that the Rangers had asked the Chief for additional men for patrol.

Blake voiced his opinion, "More like they want someone to share the blame with if something else occurs." The other men nodded in agreement. Most of the men agreed the perp must be the ex-maintenance man, Mike Reynolds. Luke had been oddly quite since he had put the latest red X on the board. Finally noticing his expression, the rest of the group fell silent as they too began to study the board.

It just took Nico about ten seconds to get it. "Well shit." He reached up and rubbed hard at the back of his neck. "I guess you guys are seeing what I'm seeing?"

Luke just got up and took a yellow highlighter to connect the X'es. It almost made a perfect letter S. To complete it, it would have to end up on one particular apartment. Shannon's apartment.

Noticing the time was getting late; he quickly called Shannon and told her he would pick her up downtown. Nico insisted on going with him.

Sherri was pissed off. She had been dating long enough to know when a man was losing interest in her. But she had thought this time it was different. Nico was different. She really thought he could be the one. A tear slid silently down her cheek. "But he had no right to talk to me like that on the phone today. He's gotta take a break sometime. Why can't it be with me?" Lately he had even been sleeping at his own place instead of hers. Without her! She decided to give him another chance. It had been several hours since she had spoken to him.

She dialed his number and was pleased when he answered so fast. "Hi, Nico. Listen, I'm sorry we fought earlier."

"Me too. But like I told you things are heating up now and we really need to close this case. People are dying here!"

"But, Nico, you can't work twenty four hours a day. You have to take a break sometime." She was quiet for a minute, "Are you seeing someone else?"

"What?" Nico groaned, "Oh, hell no, not this again. Listen, Sherri …"

"Okay, okay, you know me—I just had to ask." She hurried to make light of it. "Where are you going now? Can we meet up later tonight?"

"Sherri, I'm not kidding, I really don't have the time tonight. After we pick Shannon up, we're going by her place to pick up some of her things, and then we're getting her the hell out of there. Things are really bad, baby. I'll try to call you later, okay?" He hung up the phone before she could object.

"Man, that's all I need right now." He turned to Luke as they sped down Dallas Toll way.

"I'm starting to get that feeling. You know when your shoes get too tight and you need to get new ones?" Morosely he stared down at his shoes. "But I really care for her. I guess I'm just not sure I'm IN love with her. Sometimes I think—maybe, and then she gets like this."

Luke glanced over at him in sympathy. "So, are you trying to tell me you're still a growing boy? Or are you calling Sherri a shoe? "Nico laughed and they relaxed a little as they neared downtown.

$$* \qquad * \qquad * \qquad *$$

Sherri had a brilliant idea. If she left now, she could meet them at Shannon's place and after they collected her things, maybe they could all go out for dinner. "Hey! I can offer to let Shannon stay at my place. That way I can be in on everything. Nico and Luke would probably even stay there too. Guarding their precious Shannon. Maybe I should just put myself in harms way to get his attention." She had no way of knowing how much she was about to regret that thought.

CHAPTER 50

▼

Once he had the idea of doing something else right under their nose, he just couldn't resist. It was too much fun. Risky, but he just knew he could do it. He felt the greatness swelling up inside, "*Oh yeah, I can do this.*"

When he saw the girls' car pull up he knew it couldn't be more perfect. It was just getting dark and he knew nobody expected anything until well after dark, and especially not so soon after last night. Plus the pizza he had had delivered to the clubhouse had most of the cops on a break. The idiots never thought to ask who ordered the pizza.

Not wanting to get his clothes dirty, he had chosen another murder weapon for this special event. Besides he kind of liked the thought of changing his M.O. knowing it would drive them crazy. He had a sweet smile on his face as he tapped on her car.

Sherri hastily wiped her tears away and tried to put a smile on her face as she opened the window.

*　　*　　*　　*

It was starting to rain as they pulled into the parking lot at Sherwood Village. Nico swore when he saw Sherri's car parked across from Shannon's apartment. "What is she doing here? What? Is she stalking me now?"

Frustrated he swung out of the car and walked over to thump his hand on the hood of the car to get her attention. He couldn't see clearly through the windshield because the rain was starting to pour from the heavy, dark sky. It looked like she had decided to read a book or take a doze while she waited. He was hoping the hard thump would scare her a little bit, to go with the lecture he was going to deliver about what a dangerous place this was getting to be. When she didn't immediately jump, he felt like a cold hand squeezed his chest. He hurriedly reached to open her car door and was just in time to catch her body as she fell out into the parking lot.

He just fell with her to the ground.

He sat there holding her, in the pouring rain, knowing it was too late. She was still warm, but there was no pulse at all. He knew the finality of death when he saw it.

He turned her face towards his and smoothed the hair back from her face. Her eyes were open and staring at him accusingly. And he knew she was right. He was to blame for this. Nico threw back his head and roared to the heavens, an unearthly sound of pain and anguish that echoed into the night.

As he heard a gasp of horror, he looked up to see Shannon reach Luke's side. "Oh no. Oh no, no, nonononono! Not Sherri too," she screamed. Helplessly she looked up at Luke. "I just can't take this anymore." She fainted so fast he caught her just before she too hit the ground.

Time seemed to stand still, as the men didn't move. They stared across the pavement at each other, each holding his own fallen woman in his arms.

Then all hell broke loose as everything happened at once. Flashbulbs went off as the media and a group of patrolmen showed up at the same time. It didn't take long for Shannon to wake up and she was doubly horrified to see the photographer taking pictures.

Luckily a policeman got to him before Luke or Nico could. After making sure that Shannon was all right, Luke carried her back to the car and told her to get in and lock the doors. He hurried back to Nico in time to help convince him to let go of Sherri so that they could try to preserve what was left of the crime scene. Seeing that Nico was absolutely stunned and still worried about Shannon, he told Nico that he needed him to wait in the car to protect Shannon. Woodenly, Nico forced himself to walk over and get into the car. Everything felt surreal. For the first time since he was a grown man he felt totally helpless. Shannon crawled into the back seat to sit next to him. She held on tight to his hand and laid her head on his shoulder. As sobs racked her body, he put his arm around her and felt a large tear fall down his own face.

Luke was furious. A cameraman had already left before he could grab the film. And where the hell were all the cops and Rangers when this had gone down? After checking Sherri's body for himself he noticed as Nico had that her body was still warm. Her lips were blue and her eyes seemed to have leaked bloody tears as she was strangled to death with the thin wire still wrapped around her throat. At the angle of the wire, it looked as though she must have rolled down her window and the killer had reached in and just taken a matter of minutes to end her life.

He couldn't remember ever being this mad in his life. How the hell had things gotten so out of control? He was looking around for someone to take this out on, when Blake took him by the arm. He started to take a swing at him before he realized who it was.

"Get the hell out of here, man. Right now. I know how you feel. But right now you better go and take care of your girl and your partner." As some of the wildness left his eyes, Blake added in a low voice, "Find a safe place for them, Luke, now!"

Knowing he was right and grateful for the intervention, he decided he would just have to trust the men at the scene to take care of things here. It was good to know that Blake was there. He hurried over to the car and got into the drivers seat. After checking to make sure the two in the backseat were okay, he took off into the cold wet night. No one said a word.

*   *   *   *

Luke checked them into the Presidential suite at the Palatial Hotel. The penthouse had two bedrooms on each side of a sumptuous living area. Even though it took a special key to get the elevator to open up to the top floor, Luke had two guards posted for the night. He poured a brandy for Nico and himself and a small glass of sherry for Shannon.

Shannon sipped it and was grateful for the warmth that eased its way into her stomach. She just couldn't look at Nico yet. It was too raw and painful. She would never forget the way he had just quietly sunk to the ground holding Sherri's body in his arms. She stood up abruptly. "I need to go call Dad. I have to check on them and then tell Dad what has happened before he hears it from—someone else." She wasn't going to mention the media. There had been helicopters flying overhead as they had left the scene.

Nico got up to pour himself another drink. He took a long look around the penthouse. He downed the drink and stood looking around the place. "I guess when it comes down to it; your roots just call you home, huh, rich boy?"

Luke didn't miss a beat, "Don't even think about picking a fight with me. I know the urge, I understand the urge, but we're all hurting here, Nico."

Nico sat down his glass and ran his hands over his face. "You're right. I know you're right. I just feel so helpless. And there's not a damn thing I can do about it. I got her killed."

"No you didn't! I did!" the words were torn from Shannon as she returned to the room. Tears were streaming down her face again. "You said it before. Somehow this is all connected to me. Did I start this? What did I do to start this? What did I do?" Her face was red and strained; he could actually see a vein pounding in her forehead.

Luke rushed over and wrapped his arms around her. "Listen to the two of you! Do you think the world revolves around you? You don't control the world and you can't control a madman." He struggled with his anger and knew it wouldn't do any good.

Nico walked over and took Shannon from Luke's arms and wrapped his own around her.

"Luke's right," he sighed, "he's right again. It's not going to do us any good to waste time with blame. It's not going to bring her back. She's never coming back" he said it again to hear the reality of it. "The best thing you can do is to get some sleep, so we can face this in the morning and do what has to be done."

Luke agreed, "In the morning we'll make plans. What's done tonight is done. Tomorrow is another day." He led her into the bedroom and helped her undress and get into the big satiny bed. He left a dim light on next to the bed. He kissed her on the forehead, "I won't be long."

Shannon sat up and caught his arm, "Luke, take all the time you need. Please don't worry about me. I'm worried about Nico and you should be too. Go spend some time with him, okay?"

Luke felt humbled at her unselfishness. He walked out into the living area and found that Nico was standing at the French doors that led to the balcony, just staring out into the night. He turned when he heard Luke's return. "What are you doing out here, boy?"

Luke leaned his head towards the bedroom, "She's worried about you." He walked over and put his hand on Nico's shoulder. "So what are we going to do now?"

CHAPTER 51

▼

The next morning Shannon was up and about before either of the two men. She could hear noises coming from Nico's room and wondered if he had slept all. Her own sleep and been sporadic at best as nightmares had plagued her off and on all through the night. In her dreams, it was as if she could see exactly what had transpired the night before, from a distance. She could see Nico sitting in the rain holding Sherri's lifeless body, and nearby was Luke holding her equally limp form as the two just stared at each other. Then it was her neck that was at an odd angle, with a wire wrapped around it. Her bloody eyes flew open and she tried to gasp for air. She couldn't breath. Hands were shaking her, calling her name. Suddenly she had woken to find Luke bending over her,

"Shannon, baby, its okay. You're okay, I'm right here with you."

She closed her eyes to firmly block it out and push it to the dark recess of her mind, with the ugly memories of her childhood that she had been trying to lock away for so long. Moving quickly she picked up the phone and ordered room service for the three of them. She purposely went overboard and asked for more than enough. She ordered eggs, cooked in a variety of ways. Pancakes, pastries, coffee, juice and—remembering Nico's penchant for Coca Cola, ordered several of those as well.

*　　*　　*　　*

Nico was staring out of the window, looking at the beautiful sunny day. Everything looked so normal. Why did that make him feel even guiltier? He could still hear the frustration in her voice from the phone conversation the day before. The frustration and just a hint of fear that their relationship was dying. How could she have known how much preferable that would have been to the alternative? The worst part was that he knew, if he had it to do over again, he would probably have done everything the same way. Had he ever really loved Sherri? On some level he supposed he did. Just not on the level she wanted—or needed. Some people just weren't meant for long-term relationships, apparently he was one of those people. He knew he would do well to remember it and vowed right then and there, he would remember that. For the rest of his life.

He showered, dressed and was beginning to smell something from the other room that made his mouth water. He realized it had been about twenty-four hours since he had eaten anything, although his burning stomach could still feel the alcohol from the night before. He wondered if there were Coke machines around in digs this fancy. His head throbbed and he thought he would pay a kings ransom for at least one Coke.

When he walked out into the living area, the first thing he saw was a large white table heaped with enough food for the whole precinct. And in the middle of it all, an ice bucket filled with bottles of Coke. The joy he felt as he spied them had the guilt slamming into him again.

Luke also followed his nose into the room. "Shannon said she ordered breakfast." He stopped when he say the table. "Are we having company?"

"Um—no. I just felt like, well you know … I thought we could all use some comfort food. Plus I know we'll need to be fortified to face what ever comes next today." She was trying to keep her voice casual, even tried a weak smile. "So? How do we catch this guy?"

Luke had already filled a plate and was sitting at the table. He poured a steaming cup of coffee as he answered her. "I've been trying to figure out what he might do next. The way I see it, he was so impressed with himself for killing Katherine right under our noses. He just had to do it again. Right out in plain sight, to prove he could. To prove his superiority." He sighed and folded his lips into a thin line as he shook his head, "And so far he's right. No one expected him to kill again so fast. And certainly not so brazenly in plain sight."

Nico was also beginning to fill a plate; he had already drunk half of a twenty ounce Coke.

"We need to call Blake and get some answers. Like, where the hell was everybody when this happened? Somebody had to have seen something, right?" He looked at Luke for confirmation. Shannon's throat swelled when she heard the rawness of Nico's voice. She could see the effort it was taking him to try to appear normal.

"Yeah, absolutely." Luke pulled out his phone and dialed Blake. He pushed a button on the side of the small unit and it turned into a speakerphone so they could all hear. "Luke, man I'm glad you called. How's Nico?"

"I'm fine, John, I'm here with Luke and Shannon. Luke has you on speaker."

Blake cleared his throat, "Listen Nico, I'm real sorry, we're all real sorry—about Sherri." He cleared his throat again and got down to business. "Let me give you a quick update. First you need to know this is all over the media. There are, well, there are pictures. Its front page of the Dallas Morning News."

When no one said a word, he continued, "Well, apparently there was some kind of mix-up about pizza being delivered to the clubhouse and the agents and cops were arguing over who it was for. It was a lot of pizza and they thought it was for them. So the word went out and many of them were just eating pizza, getting ready to be real bad-asses as soon as night fell," he said derisively. I happened to get to the scene when I did because Cunningham had put in a call to me. Seems the greenest man in the field had the presence of mind to think beyond his stomach."

"Turns out it was ordered with a stolen credit card. The son of a bitch knew what he was doing and counted on no one really expecting anything else to happen so fast. There's no doubt it was the same guy, there was blonde wig sitting on the passenger seat, and you know that information hasn't been released to the public."

He paused for a minute to let that sink in. "After interviewing everybody in the area, the Texas Rangers are wondering if maybe the guy had on a cops uniform. No one saw anyone strange around except more cops than usual. Hell, Brinker had the audacity to suggest maybe it really is one of us. I damn near tore his head off. That sanctimonious S.O.B. ...."

He started to go on when Luke interrupted him, "Hold on, that's something to think about, not that it could be any of our boys, but the perp could have a fake uniform. Hell, even a stolen uniform. Damn it, that makes sense."

They heard a beep and Blake put them on hold. When he came back on the line, there was excitement in his voice. "I'll give you one thousand bucks if you can guess where the credit card was stolen from."

Luke knew the answer immediately. "The Ice House."

"Bingo! Hey you know I was only joking about the grand, right?"

"The Ice House? Shannon had heard of the trendy restaurant in Deep Elum, but she had never been there. When Luke and Nico just continued to stare at her, she got it. "Oh. Oh. Is that where Doug works?"

"Listen there's one more thing you should know, there are moving vans everywhere. Hell, some people are just loading up their cars and taking off." Blake's phone beeped again and he said he'd call them back later.

The three of them were once again silent as they digested all the new information. Shannon jumped as her cell phone rang. "Hi, Dad, what's going on? Is everything alright?" Luke could hear the slight panic in her voice and couldn't wait for the day it was gone for good.

Then she laughed. "He wants what? Why on earth does he suddenly want binoculars?" then she laughed again, "Okay, I guess that makes sense. I'll see if I can't bring a pair out there. Listen, Dad? Uhm, don't let Bryan watch any TV channels that have news events okay? Oh, you did? I'm sorry Dad. Yes, we're fine. Okay I'll tell him. I love you too Dad." Her voice had gone husky as she clicked her phone shut.

Finally Luke asked, "So I guess Bryan wants to do some bird watching?"

Misty eyed, Shannon nodded her head, "Yeah, and butterflies."

"You know, I think there may be a pair" ... then he trailed off. "You know what, let me call Sam real quick. He dialed his own phone and was glad Sam answered quickly. "Hey Sam. Did Bryan happen to say where he got the idea of binoculars? Yeah, I'll hold on."

His eyes darkened as he listened to Sam's response. "Let me call you back in a couple of minutes."

He hung up and took a deep breath. "I think we may have another problem."

As Nico and Shannon both started to talk and ask questions at the same time, Luke held up his hand as he dialed the phone again. "Blake, have you talked to the guys that are looking for Doug Collins? Still looking huh?" He quickly told Blake about his conversation with Sam.

After hanging up, Luke crossed the room, and then stopped suddenly in front of Shannon. He knelt down and took her hand in his. He looked deeply into her eyes to judge how steady she was. Reassured by what he must have seen, he sat beside her, never letting go of her hand.

"Bryan said he got the idea from the man in the boat that has been watching them from the lake, with a pair of binoculars." When Shannon didn't make a sound he continued.

"The Rangers lost Collins a few days ago.

Nico jumped up and got his phone out of his pocket; he pushed one button and began talking. "Blake, get some men out to Luke's house ASAP ... okay, thanks John, you're a good man." He looked at the pair watching him intently. "Blake's already sent men out there. He said he did it as soon as he just hung up with you."

Shannon jumped up and started to run to the bedroom. Luke stopped her. "Shannon, what are you doing?"

"Well, I'm going to get dressed of course! We have to get out there!" When she saw the look on Luke's face she began shaking her head. "Oh no you don't. Don't even try to tell me to stay here. Are you crazy? That's my son out there. And my father! I have to protect them." She threw her hands over her face trying to swallow the huge sobs that were coming up in her throat.

Nico walked over to her and put his arms around her. "Honey, think about it. There are already police on their way out there and Luke and I can be out there in twenty minutes. We'll just put the light on top of the car and drive in the HOV lanes." Then he held her back for a minute to look into her eyes. "If you go with us, you could get Luke killed."

That stopped her. She seemed dazed all of a sudden. "What?" she asked in bewilderment.

"He would be so worried about protecting you, he would lose his concentration. And this bastard has already proven he is smart. He would take advantage of that quickly. It would be a disaster waiting to happen. You know he would die for you."

Shannon suddenly sank to the floor as if her knees gave out from under her. She just sat there staring out into space. It didn't take her long to make a decision. She knew time was precious.

"You're right. She looked at Luke. "I can't put you in any more jeopardy." She looked at Nico, "Either of you."

Luke looked at Nico gratefully. Then he grabbed Shannon in a bear hug. "You are quite a woman, Shannon Walker!" he kissed her quickly.

I'm going to bring Sam and Bryan here. We'll be back before you know it. I love you—I love you!"

She smiled through her tears, trying to be brave, "I love you too."

Nico threw Luke his coat and they were out the door.

CHAPTER 52

▼

Shannon turned on the TV for company. The penthouse felt so empty without the men. She was surprised to see the noon news already on. How had so much time passed? She looked at the clock and saw that it was already twelve thirty. She realized she must have missed the news about Sherri and Sherwood Village. She could only be relieved.

"I know, I'll just call Dad and talk to him and Bryan until Luke gets there." When there was no answer she forced herself to remain calm. "Dad's smart, he's already gone to safety. Then she remembered the cop that had been staying out there with them and was grateful. She was tempted to call Luke on his cell phone, but then decided not to bother them. She knew to make it from downtown Dallas to the North side of Lewisville lake in twenty minutes, even in the HOV lane, they would have to be driving extremely fast.

She thought about what Nico had said about not distracting Luke. There was no way she would want to be the cause of Luke's death. "This is what he does for a living. And from what everybody says, he's really good at it." She didn't know why she was surprised when her hands and feet suddenly got freezing cold. She started to tremble so hard her teeth were chattering. "Well this is a hell of a time for a panic attack." Then she realized that even with everything that had been going on, even last night she had not had a panic attack in weeks. "I don't have time for this." She looked heavenward, "Please God, don't let me have one now." But she knew it was already too late. All of a sudden the TV was too loud, the lights too bright. The pulse in the side of her neck started to beat wildly; it was so hard it was almost painful.

She ran for her purse to get the bottle of Xanex. Not finding even one little pink pill just made it worse. "What am I going to do? What am I going to do? I can't lose control like this." She paced back and forth. Then she remembered checking into the penthouse last night. The man checking them in had been almost embarrassingly eager to please. He had kept repeating that if there was anything he could do, anything at all, to just let him know. Well she was going to make him back that up.

She picked up the phone and there was an operator already there, as if on standby. "What can we do for you Mrs. Manning?" That caught Shannon off guard only momentarily, "When we checked in last night, a man walked us up here ..."

"Yes ma'am that would have been Mr. Graham."

"That's right! That's right, may I speak to him please?"

It was like he must have been sitting right next to the operator, he was on the line so fast.

"What can I do for you Mrs. Manning? I hope you are enjoying your stay," he added hopefully.

"Actually, I do have a problem. I brought the wrong purse and my ... my medicine was in it." She trailed off, feeling lame at asking for drugs. She knew now it was a bad idea. "I'm sorry, I ..."

"Mrs. Manning, just tell me what you need and I can have it to you in less than five minutes."

Okay, here goes, she thought. "Well I forgot my Xanex," she blurted it out. The pulse in the side of her neck started to beat erratically now, three hard fast beats, then a long pause. Her breathing was choppy and she prayed he couldn't hear it over the phone.

"Oh, dear," he said, and Shannon just knew all was lost. "That must be dreadful for you!"

Shannon closed her eyes and prayed. Then the man continued, "I just hate it when I run out of my Xanex. I'll be right up. Just hold on tight, Mrs. Manning, I'll be right there."

*   *   *   *

True to his word, he was there faster than Shannon had thought possible. He was wonderful to her. As soon as he saw her, he was instant sympathy. "Now, now, I'm here with help. He sat her down and poured a glass of water from a nearby pitcher. When he held a large white pill she was confused. "Oh no, I think you misunderstood me. I said Xanax. There're little pink pills."

"Pink? Oh, Honey, they're for children. This is Xanax; they're for those of us that have bad panic attacks." He took a good look at her. "I'd say you qualify."

"Oh. So this is just a little bit stronger?" She knew there were times she had had to take two of the pinks ones to calm down. She swallowed the white pill gratefully hoping it would take effect quickly so she could think clearly. "Thank you so very much." She started to go on, but he interrupted her.

He put his hand over hers. "It has truly been my pleasure." He looked genuinely concerned for her. "Believe me, I understand. I've seen the news reports. Now would you like for me to sit with you? Or would you like to be alone?"

So grateful it was hard to speak, she squeezed his hand. "I can't even tell you how grateful I am, but you've done enough. I do need to be alone now."

She walked him to the door and was grateful to find her legs working normally. Then she sat down to pray for the men she loved. She thought about her son, Bryan just had to be all right. He was just an innocent boy, hardly more than a baby really. She continued to pray harder than she had ever prayed in her life. She didn't even know it when she fell asleep.

*   *   *   *

Luke was praying too. He pulled up to his electronic gate to find it had been smashed down. He screeched to a stop in front of the house. There were no less than six cop cars parked haphazardly around his land. Sam was in his wheelchair with an officer kneeling down to attend to him. Bryan was sitting on the ground next to him holding his hand. He was pale, but otherwise looked unhurt. Luke was so grateful there were tears in his eyes. He started to run over to them when an ambulance roared into the driveway. Thinking it was for Sam he was surprised when they went around to the back of the house.

"Sam, Bryan, what's going on?" He tried to keep his voice casual for Bryan's sake. Bryan jumped up and threw his arms around his waist. "Luke, I'm so glad you're here. I got kidnapped!" Somehow the words didn't go with the big grin on his face, or the excitement in his voice.

Even though the boy was right there, Luke felt his heart lurch. "What?" He looked over at Sam.

Spying Nico, Sam looked up at him beseechingly. Taking the hint, Nico said, "Why don't you show me to the kitchen, Bryan. Yall have any Cokes?" He took Bryan by the hand to lead him into the house.

Bryan laughed, "You know where the kitchen is Nico." He looked at Sam and Luke, knowing they wanted grownup talk; he resigned to try to get all the details later. "All right, come on."

Sam was apologetic, "Luke, I screwed up. Doug Collins is shot, but last I heard he is still alive. I had sent Roberts out to get the van, and I was trying to get Bryan to get his things ready so we could leave. He ran upstairs to get his backpack, and that's the last thing I remember."

The officer that had been holding a white towel to Sam's head spoke up. "He was attacked from behind, sir. There wasn't anything he could have done to prevent it."

"I should have been listening, I just thought it was Roberts coming back in." he looked up at Luke.

"Another ambulance has already taken Roberts to the hospital. He was attacked from behind too. But he's okay. He was talking to the paramedics and mad at himself as he left."

The policeman took over, "Apparently, after knocking out both men, the perp took Bryan and put him in a boat, and it's still down there. Then he must have come back to the house to finish him off." He nodded to Sam.

"He didn't know some of the officers were already here. When the young officer saw him leaning over this gentleman on the floor, he thought he was about to hit him with the baton again, so he shot him. It didn't kill the suspect, but he hasn't regained consciousness yet. Cunningham had already found the fallen officer in the front yard, so the shooting was justified. It was a good shoot."

It was hard to tell who was the most surprised to find out that the young officer that had done the shooting was Cunningham. The one Nico had said would probably piss himself in he face of action. Turns out he didn't piss himself after all, but he had thrown up.

Luckily, Bryan hadn't seen a thing. But Sam did need to go to the hospital. He was going to need stitches in his head and a good check up from the doctor. After checking in on Bryan and letting him tell his version of how brave he had been, Luke put a call in to Shannon. After three rings, the operator answered. She transferred Luke to Mr. Graham.

The man explained that Shannon was most likely asleep, and the reason why. While grateful, Luke was surprised. He hadn't known that Shannon had ever taken Xanex. Concerned, he asked Sam.

"Yes, she has had to take it upon occasion. She has a prescription for it." Sam didn't elaborate because he thought that would be up to Shannon.

Luke didn't press for details because he really wanted to get Sam to the hospital and because he was grateful that Shannon was okay. He was also grateful to Mr. Graham for being there to help her.

CHAPTER 53

When Shannon awoke, she was groggy. Noticing it was getting dark outside; she sat up quickly and had to hold on to her swimming head. Was it really dark, or was it just her? She couldn't remember what was wrong. Something was very wrong. Bryan, where was Bryan? Oh, yeah, he's with Dad at Luke's place. Why didn't that make her feel any better? She realized she had lain back down without knowing it. She started to sit back up, and passed out again.

$*$ $*$ $*$ $*$

Luke hated hospitals. He couldn't believe how long this was taking. Things were more complicated with Sam because of his paralyses. Finally after a barrage of tests, they were releasing him. They were going back to his house to pick up Nico and Bryan, then to the hotel to get Shannon. Luke had had Mr. Graham go in and check on her and he had reported that she was still asleep. It didn't surprise Luke because he knew she had had very little sleep lately and he knew how strong Xanax could be. On the streets the white ones were know as Quad-bars. They were four times as strong as the ones she was used to.

Shifting in the drivers' seat of the van, he knew he was bone tired himself. He felt like he could sleep for twenty-four hours. He looked over a Sam. "Well, it's over. We can all get on with our lives, those of us that lived through it," he added grimly. "It's touch and go with Collins, but Blake promised to call us if and when he regains consciousness.

Then he grinned. "You up for a wedding?"

Sam matched his grin. "I think you better call your family."

Knowing he was right, Luke dialed his cell phone. His Mother was thrilled that it was all over with. She couldn't believe the course of events and was sorry to hear that Sherri was one of the victims. "Thank the Good Lord that Shannon is safe. She's always been a brave girl, but this time I'm glad she didn't have to shoot anybody herself."

"What? What are you talking about, Mom?" She never had to shoot anybody. Who told you that?" Luke thought the rumors must have been running rampant, all the way to Louisiana. With his thoughts on the coming storm, he missed most of what his mother was saying. "Excuse me? Mom, I'm sure you have your facts wrong."

A loud clap of thunder sounded above them as Luke got near the lake. Great, more rain, he was thinking. Sam reached over and placed his hand on Luke's shoulder. "No, she doesn't son. Didn't Shannon tell you?"

Luke immediately pulled over to the side of the road. "Mother, I'll call you back." He took a deep breath and stared out of the windshield as the rain began. "Tell me," he said simply.

And so Sam did.

*   *   *   *

The woman across the lake had heard the shot earlier. She had thought it must mean they were coming for her and hope had her hanging on, she kept trying to loosen the ropes around her wrist. As the hours went by, the sirens had left and it was starting to get dark. The axe, the knife and various other objects that he had threatened her with were still lying in plain sight. He had left them there to taunt her.

She lost hope once more. She was just too exhausted. She had quit being hungry sometime yesterday, she thought. They weren't going to find her. She would die here, tied and gagged in the boathouse. As she let her red head drop to her chest she prayed.

CHAPTER 54

▼

Shannon was confused as she peered up at the policeman. Her head felt like it was stuffed with cotton or something. "Wha … What are you doing here?" She knew he looked familiar, but couldn't find his name in her jumbled brain at the moment. "Why can't I think straight?"

He sat down beside her on the sofa. "Well, I'm not sure about that Shannon, but it sure makes things easier for me doesn't it?

She squinted up at him again. "I'm sorry, why are you here?"

That made him laugh. "You're sorry? Well listen to that ladies and gentleman! Now she says she's sorry." He smoothed her hair back, he was finally able to get close enough. "I'm glad you let it go back to blond. It makes this more real. More like I've dreamed of … all—these—years." His voice seemed to trail off as he examined her closely. "You know, I thought you were a monster when I was a little boy." His laughter barked out again. "Now that's funny. *I* thought *you* were a monster."

Suddenly he jumped to his feet, dragging her up with him. Shannon couldn't make sense of the fact that a man dressed as a policeman would treat her so roughly. "What are you doing?" She jerked her arm free as she struggled to clear her mind.

He smiled at her and raised his brow. "Okay, let me calm down a little. We tend to get like this when we loose one of our own. And even though you didn't kill him yourself—this time—you are responsible."

"Loose one of your own—what?" She held on to the back of the nearest chair.

"Can't you see I'm a policeman? Don't you remember me?" He puffed out his chest and struck a pose for a moment. When she still looked confused, he changed his face completely to look a little lost and shy.

"I do know you. Yes of course, you walked me home that first night. Sometimes you're the cop on duty that guards us in the office. You are a cop." Then she paused as dread filled her stomach. "What do you mean you lost one of your own?"

He looked extremely sad, "Luke is dead. Your ex-boyfriend shot him dead, out at Lewisville Lake today. And here you've been, taking a nap. The world has gone to hell, and you decide to take a nap and let others risk their life." Her knees collapsed and she would have fallen to the floor if he hadn't caught her.

"Luke is … dead?" She looked around the penthouse. Pictures began to form in her mind of the recent events. She heard a high whaling sound and thought it must be sirens. Then realized the sound was coming from her own throat. The officer, what was his name? looked at her throat in distracted interest.

"I need to take you to your son. He needs you. You didn't forget Bryan did you?"

That made her stiffen her spine. She had to protect her baby. Oh, Lord, please help clear my mind. I have to think straight for Bryan. She swallowed and wiped a hand across her brow. "Yes, take me to my son." She was distraught to hear how weak and shaky her voice sounded.

They road the elevator down in complete silence. He held on to her arm as if to catch her again if she fell. As they were crossing the lobby, Mr. Graham came hurrying up to them.

"Mrs. …"

She was so intent on getting to Bryan, so devastated at the thought of losing Luke, she just held up a hand to ward him off. He stopped helplessly and watched her rush from the hotel with the policeman. Well, if there was trouble, at least she was with a cop. Uneasily he went back to work.

CHAPTER 55

▼

Luke was having a hard time getting his mind around the facts. His sweet and innocent Shannon had killed somebody? And never even thought to share that little detail of her life? Why hadn't she trusted him? She had been upset when he hadn't disclosed his wealth to her, and he had felt guilty about that. But this was on a different level entirely.

He could hear Bryan and Nico talking in the back seat, and was grateful to Nico for keeping the boy occupied. They had picked the two of them up at Luke's house after Sam had explained everything to Luke.

Sam was very quiet. He knew Luke needed some time to absorb everything. They were on the way to get Shannon at the hotel. Sam would be glad to return home and he knew when Shannon and Luke had a chance to talk, they would work it out. A love as obvious as theirs would stand the test, wouldn't it? He glanced over at Luke to see his jaw clench and unclench as his thoughts continued to sort it out.

They decided to all go up to the suite. Luke and Nico had to collect their belongings and it didn't make sense to just leave the other two waiting in the van. Plus Shannon would want a full accounting of everything. Luke thought he would see Shannon and her family back to her apartment, and then he had a strong urge to go out and get drunk with Nico. If ever two men needed it, he figured it was the two of them. Maybe he should put a little distance between himself and Shannon for a while. At least the madman had been caught, it would give them both a chance to chill out, and see if they could get past the fact that she had kept such an important part of herself from him. Morosely, he wondered if she had really ever loved him at all. She sure as hell must not trust him.

When Mr. Graham came up to them, Luke thought to just hurriedly give the guy a big tip for helping Shannon earlier, then send him on his way.

"I'm so happy to see you, sir. I must say I was a little concerned when I saw Mrs. Manning take off so quickly with that young police officer. I trust all is well?" The smile faded from his expressive face as he saw the alarm leap into Luke's eyes.

He actually grabbed the poor man by both shoulders, almost lifting him from the ground. "What did you say?"

"I ... I said I trust that all is well?" His voice all but squeaked.

"No, before that. Are you saying Shannon isn't here?"

"She left some time ago. With a police officer," he added hopefully.

"What police officer? Was he in uniform?"

"Yes sir, but just barely. He hardly looked old enough."

Luke felt a tightness in his chest. "Was he about six feet, with reddish/brown hair?"

Graham was relieved that he knew the one. "Yes sir, that's the one."

Luke dropped both his hands and turned to look at Nico. Without looking at Graham he said, "Please take Mr. Walker and this young man up to the suite and make them comfortable. See to it that they have anything they need."

He turned to Sam, "We'll go and get Shannon and bring her back."

He looked at Bryan who was looking up at him with alarm. "Hey," he knelt down in front of the boy. "You know what? You can ask this man for anything you want, video games, computer games or as much ice cream as you can eat."

Bryan looked at him seriously, "Even a banana split?"

Luke smiled and ruffled the top of his hair. "Sure you can. Right Sam?"

Trying to keep it light and simple, Sam replied, "With a cherry on top." Then he grabbed Luke's wrist, "Keep me informed. Please?"

"You know I will." Luke and Nico hurried out as Sam and Bryan started towards the elevator. Glancing back, Luke saw that Bryan was holding Sam's hand and looking back at them with worry etched on his young face. Luke knew they hadn't fooled the kid at all. Felling like a fool, he smiled as big as he could and gave the boy two thumbs up. He felt a little justified when he saw Bryan smile in return.

CHAPTER 56

▼

"No, it's not this exit. It's past the bridge." Shannon put her hand on the officer's shoulder to get his attention. He had been silent the whole trip and she had been grateful for that. It was hard enough to clear the cobwebs from her mind. It wasn't until the last minute she realized he was taking the wrong exit.

"I know what I'm doing. The road is closed at the next exit because of all the rain." Even as he spoke lightning lit the skies in several areas at once as it sometimes does in Texas. Just at its heels thunder shook the car. The strong winds pushed the car back and forth.

Too disoriented to argue she sat back and held on. The rain was coming down so hard she thought more than once they might go off the road. All she knew was that she had to get to Bryan and Sam. She kept trying not to think about Luke. Surely they must be wrong. Wouldn't she feel it if Luke was dead? That wonderful gorgeous man, he was too full of life, too smart to be taken out by a weasel like Doug. Besides no matter how bad Doug was, she just couldn't believe he was a killer.

When the car pulled up beside a boathouse, she was even more confused. "You can't be planning on taking a boat across in this weather. I mean, can you?"

"I could if I wanted too. How much does your son mean to you? I mean you haven't even asked me many questions. You know, I meant a lot to my Father. And he meant a lot to me." He sat for a minute and just looked out through the rain. "No one, in my entire life has ever loved my like that since then." He turned to glare at her bitterly.

"What happened? Is your father dead?" Shannon wondered why he was bringing this up now.

He slapped her so fast across the face that she had no time to prepare. Her ears were ringing and she thought she might be sick. The hot nausea burned the back of her throat. "Wha ..."

He twisted her long hair in his hand and jerked violently, "Like you don't know!" Then he seemed to calm down as he thought of something funny. "I have an idea, let's play a game. I am going to kill you tonight, but first let's say I give you a fighting chance." Shannon just sat there and looked at him, thinking he had gone crazy.

Tears blurred her eyes as he dragged her across the console in the middle of the car and threw her to the ground. Her head was spinning as she tried to sit up. He grabbed her by the hair again and pulled her to her feet. "Run, Shannon. Run for your life. I'll even turn around and hide my eyes. I'll count to ten." He giggled, delighted with himself.

Shannon didn't waste anymore time. She ran into the cover of nearby trees. The wind was blowing so strong it whistled through the autumn leaves in a mournful sound. The rain had taken a break, but the ground was still muddy and slippery. Was that already footsteps behind her, or the sound of her heart beating wildly? She felt like she was caught in a nightmare, made even worse by the strong dose of Xanex.

The lake appeared before her suddenly as the ground came to an abrupt end. "Shannon." He called out in a sing song voice. "Shannon, I'm coming to get you." The voice came from her right, which confused her. She thought she had left him straight behind her. She looked up, wondering if she could just climb a tree and hide until he left. Maybe from up in a tree she could even watch him to see where he was going. Choosing the biggest nearby tree, she grabbed it and tried to climb. Because everything was so wet from the rain, her foot kept slipping off.

"Shannon," he sang out again, this time closer. With fear clogging her throat, she tried not to whimper. She turned blindly, the wind whipping her hair into her face and eyes, even into her mouth as she tried to gulp for breath. She ran from tree to tree, trying to be quiet now as he got closer. She pressed herself behind one of the trees, holding her hair in one hand, so he couldn't see it blowing and give away her position. Heavy clouds raced in front of the moon. One minute everything was bright, the next very dark.

"Do you know how many girls I've killed now Shannon? I've even killed a man, but I have to admit, that wasn't as much fun. I've done it all for you Shannon." She could feel him getting closer. "And I'm gonna fuck your brains out." She could hear him breathing hard, even above the howling winds. "Before and after you're dead. What do you think about that? Oh, I've got so many plans for you; I just hope I can fit it all in this one night. I can't afford to keep you longer than that. But don't worry, you'll be praying for death by time it comes."

Shannon was frozen, not daring to move. If she tried to run now, she knew he'd be right on top of her.

He too had gone very still, looking for the slightest movement. Finally she heard him move off in the other direction. She closed her eyes and counted to sixty before daring to peek around the tree. His hand was around her wet throat before she even had time to scream.

He tried to grab her hair and wrap it around his hand but this time she was ready for him and she quickly darted out of his reach. She twisted her hair into a rope and stuffed it down into the back her blouse. He stood there amused as she got into a fighting stance, crouching with her knees bent and her fists ready.

Laughing, he feinted to the right and tried to trick her by jumping quickly back to the left. But instead of moving left or right, she just moved further back from him, bouncing on the balls of her feet. The adrenaline was surging through her blood and she felt ready to kill.

"Well, well, it looks like someone has taken self-defense classes. Do you really think they'll help you now, Shannon? I'm bigger than you are. I out—weigh you. And you know what else? I'm smarter than you. I'm smarter than the whole fuckin' police department." His voice was getting louder and louder until he was all but screaming at her.

Shannon didn't say anything; she was waiting for his next move.

"Come on Shannon, you must be dying to ask me all kinds of questions. Like how did Luke really die? Is Bryan really still alive?"

At the thought of that, Shannon made a mistake. She was so stunned she relaxed her guard for just the second he needed. In an instant he was on her. Jerking her hair out of her blouse he wrapped it tightly around his hand he started dragging her back towards the boathouse. She grabbed wildly with her nails, trying to scratch or gouge, but he had her at such an angle that it was useless. He just tightened his grip on her hair making her cry out in pain. Before she knew it they were at the boathouse. Her heart was racing.

"Aha! Now I've got you. See? I out smarted you, just like everyone else. I always know what buttons to push. But don't worry; I have a little surprise for you. "I've planned a little reunion for you Shannon. I hope you'll be grateful." He threw the door of the boathouse open and shoved her inside.

CHAPTER 57

▼

Nico was on the phone with Blake as Luke headed North on the toll way. He cursed when he saw there had been a wreck up ahead and the traffic was narrowed down to one lane.

Nico hung up to relay the news to him. "Apparently Cunningham was told to go home for the rest of the day after he shot Collins. He's on paid suspension pending an investigation, although everyone there thought it was a good shoot. No one's spoken to him since then. And get this, they found Mike Reynolds today."

"You're kidding? Now they find the guy? What did he have to say for himself? Nobody goes into hiding as good as he did without a reason." Luke slapped the flashing light on the dashboard to see if they could get around the traffic.

"Oh, he had a good reason alright. He's dead. Been dead for some time by the sound of it. They found him in a motel room in Mesquite. It's the kind of room you can rent by the month." Nico wished he had a cigarette. The cold wet night, the stress of this never-ending nightmare was starting to take its toll.

As if he read his thoughts, Luke handed him a stick of gum. "I guess that explains it, huh?" They were both quiet for a moment. "That must be how Collins got the fingerprints on the glass and the name tag. I gotta admit it threw us off for a while. Did Blake have any ideas where Cunningham might be, or why he has Shannon with him?"

"He's pulling up his file right now; he'll have it printed out when we get there."

*   *   *   *

Through the gloom Shannon could see a small woman tied up in the corner. She looked lifeless; her head was slumped on her chest. As Shannon turned to stare accusingly at him, Cunningham grabbed her hands and roughly tied them behind her. Shoving a filthy smelling gag in her mouth he threw her roughly to the floor. Shannon spit the nasty gag out of her mouth, but he didn't seem to notice.

He walked over to the other woman and grabbed her by the hair. As he yanked her head up her eyes opened weakly. He slapped her across the face. "Don't you dare die on me yet." Then he laughed. "This is the good part. This is what I've been waiting for most of my life."

He pulled up an old wooden stool and sat between them, looking back and forth like he was watching a tennis match. A high pitch giggle escaped his lips; he clapped his hands like a kid at the circus.

"Well, aren't you going to say anything to your best friend? How many years has it been since you saw each other?" He mused. "Oh yeah, I remember, it was the day that ruined my life—forever." He snarled the last word.

Shannon gasped as he lit a kerosene lamp and the light fell on the face she used to know so well. "Jill? Oh my god, Jill!"

The two women stared at each other in disbelief. Even with the passing of so many years, it was easy to see the little girls they had once been.

He moved the light closer to Jill's face. "Look Shannon, I didn't hurt her face yet at all so you two could recognize each other." He frowned for a minute as he saw the bruise that was already starting to swell on Shannon's cheek. Then he giggled again, "Oops, guess I got carried away with you. But you have to know it's you I hate the most," he explained, as if he really wanted her to understand. "You know, because you killed my Dad." He said conversationally. Then he swung back to Jill. "Do you know how long I waited for my Dad to come home? Your Dad put him in prison, and then when he finally had a chance to come home," he turned to Shannon, "you killed him." His lower lip trembled, "Why'd you have to go and do that? Huh? Why?" He looked like a five-year-old boy that was about to cry.

"I know, I know, he shot your Dad first, but he didn't kill him. Plus her Dad started it!" He pointed at Jill accusingly. "So I have to pay you back, you know? Both of you. I planned it all this time. You wanna hear about it?"

Jill's eyes had drifted shut again. She looked so bad, Shannon was afraid she would die any minute. The man jumped off the stool and screamed, "Okay, quit looking at her now, look at me! Don't you want to hear about all this?" Then he looked at her slyly, "Don't you want to hear how I'm gonna kill you?"

*   *   *   *

Luke, Blake and Nico were busy going over Cunningham's file. His innocent looking face beamed up at them proudly from six months before when he had graduated from the academy.

"Some of the guys gave him a hard time today for throwing up after he shot Collins. But I think most of them felt sorry for him. Jimmy's always been a good kid. I just can't figure out why Shannon is with him." Blake sounded perplexed.

Luke was staring at his full name. Why did it sound a little familiar? James Earl Cunningham. Date of birth June '88. Parents Fred and Marcie Cunningham. Both had died in a house fire when the boy was eighteen.

"Hey, this is interesting, they had only been married for ten years. Jimmy must have been from a previous marriage. Yeah, look, he was adopted by Fred the first year they were married." He flipped through the next few pages, but page three was missing. "It doesn't say what his real last name is," he said as a terrible idea was starting to form in his mind.

Pulling out his cell phone, he called Sam at the hotel. "Hey, Sam … No, no we haven't found her yet. I guess that means you haven't heard from her either? Listen Sam, about that story you told me earlier, what did you say the man's name was? Yeah, that man. Okay, thanks, no, no I'll call you back." He shut his phone slowly. He said, almost to himself, "James Earl Cabot. Oh—God, no,"

"What?" Blake asked.

Luke repeated louder, "James Earl Cabot. Jimmy is a nickname for James."

Suddenly Blake remembered the name. "Hey, that's the name of the man that was shot and killed by that little girl up North. What was her name?"

"Shannon." Was all Nico had to say. "Guess it wasn't Collins after-all.

CHAPTER 58

▼

"Well like I said, I've been planning this all my life; well it seems like my whole life. My Mom never could understand why we couldn't keep any pets around. She thought they kept running away." He giggled again, thoroughly enjoying himself. "One day she caught me trying to garrote—that means strangle—the cat. I couldn't believe how mad she got at me. She looked at me like she didn't even know me. She screamed at me that I was just like my Father." He was staring off into space as if part of his mind was still there. Then he shrugged. "Anyway, that night I burned the house down. Of course I had hit Mom and my fake Dad over the head first. Everybody said how lucky I was to have survived. No one has ever understood how smart I am. I took the insurance money and put myself through college. Then I joined the police academy and … here I am! Just like I planned."

Then he looked at Shannon slyly again. "Oh yeah, I guess I left something out. You see, I learned how to do research in college. But I couldn't find you, Shannon. You and your Dad hid pretty good. But I did find your Mom, and that's how I finally found you!" he said proudly. "I didn't think it was really you, cause you didn't look like I thought you would. Then I figured out you dyed your hair and stuff."

"I was even smart enough to pay that black kid to take pictures of Bryan to freak you out." He laughed, "Worked, didn't it?" He grabbed a nearby Polaroid camera and took a few pictures of both women.

He was swinging them back and forth in the air to speed up drying, when Jill made a harsh gasping noise and fell over. "Well, hell, I guess she died already. She was hardly any fun at all. But she was easy to find, cause you know, her parents and all. Oh yeah, I forgot to tell you, I had to kill your Mom. And it was only fair you know. Cause I kinda killed my Mom because of you."

Hearing about the death of her own Mother and seeing Jill die right before her eyes pushed Shannon over the edge. She tried to jump up and go after him, knowing the best she could hope for was for him to kill her quickly. When she was jerked back suddenly, he cracked up, laughing until there were tears in his eyes. "I threw the end of your rope over that anchor. I told you I've been planning this for a long time."

He got silent for a while. "Don't you want to know why I killed all those other girls?" Suddenly he looked older, almost completely different. Different, even from the young cop she knew as Cunningham.

"I was practicing. I wanted to know the worst way for someone to die. Plus it was fun fuckin with the cops. They never treated me like a real one. They even believed it when I stuck my finger down my throat and threw up after I shot Doug Collins today. I knew he had been stalking you; he's been waiting for a chance to steal the kid."

"What?" Shannon almost screamed the word.

Don't worry, I was a hero and shot him today before he could get away with the kid. I thought it was funny that every move he made just made him look like he was also the killer. Everyone's always treated me like a kid. Except I didn't have much of a childhood, did I Shannon?" He picked up the axe she had just noticed and slammed it into the old wooden table.

*   *   *   *

On the computer, Luke had pulled up the central appraisal districts for Dallas, Denton, and Tarrant counties, trying to find out if Jimmy had bought a house lately. His address listed on the application was an apartment in Mesquite, but he had moved out of there several weeks ago and told the Manager he had bought a house.

His heart took a leap when he finally found a match. Recently, he had bought an old house—on the south side of Lewisville Lake. Luke clicked on the address and the map showed that it was just across the lake from his own land, his own house.

Not waiting for it to print out, he grabbed his keys on the run, Nico on his heels. Blake was yelling after them. "I'll be right behind you, let me round up the troops!"

CHAPTER 59

▼

It was silent in the old boathouse, except for the patter of rain on the tin roof. It felt like it was freezing and Shannon started to shiver uncontrollably. Finally the effects of the Xanex had worn completely off. She thought of Luke, she couldn't believe he was dead. She thought of Bryan and Sam, fearing she would never see them again. She remembered Bryan's first shaky little first steps, the first time he threw a football and Sam's proud smile. She put her hands together to give thanks, one last time for the wonderful life she had had.

"What are you doing? Praying for your life? It won't do you any good." He was standing there watching her, his head tilted to one side as if watching a specimen, his thumb slowly caressing the edge of the axe. Her face was tear stained and bruised, but some how she didn't look as scared as he wanted her too. It was that stupid Jill's fault. He had planned to rape and kill her in front of Shannon. He wanted her to see what it had been like for those other girls. Stupid, dumb Jill had to go and die on him.

Oh well, he'd just have to give Shannon all the details—as her raped and killed her.

*   *   *   *

Luke had never been so scared in all his life. He had even agreed to let Nico drive so they could get there in one piece. The worst of the storm had moved away, but it was raining again. They parked down the street and ran through the woods to the house. It was completely dark. No lights on at all. Then Luke noticed a light on in the small boathouse near the water. Motioning to Nico he put his finger to his lips and pointed.

Cunningham was describing to Shannon exactly how he planned to kill her as he advanced on her. He had removed his gun and laid it on the table; he unbuckled his belt, ripped it free of the belt loops, and wrapped it around her neck. "I kinda like it when the girl is half dead, so I'm gonna strangle you just a little bit while we have sex, you won't believe this, but I think they kinda like it when I do that. He squeezed it tighter, enjoying the choking sounds she was making. He used one hand to rip at her pants, prodding her between the legs with his penis. Shannon's head was spinning and she was praying for darkness to take her when she heard a shot ring out. She felt his body jerk and the pressure around her throat was suddenly gone.

There was disbelief in his eyes as he spun around and saw Jill holding a smoking gun. Just as he was falling, clutching at his throat, Luke and Nico came crashing through the door. Luke ran to Shannon to untie her arms and remove her gag.

Nico quickly put his booted foot on Cunningham's chest. Jill was standing very still, the gun falling out of her numb fingers.

"Shannon you always stood up for me, even when it ruined your life. It was my turn to stand up and protect you." The two women crossed the room to each other to embrace and hold on tight. The nightmare was finally over.

CHAPTER 60

▼

The two men had brought Shannon and Jill outside to wait under the covered porch of the house. They could hear the sirens coming closer as Luke was answering questions for Shannon about Sam and Bryan. Nico was sitting on the steps holding Jill in his strong arms, she was so weak she couldn't walk on her own and she was shivering badly.

Luckily, Blake had thought ahead enough to put in a call for a couple of ambulances. Shannon had protested, she wanted to stay with Jill, but the paramedics had insisted on putting her on a stretcher too and into another ambulance.

"Honey, Nico can stay with Jill. Let's just get the two of you to the hospital and then we'll see about getting you together again. He was using a towel to dab at the various places she had scratches and wounds.

Shannon reached a hand up to his cheek and was devastated to see tears in his eyes. "Luke, he said you were dead. I didn't think I would ever see you again. I'm sorry Luke. I'm so sorry! This is all my fault. I never told you, I should have told you ..." she choked, still unable to get the words out.

"It's okay now Shannon. We can talk about it later," Luke just wanted her to calm down.

Realizing his concern for her, Shannon took a deep calming breath. "No, Luke this can't wait. I should have told you. I—I killed a man when I was young." She stared into his eyes, desperately trying to gauge his reaction. She was confused when his expression didn't change at all. "Luke? Did you hear me?"

"What were you expecting from me Shannon? Did you think that would change my feelings for you? Is that why you didn't tell me? You thought I wouldn't love you anymore or what? I thought we trusted each other more than that by now. You couldn't bring yourself to tell me because you couldn't trust my feelings for you." His eyes were locked on their clasped hands so she couldn't see how much that hurt him.

'No! No, Luke that's not it at all, I couldn't tell you because I was ashamed." She said it quietly, willing him to look at her.

"Ashamed? Of what? Saving the lives of your Father and your best friend? Your Dad told me the whole story earlier today." Of all the reasons Luke had thought of, shame wasn't one of them.

Taking another deep breath, Shannon admitted, "There's something I've never told anyone. Not Dad and, and not the ther—therapists." She swallowed audibly. "I think I could have stopped it. Just like now, like this. I could have stopped it." Her breath caught in her throat as the ambulance screeched to a halt at the emergency room doors. As they wheeled her into the hospital the Doctors took over and Luke was more at a loss than ever.

An hour later they had cleaned Shannon up and decided to keep her over-night for observation. There were no broken bones, but she had taken some severe blows to the head and had plenty of cuts and bruises.

Jill was in a far more serious condition. Jimmy had tracked Jill to Colorado, where she lived in Boulder. It had been way too easy for him to kidnap her and bring her to the Dallas/Ft. Worth metroplex. He had been holding her in that boathouse for almost a week. During that time he had given her just enough food and water to try to keep her alive until Shannon got there. She was suffering from dehydration combined with wounds from the various beatings she had taken. Miraculously she had not been sexually assaulted and was expected to make a full recovery. The doctors told Shannon that Jill had been given a sedative and was sleeping. She would have to wait until morning to see her.

Nico had agreed to go back to the hotel to talk to Sam and Bryan; he would also stay the night there with them. Shannon had just gotten off the phone with her Dad and her son after assuring them that she was fine.

Finally she was alone with Luke. He sat on the side of her bed, holding her hand. Bending down he lightly touched his lips to hers. "Do you feel up to finishing your story?"

They were in a private hospital room on the third floor of Lewisville Hospital. It was quite at that time of night and the room was dim. The smell of antiseptic was strong as it is in most hospitals.

Shannon struggled to sit up better in the bed, she felt sore all over. "Yes, Luke, I need to get this out. But first can you tell me how you found us, out in that boat house? You said that my Dad had told you the whole story earlier. How did you put the pieces together so fast after that?"

"Well actually it was my Mom that first said something. We thought everything was over with after Doug Collins was shot by Cunningham earlier in the day out at my place. As I told you earlier, Collins tried to kidnap Bryan and somehow Jimmy was one of the first cops at the scene. I think Jimmy had been pulling Doug's strings all along, somehow making him think he was working with him as a wronged Father just trying to get his son back. I'm still not sure how they found out that Sam and Bryan were at my place. I guess there are some things we'll just never know."

"Anyway, I called my Mother to tell her everything was over and she said that she was glad that you didn't have to shoot anybody this time. I thought that surely she was mistaken, but she remembered the whole story of what had taken place back in '93. She even remembered what you looked like and it seems she knew all along who you and Sam were and just assumed that I did too. Sam filled me in on all the rest of the details."

"When we got to the hotel, the concierge told us that you had left with a young policeman just before we got there. The description matched Cunningham, so Nico and I called Blake to see what he made out of it, and at the station we looked into Cunningham's file. We discovered that he had been adopted, and that his real Fathers name was James Earl Cabot. Jimmy is a nickname for James, and after the story your Dad had just told me it just clicked into place for me. We looked through the local appraisal districts on-line and found that a James Cunningham had just bought property out by Lewisville Lake. I don't know if it was a coincidence that it was close to my property or not. Like I said there are some things we'll never know for sure."

By the time he was finished with his story, there were tears streaming down Shannon's face. "I knew it. It's all my fault. I could have stopped this sooner if I had just told you about my childhood. I'm just so used to trying to block it all out and try my best to never think about it, that I couldn't bring myself to say it out loud. I never thought there could be a connection, so I never said anything. Just like I never said anything to my Dad all those years ago." She threw both hands over her face and cried as if her heart was breaking.

Luke pulled her into his embrace and just let her cry for a while, knowing she needed to. Finally he asked, "Shannon, what are you talking about? What did you keep from your Father?"

Taking a deep breath, Shannon wiped her face with the tissues Luke had given her. With her eyes downcast, she finally said out loud what she had never told anyone. "I met James Earl Cabot the day before he shot my Dad and tried to take Jill. It was a beautiful fall day and Jill and I were playing in the leaves. Throwing them up in the air and just having fun. Then we noticed a strange man taking our picture. He said he was working for a newspaper and wanted to put our pictures in the paper."

"We were scared because we weren't supposed to be messing up all those piles of leaves; actually we were supposed to be in the library. We had snuck outside, and we knew we would be caught if the picture came out in the paper. Jill was afraid that her parents would send her away to a private school. So I yelled at the man and told him that Jill's parents would sue him if he used her picture, and he just backed off and said okay. But Luke, I knew something didn't feel right. The man scared me. I almost told my Dad about it at dinner that night. But I didn't want to worry him because he had a big game to coach that night, and—I didn't want to admit I had broken the rules again." She shrugged her shoulders, "I did that a lot when I was little."

"If I had just told my Dad, maybe I could have stopped it. Just like if I had told you earlier about that incident when I was a child, you could have put the pieces together sooner and maybe some of those girls wouldn't have been killed. Don't you see? It's all my fault—again!"

Her face was so pale, the devastation so clear in her eyes that it almost broke Luke's heart. "Oh, sweetheart. Is that what you've thought all these years? Why didn't you discuss this with a therapist? You could have saved yourself a lot of torture."

He took her by the shoulders and looked deeply into her eyes.

"Shannon, none of this, past or present—is your fault. You developed this sense of guilt when you were just ten years old and you've got to let it go! Even if you felt like that Cabot man was a bad man, there was no way you could have known what was going to happen."

"And even if you told your Dad about it, nothing would have changed. He couldn't have had a clue what the man was up to either. The guilt you've been carrying all these years is the guilt of a ten-year old, don't you understand that?"

Shannon blinked rapidly. Could that be true? She had never thought about what her Dad could have done to stop it if she had told him the night before. Luke was right; there couldn't have been anything to stop it. But what about now?

She nodded her head slowly, "Okay, okay, I do see that you are right about that. But what about now? If I had told you all about it, maybe you could have stopped him sooner. Maybe some of those girls wouldn't be dead now because of something I did all those years ago."

"Why are you determined to blame yourself for everything? You are not responsible for all the lunatics in the world. But you are right. I would have checked into it and done a search on the name Cabot. Shannon, I wouldn't have found anything. I still wouldn't have suspected Cunningham. There was no reason to suspect him until that concierge …"

"Graham" Shannon supplied his name.

"Yeah, until Graham came up to us at the hotel and told us you had left with him. And the only reason we knew which young cop you had left with so fast was because he had just shot Collins hours before so he was on our minds. Normally we didn't usually notice him. Don't you see, I could just as easily blame myself? Why didn't I notice a weirdo cop right in front of me all this time? The blame game could go on and on. Do you know that Nico blames himself for Sherri's death?"

"Things happen for a reason that we human's don't always understand, we are not perfect. None of us are perfect."

Shannon was trying to wrap her mind around all that Luke was saying. He made perfect sense. "Can it really be that easy?" There was so much hope in her voice, in her eyes, that Luke was humbled that she would put so much faith in his words.

"I know how to make it perfect. If you're not perfect, and I know I'm not perfect, there is one way to get closer to perfection. Shannon …"

Luke got down on one knee beside the hospital bed. "Shannon, will you marry me?" He took her left hand and placed a beautiful diamond ring on her finger. "Together we can always talk things out. We can be two halves of a whole."

Shannon couldn't believe it. She was so happy she wanted to burst with it. She tugged at Luke's hand until he was up on the bed with her again. She was laughing with sheer joy as she threw her arms around his neck. "Oh Yes. Yes! Yes, Yes! I will be so happy to marry you! I need you in my life, Luke.

"Right back at you, sweetheart.

Don't miss
Nico's Guilt
Coming this Fall 2008

Nico Tribiani sighed as he put the last picture down. It already seemed that the wedding was a long time ago. His best friend and ex-partner on the Dallas Police Department had gotten married and settled down about six months before. The whole family had been through so much trauma at the hands of a serial killer, that when it was over with, Luke had finally succumbed to his father's wishes and taken over the family business. The Manning family was one of the wealthiest in the country and no one had really thought Luke would stay a cop for as long as he did. Of course it had been different when he was single, but now he had a wife, and her family to take care of. She had a son and a handicap father. Luke had adopted her son Bryan and now along with the wedding pictures, was news that another baby was on the way.

Nico picked up the glass of whiskey and saluted the picture of a grinning Luke. "Congratulations, boy. I'm happy as hell for you." Happy. Now, there was a thought. When was the last time he had really been happy? His girlfriend Sherri had been murdered by the same killer that had terrorized Luke's wife, Shannon, all those months ago. The guilt of feeling like it was all his fault for not paying enough attention to her ate at his gut on a daily basis. He looked at the bottle of whiskey and noticed it was already near empty. Well, that was okay, he patted his shirt pocket, and he was almost out of cigarettes too. He'd just go and get some more.

The phone rang and he ignored it, as he had been doing a lot lately. It was probably Shannon or Luke again. They had been trying to get him to come visit them in Louisiana. He knew they were worried about him. Hell, sometimes he was too. But he just wasn't ready. Although he felt like he needed this time alone, he knew he would have to rejoin the living sooner or later.

When the answering machine came on, it took him a few minutes to realize it wasn't Shannon's voice.

"Nico, listen." The voice was speaking quietly. "I'm in trouble …" she paused.

Recognizing his little sister's voice, Nico lurched to grab at the receiver.

"Toni?"

Sighing with relief, Antoinette laughed a little shakily. "Hi! I'm so glad you're there. I need you to come to New Orleans—tonight. I hate to ask but, I … Oh, God! Nico!" She screamed as the line went dead.

Nico just stood there, holding the receiver. His heart in his throat.

978-0-595-50904-1
0-595-50904-5

Printed in the United States
117559LV00003B/199/P